GOING OUT LIVE

Mark Lawson was born in London in 1962. He is the author of *Bloody Margaret: Three Political Fantasies*; a travel book, *The Battle for Room Service*; and *Idlewild*, a novel. He is an award-winning journalist and broadcaster and currently presents Radio 4's *Front Row* and BBC 2's *Review*.

MARK LAWSON

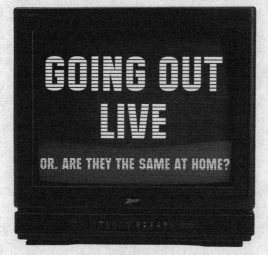

A NOVEL

PICADOR

First published 2001 by Picador

This edition published 2002 by Picador
an imprint of Pan Macmillan Ltd
Pan Macmillan, 20 New Wharf Road, London N1 9RR
Basingstoke and Oxford
Associated companies throughout the world
www.panmacmillan.com

ISBN 0 330 48861 9

1 3 5 7 9 8 6 4 2

A CIP catalogue record for this book is available from
the British Library.

Typeset by Intype London Ltd
Printed and bound in Great Britain by
Mackays of Chatham plc, Chatham, Kent

For

R.L.R.

and in memory of

ANTHONY BEVINS
(1942–2001)

and

SALLY PAYNE
(1956–2001)

Contents

PART ONE

PRESENT

present pri'zent v. . . . (of a performer, compere etc.) introduce or put before an audience . . . exhibit (an appearance etc.) . . . *Med.* (of a patient or illness etc.) come forward for or undergo initial medical examination.

Oxford English Dictionary

1. OPENING LINKS

I have voices in my ear and urgent messages surge before my eyes in flickering green type. And yet no one thinks I'm insane. When I pass my hidden whispers and secret sentences on to them, they like me for it. Some would go as far as love. They invite me into their homes.

This invitation is metaphorical, although some of them would like – even desire – an actual visit. Others, admittedly, detest me, sending letters containing sentences which are, curiously, often also green, though still and scribbled on torn-off looseleaf, not floating in the air like mine.

The letters distressed me at first. Communications of such hatred would normally be sent only to the paedophile wing of a prison. But everyone just shrugs and says there are always nutters: 'Nobody wins them all over.' They point, like a politician, to the majority. My OK-postbag is fatter than the anti-sack.

'*Happy, Richard?*' is the latest question in my head.

In an average week, there are seven or eight different voices in my ear – or in both ears if it's the afternoons – but it's Lucy's I like best. I may soon have to make a television programme called *I Don't Love Lucy*. I can't see her but know that she's watching me from above. I nod.

'*Coming in two minutes,*' she breathes.

I smile, trying to look less frightened than I am.

And now the green words start to appear. They scroll

past too fast to read at first but then there is a moment of
sharp focus in which I can make out three phrases:

IS THERE A GOD?
IS SEX WRONG?
WHEN WILL
THE WORLD END?

Christ, I think, it's the big questions tonight.

'*What are you smiling at?*' Lucy whispers down.

I shake my head and lip-mime, 'Tell you later' up at what
they used to call the gods.

'*That's OK. We like you smiley.*'

The three big queries speed away from me and, as the
scroll slows down, a lone green word flutters at eye level,
like an alien communication from outer space:

HELLO

The biggest rule in this is that you mustn't ever think
there are millions out there. Look through the words and
imagine someone who loves you, listening to what you have
to say. I close my eyes. Tonight, I really have to feel and
listen for my heart before I find it. On a bad night, it's like
a rat inside the ribcage trying to claw out.

I count the heartbeats. A little fast. I breathe in short,
fast, quiet gasps to bring it down. The problem when an old
pro first taught me that trick was that I always thought of
when the girls were born, telling Imogen to pant. Among the
many conversations we had which ended in screaming, only
that one turned out happily.

When people ask me why I always shut my eyes just
before, I make out that it's some kind of vaguely Buddhist
thing. Meditation. But, in fact, it's ex-Catholic. How ex I
don't quite know. What I say inside my head is: *Please, God,*

let this be all right. My mother always said a Hail Mary before she had to drive on motorways and this is my equivalent. But my mum was betting on her favourite. For me it's longshots, a horse so dark you can't see it; a ruined gambler betting because he remembers what it felt like to win.

I open my eyes.

'*Coming*,' says Lucy softly in my ear. '*You'll be marvellous, darling.*'

And then the voice is not Lucy's but Helen's, which isn't as nice.

'*Ten, nine, eight* . . .'

The moon-shot moment. At the age of fourteen I was dragged downstairs in a half-dream in my pyjamas to watch Neil Armstrong on weightless feet speak what no one called a sound-bite then. I wanted to be an astronaut and never made it, but – unlike the other frustrated spacemen of my generation – I get countdowns almost every day.

'*Seven, six, five, four* . . .'

It's still a source of slight regret to me that four is followed not by 'commence ignition sequence' but –

'*Three, two, one, zero* . . .'

And the roar is not the explosion of rocket fuel but the colliding hands of 500 people who earn in a year what I get for a week and are being encouraged to clap by a man waving his hands above his head like a stockbroker on the day the president is shot.

The extraterrestrial welcome flickers in front of me:

HELLO

'Hello', I say, the Ambassador from Planet Fame.

Interviews 1: The Sun's Moved

ROLL 1 – DEAD ON LIVE TV – INTERVIEW 22/11/99

(General indistinct chatter.)

Man's voice: OK. I'll just ident this. *Dead on Live* TV – roll 1.

Woman's voice: Jesus f***. You're not calling it *Dead on Live TV*, are you?

2nd Woman's voice: It's a working title. Our insect (?) prod's keen. But . . . I hear what you're saying. We're almost bound to change it.

2nd Man's voice: Up to speed. And running, Agnes . . .

2nd Woman's voice: OK, we're rolling. Could I first just ask you to state your name – spelling anything unclear – and how you'd like to be described.

Interviewee: Right. I'm Lucy Brooks. L-U-C-Y perhaps I ought to say. There's one with an I-E in my son's class. I'm a BBC television producer. I was the producer of Richard Fleming's chat show, *Fleming Faces*, for seven years.

2nd Woman's voice (*from here* Interviewer): We can Aston you with your new job if you want.

Interviewee (*from here* Lucy Brooks): No. You know, I'm just doing pilots . . .

Interviewer (Int): OK. Well, let's just, uh, start with the, uh, obvious stuff. When did you meet Richard Fleming?

Lucy Brooks (LB): Well, it was . . . Hang on, I should have asked . . . Are you in this or is it self-contained answers?

Int: Oh, er, self-contained ... When did you first meet Richard Fleming?

LB: I first met Richard when he got the Friday peak-time chat-show on BBC 1 seven years ago. He'd been doing a late-night sort of satire thing on BBC 2. The insect (?) prod of that—

Int: Lucy, could you just spell that out for people who don't know television?

LB: What? Oh, exec prod? Yeah, sorry ... The executive producer of that, Tom Ogg, who's now Managing Director of Broadcasting, asked me to produce it.

Int: Lucy, this is great. But maybe you're giving people more detail than they strictly need. It's just the slot we've got ...

LB: Yeah. What have they given you?

Int: 22.00 Friday.

LB: Christ. That's our old slot. There's BBC shrift (?) for you. They'll always get another programme out of you.

Int: OK, should we go back? How much did you know about him before you met him? And – remember – self-contained if you can ...

LB: Yeah ... Before I was asked to produce his chat show, I knew Richard from his BBC 2 show, which I'd liked. I'd read his *Observer* column in the 1980s. That had been a bit of a cult thing at university.

Int: Where was your first meeting?

LB: We had lunch at Julie's in Holland Park, which was the BBC canteen at the time. That was before they opened Orsino next door. And who'd have thought then that Alastair Little would open up in Ladbroke Grove? ... Hang on, can I do that again? I don't want to give the impression that the licence fee is spent entirely on Mediterranean cravats (?) in a reduction of lentil ... We had lunch at Julie's restaurant in Holland Park.

Int: What was your first impression?

LB: He seemed surprisingly – and this really isn't just brojecting . . . sorry . . . and this really isn't just projecting backwards – vulnerable. I remember saying that I'd thought the week before last's show in his satire series had been just superb. And he said, 'What was wrong with last week?' He really looked crushed. But I've since realized – not just because of Richard, but because of all the people we had on the show – that this idea of stars being arrogant really isn't right. They have to appear confident, because performing is about that, but underneath they're generally more insecure than the rest of us. People think it's mad when you say it, because why would you go on stage or do television or movies or write books if you were shy? But – with the obvious possible exception of Lord Haydon of Hitchin – they do it not because they think they're brilliant but because they need to prove to themselves that they are.

Int: Lucy, could you do that again without the sneering reference to Lord Haydon?

LB: Why?

Int: It's just kind of a dog-leg. And the audience we're aiming at would probably read his books.

LB: I'm really not pandering to that talentless a***hole. I'll tell you later what he did in the lift when we had him on the show.

Int: OK. OK, we can come back to that. Lucy, when you had lunch that time – or subsequently – did Richard go to the loo a lot?

LB: What?

Int: Did Richard go to the loo a lot?

LB: No. What is this?

Int: There are just these persistent rumours that he was no stranger to the porcelain. For whatever reason.

LB: Jesus.

Int: You were never, um, um, aware that he went to the Gents more, er, often than would be considered normal?

LB: Well, I don't have the national pissing statistics . . . Look, can we stop this for a minute . . . Are you trying to suggest he was gay or something?

Int: Hardly gay. Oh, I see, hanging round lavatories. No. There are at least two other media uses of loos. I mean apart from the primary one.

Man's voice: The sun's moved. I'm sorry. The sun's moved.

Int: Can you, uh, cheat it?

Man's voice: No. She's in shadow. I'm going to have to reset.

(Tape break. Tape resumes with general indistinct chatter.)

LB: *(indistinct)* . . . going to be a serious interview . . .

Int: It is . . . We want to give as full a picture of Richard Fleming as possible.

LB: Right. You realize that, apart from anything else, *Dead on Live TV* is wrong as a title because Richard's TV show wasn't live.

Int: Yeah. But 'as-live' . . .

LB: 'As-live' isn't live, though.

Int: As I say, it's a working title. Now you understand I have to ask you about Matthew Harding (?) . . .

LB: Yeah.

Int: When did you become aware of his name?

LB: Oh, not until . . . not until his picture was on the news, to tell the truth.

Int: But he'd been writing to Richard for some time?

LB: Apparently. So it turned out.

Int: But Richard never, uh, mentioned him?

LB: No. But then he wouldn't. That kind of thing. He wouldn't have wanted me to worry.

Int: There's a rumour that Richard was writing some kind of memoir towards the end . . .

LB: Yes, I'd heard that. I read that. But with a lot of what's been written about Richard, it's a matter of divide by five while pinching salt. I have to say I think it's unlikely, because he was very down on the celebrity memoir as a form. Because plugging books was the main reason stars would come on the show, he was reading two or even three a week sometimes. Richard used to say that an autobiography is God's way of telling you how dull and smug you are.

Man's voice: Sorry, Agnes. Tape change.

(Tape break. Tape resumes.)

LB: Could I have some water please?

Int: OK, that's great, Lucy. Uh, while Holly's getting you some water, obviously in the documentary we're going to have clips from Richard's shows. Are there, you know, particular, um, ones you'd suggest?

LB: Well, you'll be using the Alice Jackett one obviously? I mean the *first* Alice Jackett one, that is . . .

Int: Yeah. We've got that.

LB: Well, that's a good one to have. Richard always said – long before it actually happened – that that was where it started to go wrong.

2. ALL WE'VE GOT TIME FOR

I should have realized it would be a significant day when Fiona held the razor at my wrists.

'Is it OK if I shave your hands?'

'What?'

My perplexed face was reflected in the mirror ringed with bulbs, an intended touch of Vegas which had failed because Television Centre is located between railway tracks and used-car lots in west London.

'Why do you want to shave my hands?'

'It's their latest thing,' said Fiona. 'We've had a circular.'

Fiona's make-up case opens, like a doctor's, into canti-levered trays. There are pots of powder in different shades of orange, an unnatural skin tone needed to counter the equally inhuman bleaching effect of studio lights on faces. She handed me a sheet of paper embossed with the three letters: BBC. An expensive team of outside consultants had recently redesigned the corporate logo. On my first contracts – in the 1980s – the letters had sloped slightly. Now they were straight. For nudging three letters upright, the consult-ants had taken home several zeros.

From: MD.BRO
To: Coordinator, BBC Cosmetic Resources

Recent feedback from focus groups is that many viewers – particularly ABC1 women in the 35–45 age groups, living in the South-East corridor – find excessive hairiness on the backs of the hands of male on-screen talent unsightly and off-putting. Therefore – with immediate effect for all programmes broadcast in or after Week 9 – the hands of all men presenters should be shaved to standard cuff-level. In the case of outside broadcasts in summer or from hot overseas locations – where short-sleeved shirts may be worn – consideration should also be given to the arms. Waxing may be offered as an alternative to shaving. The names of any talent refusing to comply should be passed in the first instance by cosmetics operatives to their Coordinator, who should collate them for the Deputy MD.BRO in this Directorate. I thank you for your cooperation in serving our customers in this way.

For two decades, the BBC habit of identifying officials by initials had seemed like dinosaur corporatism. Now, suddenly, these middle-aged men addressing each other as MD.BRO or DD.RAD had the modish ring of gangsta rappers. But even by the standards of the bad ideas they were famous for, this wanker's bikini wax was absurd.

'I think we'll tell MD.BRO where to go, Fiona. Has anyone let you shave them yet?'

'Well, Cornelius Raven was really keen. But more for the sensation than anything else, I think. His whole body's like a baby's bum. Thankfully Craig McCrae was as rude as you about the idea. I mean, the girls here call him the missing link. The floor would have looked like the grooming room at Crufts by the time we'd finished. And the sports boys, I mean, they've hardly come to terms with mascara yet.'

Fiona shifted her electric razor to the less controversial territory – at least for her – of my face.

'Tried to kill yourself again, Richard?' she asked.

'What?'

'Your chin's all cuts again. Four, five years I've been doing you, is it?'

'Seven . . .'

'God, it just goes, doesn't it? And it's as if somehow you've just forgotten how to shave.'

'I know, I know. I was never very good at it, actually. I had a beard until I was thirty-two. But they have this thing against facial hair in television.' I stroked my hands. 'In fact, they now seem to be hostile to any bodily fluff at all.' I thought of joking about it being pubes next but, though I guessed that Fiona knew me well enough, if you said anything even slightly sexual at work these days, you could be ringing your solicitor from a desk at home.

'I always think that men with beards have something to hide,' said Fiona.

It was impossible to tell her the truth: that the more I came to hate my face, the worse my shaving was. The first sign had been a stubbly under-chin, the result of nerves about my rounding jowls. Then, unable to tolerate my mirrored image in the unforgiving morning strip-light, I had begun to shave while sitting in the bath, relying for guidance on the flattering reflection from the tiles, Vaselined with steam. I judged the success of my efforts from the blood in the water. That morning, the bathroom had resembled the death of Marat. (On television or radio, I would have thought Marat but said the shower scene in *Psycho*. Broadcasters learn to adjust their references to what they have been told is the audience's level of intelligence.)

Even after submitting to cosmetics at least once a week for a decade, make-up still feels strange. A lurking terror of effeminacy cancels out my liking of disguise. The nasal strips are the strangest. An adhesive bandage is stuck across the middle of my face, creating the appearance of a boxer leaving hospital. When the material is peeled away, the dirt has been drawn out of the pores in stalks so that it looks like hedgehog skin.

Now Fiona began to press the orange powder across the scars from my blind shaving. Then I felt the patting on my scalp. While powdering my bald spot – a process which dismayingly took longer each week – Fiona usually began a conversation to distract from the embarrassing intimacy of the action. It's probably the same at the end when the home help is lifting you on and off the commode. And, in that case too, you'll talk about what's on TV.

'Who have we got tonight?' asked Fiona.

'A film star and an archbishop for starters,' I replied, a deliberate feed-line which she fielded.

'If there are no jokes in that, you should go home. Who's the actress?'

'Alice Jackett.'

'Oh. I liked her as Shakespeare's wife. Do you think she'll bring her Oscar? And which bish?'

'The biggest. Canterbury.'

'Ooh, you'll have to be careful not to swear tonight when you screw up Autocue.' She must have felt my flinch under her improving hands. 'Not that you usually do.'

'And a rock star,' I added, now seeking double diversion from the attention to my hairline and the damage to my ego.

'Oooh. Who's that?'

'Marty Stark.'

'I bet I don't do him,' predicted Fiona. 'He'll bring someone of his own to do his hair at least. The last few years he's been spreading it as thinly as butter in a wartime boarding house.'

I laughed, but not without thinking of the jokes about

my own lost crown she would tell other sitters in her trans-
forming chair.

*

Face and tonsure orange, I always go back to the dressing
room after make-up, to check over my notes on the guests.

At Television Centre, the dressing rooms resemble the
kind of cell you might get if sentenced to an open prison for
embezzlement: desk, penitentially plain chair, rug, narrow
mauve sofa-bed, wardrobe and a cramped toilet and shower
cubicle through a door in the corner. A worn brown towel
shrouds a rattling radiator. And – above the desk – there's a
mirror, which is losing its looks, rashed with coppery spots.

From my briefcase, I took a sheet of brown wrapping
paper and a roll of Sellotape. This masking started when I
was a newspaper reporter, typing (as it then was) on assign-
ment in hotels. The sort of room you got on Fleet Street (as
it then was) expenses usually had a mirror screwed to the
wall above the bump-knee desk.

I have known only two writers in my life – one a war
correspondent, the other a poet – vain and pretty enough to
be able to stand the unvarying sight of their own face during
the long hours of composition. Most of the rest of us, staring
at the hotel mirror, would get nothing written except a staccato suicide note.

As deadlines approached, I could be found searching
stationery shops in Washington, Delhi, Bilbao and Berlin
for wrapping paper and tape. Soon it became as fixed a
part of my travelling kit as toothpaste, short-wave radio
and strong mints. Occasionally, a maid would look strangely
at the parcelled glass. They seemed to assume it was something sexual, although the only erotic use of mirrors I know
demands them naked.

The gift-wrapping of mirrors dates from before I started shaving in the bath but both are elements in the same defence. As long as I avoid the monitors in the studio, I can go a whole day – even one on which I appear on television – without seeing my face, although it is sometimes necessary to glance away from highly polished doors or tables and shop windows.

Most of us flinch when we hear our own voice recorded – on answering machines, most often these days – or see our bodies moving – usually in home videos now. Our sense of the sound and pictures we transmit is a flattering fantasy. These civilian humiliations are multiplied for broadcasters.

The repeat-record facility is set on my study video for every Friday of the run. You have to try to watch yourself. Looking at a camera for long periods is so unnatural that defensive flinches develop. Peter Pennington – my main rival on the other side – began last Christmas to jerk his head to the left at the end of sentences. Soon a critic will point out the tic and he'll become stiff and self-conscious on screen.

I picked up a nervous blink during series two, and an involuntary wrinkling of the nose to celebrate the hundredth edition. I force myself to watch every twentieth show, registering the image, then glancing away, like a liberal watching a snuff video. When my wife finds me watching myself, she calls it vanity, but my self-inspections are the damage limitation of a desperate man.

Having turned the dressing-room mirror into an improbably thin, flat package, I plugged my laptop into the telephone. A notice warned that – in the BBC's latest cost-saving measure – it was barred to international calls. I was about to open my electronic letter box when I heard the signature tune of *Fleming Faces*, not the vast brassy sound to be played in the studio in thirty minutes but the thin trilling of the version in the memory of my mobile. My producer, Lucy, programmed it in as a joke once and I've never been able to change it. I have to tell people it's ironic.

The caller read-out, which I have in case a fan or worse than that pulls my numbers from some Internet celeb site, showed a Docklands code.

'Yeh,' I said, a short enough response to be able to deny my identity if I have to.

Voices you don't recognize are usually a newspaper doing a ring-round. When and where in your life were you happiest? Do you believe in God? Which film star would you most like to fuck? (Primary school, sometimes and Alice Jackett are my answers, incidentally.) It's the celebrity equivalent of double-glazing sales.

'Gordon Bannoch.' The caller gives his name. '*Daily News*.'

The voice was cigarettes and menace combined with a Scottish elongation which made the first name Gurr-ud-un. I knew who Bannoch was. If you had a name which even a few strangers might recognize, he arrived at your door shortly before your wife's divorce lawyer or the fraud squad.

It was two weeks since he had broken the story that Peter Pennington – two years into his third marriage – had given cunnilingus (well, 'a disgusting sex act', the paper called it, with coy misogyny) to a fifteen-year-old fan while wearing her briefs. These were liberal times and the view in the industry was that, if he had waited another year and restricted himself to his own knickers, he could have screamed invasion of privacy. But Pennington had lost his advertising contracts, and a lucrative set of audio-book readings of Beatrix Potter had been withdrawn from sale.

When Bannoch rang, skeletons rattled. But I was sure enough that mine were secure.

'I know your stuff,' I said as coolly as if we were meeting at a seminar on the contemporary press.

'I know you're stuffed,' Bannoch rasped.

'What?'

'How's Charlie?'

'Who?'

'Your mate Charlie. Don't be sniffy with me.'

'Look, Mr Bannoch' – in media etiquette, the titles of polite address are now used almost purely for rudeness – 'I'm on air in twenty-five minutes.'

'In the air, I hear. High already. Are you denying that you use cocaine?'

'Of course I am.'

My relief emerged as a triumphal sigh. Wrongful imprisonment is a common fear, but false arrest a general fantasy. Proven innocence is dizzying.

I thought of making a joke about being able to run for American president but feared that Bannoch would use it as an excuse to sniff my sheets. Since the newspaper watchdogs had started yelping privacy – trying to give the princes in the glass tower an even slightly standard adolescence – the trick was to try to win from celebrities some home-is-my-lodestone quote and then monster them for hypocrisy.

'Ricky' – a diminutive no one had used except a college girlfriend who gave cutesy names to her car and pencil case as well – 'let me level with you. Since the Junkie Bunny business' – the actor playing Rabbie Rabbit in the pre-school TV hit *The Fun Buns* had recently been exposed by Bannoch as a coke dealer – 'we're doing an investigation into just how much snow business there is in show business.'

It amused me that Bannoch spoke in tabloid prose. Perhaps it was like the way in which, if you're chatting to someone with a strong accent, you inadvertently imitate them. I was having to concentrate on not going Caledonian.

'So you're doing a random ring-round of television asking people how their septum is?' I asked, as Englishly as possible.

'Not random, no. And you seem very up on the parts of the nose, Ricky. That wouldn't be from conversations with a doctor?'

'Oh, for fuck's sake. And what do you mean by not random?'

'The gossip in the world of the box is that you head for the heads, as it were, at every chance. You frequent the Gents at a level which could only be accounted for by rent boys or dysentery. And I can't vouch for your stomach, but I've checked out the other and you seem to be entirely vaginal. And one of those only, as far as we know.'

Even when the tree they're barking up is the wrong one, it's a shock to find the tabloids in your garden. I was appalled at the thought they had been investigating me.

'I'm now – very politely and reasonably – going to put the phone down,' I said. Although you didn't put a mobile down, the phrase would remain in the language for another generation or so. Hanging up – from when the instruments were vertical – still survived. And Bannoch would tell his readers that I slammed my phone down. Tabloid journalism is about choosing the verbs which sound worst.

'Ricky,' he wheedled, 'you used to be a journalist. I read your stuff. Few too many long words but there was ink in your blood. What about turning Queen's evidence? And let me tell you what a relief it is to use the word queen without prejudice in one of these calls . . .'

I stayed on the line only to find out if he was really offering the bribe I thought he was.

'What?'

'I'll offer you a deal. We accept you're clean, but you no more want your children – well, stepchildren in your case' – I thought of Bannoch's sweaty, yellowed fingers grubbing their way along my lines in *Who's Who* – 'growing up with a needle in their arm than I do. So you join our crusade against drugs. You slip us the names of the famous presenters who sniff when it isn't winter and we run one of those The Water He Walks On-type profiles when you've got a series or a book out. How does that sound?'

'I am putting the phone down,' I said, in fact pressing the little red picture of an old-fashioned telephone which, on my mobile, kills calls.

Television Centre is built in a circle. In the innocent, hopeful early days of the medium, the staff called it a doughnut. In recent times – as hope and finance have drained away – tourniquet seems more appropriate. The dressing rooms are arranged around the ground-level ring. As they wait to be admitted, studio audiences queue around that lowest level. There's only one slit window at the top of the wall – another similarity with prisons – so they can't see you. But, as presenters wait to be led under the lights, we listen to the anticipatory babble. Sometimes you hear your name – in general, the women seem to call me 'Richard', the men 'Fleming' – though thankfully not details. I always draw the short brown hessian curtain because they feel so close.

The virtual postman had only one letter for me that evening.

From: lucy.brooks@bbc.co.uk
To: rgfleming@newtalk.com
Subject: Luck
Time: Friday 19:48:41

It's going to be a wonderful show tonight. Again. I will be

whispering sour nothings in your ear soon but see you in
the Green Room afterwards to celebrate another ratings
triumph.

Good Luck. Lots of love, L XXX

I had seen Lucy forty-five minutes earlier at rehearsal.
She would be speaking in my ear in another fifteen. But this
was a ritual. On the night of the pilot show for *Fleming
Faces* – when I had to keep my hands in my pockets all
afternoon so that the crew wouldn't see them shaking – I
tried to distract myself in the dressing room with e-mail – six
attempts to enter the password (S-O-P-H-I-E) with skittering
fingers – and found a message from Lucy.

I scarcely knew her then. I scarcely know her now. It's
fair enough – linguistically at least – that people call us
'luvvies'. We bring the vocabulary of romance to a business.
When the series was commissioned, I jokily insisted that
these messages should be our high-tech lucky heather, and
she had sent the same greeting now on 211 Friday evenings.
We prefer to think of our show as journalism but all television, finally, is showbiz.

The mobile played its post-Schoenberg version of my sig
tune again. I briefly panicked that it was Bannoch with new
ammunition or innuendo, but this number was a cell-phone,
which I recognized as belonging to Tom Ogg, the BBC's
Managing Director of Broadcasting, or, in his bureacratic
gangsta tag, MD.BRO.

'Richard, it's Tom Ogg. How's tonight shaping up?'

'Tune in and you'll find out what the archbishop said to
the actress.'

'That's good. I hope that line's in your script.'

I waited. Ogg never rang you with neutral news, only
good or bad: buy-a-car or sell-your-house.

'Richard, this is probably nothing. But you were down point eight last Friday.'

'Is that bad?'

'We're viewing it as turbulence. Nobody here sees it as freefall. Everyone was down right across terrestrial. Not as low as you, but down. So you still did a twenty-one share in your slot, even with point eight slippage. But you'd been twenty-two the week before. Tentatively, Richard, we think it's seasonal. Research have checked with the Met Office and it was the warmest Friday in February for forty-seven years. We think people went out, a helluva lot of people just *went out*.'

Nobody in television really understands why anyone watches at all. So when viewers are suddenly missing, executives set out, like the good shepherd, to try to bring them back. When guys like Ogg came into the business, there were three channels available in Britain. Now there are hundreds. But we apparently needed weather charts to explain the absentees. I suddenly resented the pressure.

'Are you sure that's right, Tom? Shouldn't you cross-reference the meteorological reports with data from the leisure industry? Were restaurant takings up last Friday? Did cinema box offices show a rise? If so, does the increase add up to the 800,000 people who didn't want to watch me last week? Shouldn't you check the national incidence of stiff dicks and wet pussies against the seasonal norm? Perhaps a lot of people just went to bed early for a fuck.'

Having been with Ogg at Oxford, I could be cheekier than our places in the food chain would usually decree. But I knew that he would be thinking of Peter Finch in *Network*. Every television executive dreads the moment when the presenter goes demented. Live broadcasting is about appearing normal under disturbing circumstances and everyone's fear is that the illusion will break down.

'I know that the talent is uneasy about audience research,' said Ogg, 'but if your local supermarket didn't ask its customers questions, you'd soon be buying your ciabatta somewhere else.'

'I don't think of broadcasting as a bakery, Tom.'

'Maybe that's your problem, Richard. You should regard the BBC less as a temple of culture and more as a media megastore. I understand that presenters get defensive. But you've nothing to worry about. Your latest focus group findings are . . . but I'm trying to give up the word "sensational" for Lent.'

'Tom, I don't . . .'

'Eighty-seven per cent of the sample, Richard, would like you as a friend. Three-quarters of those asked would rather that you moved in next door to them than Peter Pennington, Richard Rennie or Agnes Kerr.'

'Tom, when we met, you were going to make documentaries that changed the world. Now you're playing hypothetical estate agent to people from Wolverhampton with nothing better to do in the afternoons.'

'Richard, in broadcasting, statistics are the new intuition. Let me just quote you this from the sub-sixteen data. Seventy-six per cent of sub-sixteen viewers questioned would be very pleased or quite pleased if it turned out that you were really their natural father.'

'Jesus Christ, who does the questions?'

'Be against focus groups if you like, Richard, but this one wanted to have your babies. If this was the New Hampshire primary, your opponents would be taking cyanide pills. Just listen to this stuff. Asked to choose adjectives to describe you from a pool of a hundred words, almost eighty per cent of the sample ringed "friendly" and "eloquent". Friendly and eloquent, Richard!'

'Fuck off and die, you little piece of shit.'

This was a joke: a perfect chat-show bounce-back in everything except the language. But the spluttering it prompted was electronic, not human. Ogg, who had been using mobile phones since the days when it took two hands to carry them, had obviously entered a tunnel. I waited.

'Hello? Hello? Sorry. Marylebone underpass. I'm being driven back from the Joanna Fitch private view.'

Ogg was famous for not so much dropping names as building them into towers, like a child with plastic bricks. Joanna Fitch had done me for the National Portrait Gallery. I had gambled that, with my face, I was safer with an abstract expressionist. One of my chins might be taken as modernism.

'It was a joke,' I explained.

'What? . . . Hello, hello . . . You're breaking up,' he battled through static.

' "Fuck off and die, you little piece of shit",' I quoted myself as perfect clarity returned.

'Yes, well, I understand it's not nice to be measured against ratings every week like the smallest kid in the family against the door. Look, I've seen the hold-the-nose moment happen – that week when viewers suddenly think "This one's turned" – and that's not what's happening here. Still, I think it would be good to do something share-positive.'

'Is that a medical condition?'

'What? . . . Second left, no this one, *this one* . . . Sorry, is there anyone you'd really like as a guest?'

'Anthony Stubbs is interesting.'

'Remind me.'

Those two words are the favourite media device for concealing ignorance.

'He's Chief Secretary to the Treasury, but a decent bet for next-but-one PM.'

'Look, Richard, on your radio show maybe – I held you up at a conference the other day as a wholly successful example of bimediality – but that's not gonna be share-positive at twenty-two hundred Friday.' Ogg had been born in Yorkshire but, like all British television executives now, spoke a London dialect of American. 'I'm kinda thinking Lindsay Lennox.'

A talk-show guest I'd only want on an *electric* chair. A blonde movie star – ditzy single moms her speciality – who was reputed to drink her own piss every morning and to have jerked off President Riley into her stiletto under the top-tablecloth at a White House dinner for the Emir of Bahrain. But her people would slap a pre-nuptial on us, preventing any mention of the President. All I'd get was how her latest movie was, like, a fascinating challenge. It was bad enough having Alice Jackett tonight, but at least the researcher reported she'd spoken coherent sentences.

'How fruitful, finally, are actresses, Tom?'

'Well, people switch on televisions to see them, which is rather the point. And I've heard the new movie's interesting.'

Christ. In the media glossary, 'interesting' means, with regard to mainstream work, terrible but profitable; in an art-house context, tedious and unseen. With Lindsay Lennox, it would be the first definition. The word also has a third interpretation. Spoken to a senior about an idea of theirs, it means that nothing will be done.

'That's an interesting thought, Tom.'

An electronic coughing fit again. 'This is always a bad reception area. I'll call you tom—'

Ogg was gone. Through the slit window, the sound of my waiting spectators rose in a pitch of excitement and then drained away. They were being shepherded towards the terraces of plastic seats. My watch told me that in fifteen minutes our eyes would meet. I picked up from the desk a manila envelope enclosing ten smaller ones of different shapes and colours. A compliment slip from the Correspondence Unit fell out. This was the week's post from viewers.

The letters had been opened. Everything sent to a presenter is checked. The theory is that you see nothing too threatening or begging but, judging from what I got, I suspected that the mail room was staffed by members of the Peter Pennington fan club.

In this batch, for example, were two letters accusing me of being a smug, fat bastard who waved his arms around too much, and two seeking telephone numbers for guests (the comedian Cornelius Raven, the crime writer Dame Felicity Hatch) who had recently been on the show. These – in solidarity with ex-directory celebs – I balled together with the loathe-notes and dropped in the plastic bin.

There were three requests from charities: cardiac, cancer, stillbirth. Since the death of the Princess two years before, Britain's guilt organizations faced a figurehead famine. There was also a list of ninety-three paragraph-length questions from a student in Coventry writing a thesis on the rise of tabloid television in Britain. The covering note failed to make clear if I was being subpoenaed for defence or prosecution.

If I want to reply, I write a number on the letter from 1 to 5. My PA has template letters in her computer. The Midlands undergraduate, for example, would receive Standard Answer 5. ('Richard Fleming regrets that his schedule does not allow him to give lengthy written answers to correspondence. However, I enclose a copy of his 1998 Royal Television

Society lecture, "Poppy But Not Pappy", from which you are welcome to quote.')

I put the three pleas from charities on the table, shut my eyes and shuffled them, playing a kind of Compassion Patience. Stillbirth would receive a 3 ('Richard Fleming is happy to become a patron . . .'), while cancer and cardiac were graded 4 ('Richard Fleming is reluctant to become merely a name on a letterhead and therefore, given the several charities to which he is already committed . . .')

The ninth letter was from a private address but neatly typed and therefore unlikely to be abusive. It's odd. A sensible lunatic these days would use computers. The surge in word-processing has made it virtually impossible for police to trace an anonymous letter. But hatred and envy still seem to favour ink. Or perhaps hostile correspondents like to tighten their fingers around the neck of a pen.

As I said at the beginning, the nutters really do use coloured ink; frequently, indeed, green. I suppose it's a sign of a mind which rejects the conventions: the communicational equivalent of odd or brightly coloured socks and clashing ties. Another clue, I find, is that the letter O is often scored right through the paper – where the writer has pressed down hard with the pen – like a bullet-hole.

But this letter passed every weirdo screening. It was computerized and signed, and no columns of light streamed through the creamy paper.

Dear Mr Fleming,

I thought you did really well with Lord Haydon of Hitchin. I hate his books and films too! And why can't he shut up about how much money he's got? You got much more out of him than Peter Pennington on Channel 4 last month. You're a 'celebrity' but you're also 'normal'! Now, can I ask you something? I think you must know – because there was something on your radio show, which I also always enjoy! – about events at Plasco in Solihull. A light engineering company bought by one of those Seattle nerd-firms because we had one patent which might make mobile phones quicker or lighter or both. But they wanted the part not the staff! Five hundred people – as you accurately reported on your 'show' – 'let go'. And guess whose name was on the list.

That was a year ago. But, as you probably know, Lucas Quinney doesn't wake up every morning at Quinney Com in Seattle shouting, 'Bring me forty-four-year-old accountants from the English Midlands!' I've missed six payments at the Nationwide now and, although my 'loan agreement' allows a 'holiday', I'm about to 'trade down' to a 'smaller property'. I was just writing to ask you – as someone who took an interest in what happened at Plasco – if there was any chance at all that there might be an opening in the 'media' world. I would be useful as a researcher (accountants are pretty good at poring over dry documents!). I wouldn't, of course, expect a busy man like yourself to deal with this personally but perhaps you could nudge it in the direction of the powers that be at the BBC!

My contact details are on the attached sheet.

Yours in admiration and gratitude,

Matthew Pardon

I would normally have written a 2 on the letter without hesitation. ('Richard Fleming is an employee of the BBC and, though it may surprise you and has occasionally surprised him, has no power to hire staff.') It was my belief – kept deeply secret in an all-the-same age – that people who worked in television were special: how would a Brummie number-cruncher get in? Also – while he had not used a coloured pen and no O was hollowed – Matthew Pardon displayed two of the traits I associated if not with mad writing then with bad writing: superfluous quotation and exclamation marks.

The child of two English teachers at what were still then called grammar schools in Bolton, I have always been a language queen. (Note in that sentence the careful avoidance of a dangling participle, the 'child' of the sub-clause qualifying the 'I' of the main sentence. Participles now dangle all over the press. 'Dreary, repetitive and well past the sell-by date, I switched off the new series of *Fleming Faces*,' wrote a television critic recently. My only sadness being that just a few pedantic over-forties would even realize that he had skewered himself.) For me, noticing English is like laying flowers on my parents' graves.

And yet against this should be balanced the fact that Mr Pardon had spelled 'poring' correctly, which is practically unread of now. I was also drawn to what he was called. You had to feel sympathy for a man who had endured decades of hotel receptionists, bank clerks and *maître d*'s repeating, 'What name was it?' in a slightly louder voice.

And there was another factor. I disliked hearing of careers ending, even in quite different fields. It was part of my defence against the depressions of middle age to believe that people of reasonable diligence, once established in a job, survived until retirement.

Once – on Shepherd's Bush Green – I walked past Tony Andrews. If you're under forty, you won't remember Tony, but when I was growing up in the 1960s, he was the star reporter on *Britain After Six*, the show that followed the *Six O'Clock News* in the days when the hard stuff and the soft stuff were on different programmes. Tony was the mad-for-it one who did the sky-diving and talking-dog items.

He was promoted to his own chat show: Friday nights, this country's first go at a Carson or Cavett. We'd only ever seen photographs of most of the American stars and here they were on a padded chair in London. Tony used his power to win a spin-off series, fronting a studio shout show on the 'controversial issues of the day', based on some late-night beer-spiller he'd seen on holiday in LA. They commissioned six but shelved it after four when he asked a Catholic priest – live on air – if he wanked. Now, of course, they'd give you an award.

A decade after his fall, I was driving one day when the radio jumped to a Midlands local station on which Tony was fronting a hits-for-wrinklies show. His voice had a hangover croak. Then, about a year ago, I saw him weaving through the needles and condoms on the Green. You had to look twice to recognize, under the two-week stubble and ruddied cheeks, the face that did those pop-eyed double-takes on cutaways. It was eleven a.m. He had two supermarket bags. Their weight made him stoop. As he trudged away, I heard the lush's percussion from the bottles.

I imagined Matthew Pardon one day passing me with my shoulder-straining cargo of Special Offer Own-Brand bourbon. But I was the oldest person who worked on any of my shows. Did he really think there was work in the media for a middle-aged accountant kicked out by the plastics industry?

As I waited in Dressing Room 1 to host the series named after me, I hesitated. I was so nearly nice to him. But then, just beside the neatly printed [1] of Matthew Pardon's page-numbering, I added a handwritten 2. 'Richard Fleming is an employee of the BBC and, though it may surprise you and has occasionally surprised him . . .'

The tenth and final envelope in my post seemed to be empty. But, from previous experience, and with a trepidation caused by those occasions, I squeezed it between my hands. The fish-mouth I made spat out a thin slip of paper.

> This letter has been passed to the BBC Security Unit, who will be in touch if further action is considered necessary.

Another death threat, then. My third in ten years. It was typical of the BBC's rigid systems that, even when they held back a threatening letter, they sent the useless casing stationery to the recipient. Some sixth-floor shit-head must have found a clause in the Postal Communications Act about ownership of receptacles and sent a memo. But, for presenters, being sent an empty envelope was like coming home to find the face of a Derby winner dripping blood down your pillow. I checked the postmark. My most prob-lematic correspondent of the past had come from Leicester. This envelope had been posted in Exeter.

Next I spent the usual pre-show ten minutes in the cramped lavatory. But – as I have not yet finally decided whether this memoir will have other readers – that door stays closed.

As I was swilling out my mouth with water – there have been presenters on live TV whose lips literally stuck together: we call it studio stroke – there was a knock on the dressing-room door. I assumed it would be the assistant floor manager with the shuddery injunction, 'Five minutes!' But I found a big man looking uneasy in a shiny blue suit, as if he were used to uniform.

'Mr Fleming? Gerry Armstrong, director of security. Do you have a minute?'

'Well, literally that. We're about to go on,' I said, popping a strong mint in my mouth.

'I won't detain you, as the New Labour prime minister said to the IRA terrorist.'

The security men tended to be ex-coppers or old soldiers. Armstrong, I guessed from that gag and his military build, had served in Belfast. It's a drawback of show business that all employees feel they have to be comedians.

Armstrong closed the door. He scanned the tiny room, a reflex professional gesture surely, as even an untrained eye could tell we were alone. He nodded when he saw the brown paper.

'Ah. You've been on the war correspondents' course, sir?'

'No. Why?'

'Draw the curtains and insulate the mirror. Flying glass . . .'

'No. I just don't like seeing my face.'

'You're in the wrong job then, aren't you?' Yes. Probably yes. 'Now, you may be aware, sir, that you have a couple of people out there. From the letters—'

'Well, strictly the envelopes . . .'

'What? Yeah, well, we see the letters, of course. There's a new one, sir. The thing is – well, two things actually – they normally start off friendly and then turn nasty when they realize you won't be coming round for Christmas. Now this one started nasty. And – which is the other thing – it's normally about once a week to start with. And this is every day. Have you ever had trouble before?'

'There was a woman from Leicester early on, claimed her periods had stopped while watching me. She had this obsessive thing about wanting to be married to me. Which almost certainly was a sign of madness, because the women who have been my wives have usually soon wished they weren't.'

Armstrong showed louder delight in my wit than anyone since my kids. Five hundred of him in the studio audience every week and Lucy wouldn't have to cheat the soundtrack in post-prod.

'She used to write to me as Mrs Fleming, which she could also of course have been called, except that the police discovered she wasn't. She'd tell me what she was cooking for my dinner and where she'd booked for our holidays.'

'How did it turn out?'

'She got this thing that my wife – my second wife – was an impostor and used to ring up and abuse her. Then the calls just stopped.'

In fact, the truth about that house – as it has turned out – is that Mr Fleming is pretending to be a husband.

'Can I see the letters?' I asked Armstrong.

'Legally, sir, you could of course. They're your property. And you'll get them back afterwards.' After what? I had a morbid vision of the bundled papers being handed over to Rachel in a leftover packing box from the BBC shop. 'I wouldn't recommend it, though. You'd be looking over your shoulder all the time. And that's *my* job.'

And now Armstrong made precisely the movement he had just described because the door was pushed open.

'Five minutes, Richard,' said the AFM.

I pointed to the door as it closed again.

'But if that had been them – or if it had been them instead of you at the door just now – what would I actually have done?'

'Oh. No nutters are going to get into the BBC, sir. Except the ones that have their own programmes.'

A self-satisfied smile at his own joke suggested that he had tried it out on other worried talent.

'But I have a studio audience. Most of the other shows here have one. You'd have to be mad almost by definition to spend a Friday evening queuing in the cold to see a programme. So how would you stop them?'

Armstrong's obvious unease at my slightly aggressive tone – he raised his arms slightly in front of him – prompted doubts about his effectiveness if faced with a homicidal viewer.

'I wasn't meaning to frighten you, sir. I just wanted to get a few things straight. Is your home address in reference books?'

'No.' Although the reason had been fear of tabloid attention rather than assassination.

'Where is it you live, sir?'

'Perhaps I'd better not tell you, had I?'

A lift of the shoulders and flash of the eyes suggested that, in his army days, Armstrong would have responded, 'Don't get smart with me, sonny.' But, in their new lives in the private sector, these cops and soldiers found themselves in the odd position of having to be deferential to the public. Armstrong rather jerkily smirked.

'Holland Park,' I admitted.

'And how do you get here?'

'I sometimes walk across the Green in the summer.' Tony Andrews with his supermarket bags of celebrity anaesthetic. 'Otherwise I drive up and park in the horseshoe.'

In fact, I drove the mere mile most days. The stares had become too much. I was as frightened of those who might like me as of those who might not.

'From now on, you'd be smart to stick to the car. Maybe alternate the Westway and the Green. Even up round Acton

some days. And don't always use the main gate. Ring exten-
sion double six double six before you come in. There are a
couple of routes we use to get the management in without
the staff seeing them.'

I noticed that Armstrong was holding a large red album,
which triggered my habitual resentment about not yet having
been featured on *This Is Your Life*. Unless this was part of
the pounce . . .

'What's that book?'

'Oh, a lot of the presenters get them. We reckon it's
harmless enough.'

He showed me a cheap family photo album, filled with
sheets of plastic pockets spaced four to a page. When Armstrong flipped it open in the middle, I saw eight frozen images
of myself on colour Polaroids. It was not my daily face but
my television one: cosmetic tan, sprayed thatch, sparkle
eyes. The open mouth on every portrait made you think of
Munch. My lips were similarly parted now as I looked
questioningly at Armstrong.

'It's a couple in Dalston. Brother and sister. Never
married. They watch the telly with a camera, shooting the
presenters they like.' We both flinched at his verb. 'As it
were. Then they send them in.'

'Like a dog laying a dead bird on your step.'

'Well, I don't know about that, sir. I suppose it's more
like taking holiday snaps of your friends.'

*

For the two hundred and eleventh time, I hear the warm-up
man – one of the few cockney comedians who never quite
got his own series – deliver the traditional final pre-show
joke: the one about being careful of the cameras if you're
there with anyone you shouldn't be.

As I'm led to the studio – Barry, the assistant floor manager, clearing the corridor with 'Live man walking!', his usual Death Row joke – I pass the banks of screens showing what is going out at that moment. 'Please don't go away,' begged a continuity announcer as a sitcom ended and a game show approached. As we worried increasingly about losing viewers not just to other programmes but to rival screens – computer, video-game – these pleas sounded ever more desperate. *Please don't go away*: the silent prayer of every broadcaster to their audience and fame.

We use the term 'live' very loosely in broadcasting. There's live-live, where the programme is actually transmitted as it happens, and as-live, where it's recorded but only stops in emergencies. My radio show was live-live, my television series as-live.

These distinctions matter greatly to presenters. 'He can't do *live*,' we'll sneer, subdividing courage like stuntmen. But, like the shoppers in the margarine commercials, the public can rarely tell what we're selling. No one ever seems to know if a programme is actuality or edited. Friends invite me to meetings at the time I'm on the radio, convinced we tape them in batches like morning loaves. But others have squealed if I've phoned them on a Friday night while I'm also talking from the corner of their room.

Some of this confusion results from the deliberate vagueness of presenters about what's taped. It's vanity and machismo. We like to play up this commando side of art.

In the studio, we're about to go live. OK, as-live. While the warm-up man signs off by telling them what a great guy I am – 'your friend and mine', twice a lie – the lights over the dutifully amused audience dip. They will be looking now at a stage with two black leather chairs arranged in front of high wooden screens painted with the faces – or rather their eyes, jowls and noses in swirls of primary colour – of the famous who have sat stage right during six previous series. Centre-stage stands one of those low-rent Picassos of myself.

I'm behind that hardboard flat. The audience can't see me but I can look down the steps which I'll descend in a few minutes' time. If I squint behind my contact lenses – dating from a 1997 focus group which expressed reservations about presenters wearing spectacles – I can see my camera – Camera 2 – which will follow me all evening: like a detective or a stalker, depending on whether you're an optimist or a pessimist. Even when Lucy chooses shots of the guests – most of the time, I hope – Camera 2 will be watching me. On the Autocue, my opening word hovers in green. A message from ET, I always think:

HELLO

I learned to read Autocue from Dr Seuss. You may envisage from this name some veteran mittel-European voice coach borrowed from the theatre, but I do mean the children's author. During my first guest spots on television – *What the Papers Say*, *Pebble Mill* – I had the beginner's passport-photo pop-eye, frightened to look away from the rolling prose in case I lost the place. Then one night – reading the speedy nonsense of Dr Seuss to Isabelle and Sophie – I turned these rare moments with my children into Autocue tuition.

The challenge was to turn at random to a tongue-twisting page and speak it without stumbling:

> WHEN BEETLES BATTLE BEETLES
> IN A PUDDLE PADDLE BATTLE
> AND THE BEETLE BATTLE PUDDLE
> IS A PUDDLE IN A BOTTLE . . .

Forcing the eye to see the tiny differences between these sound-alike nouns, you sometimes got the lines which seemed to signal the mind's resistance to this artificial task, the silent prayer of the presenter:

> PLEASE, SIR. I DON'T
> LIKE THIS TRICK, SIR.
> MY TONGUE ISN'T
> QUICK OR SLICK, SIR.

One Saturday night, I completed *Fox in Socks* – the Grand Prix track among Seuss's rhyme schemes – without a single accidental transposition. Isabelle and Sophie were restless and unimpressed and mystified by my high spirits on the final line. It was one of the last times I read to them.

The two sound guys walk towards me and I do my Jesus thing, stretching out my arms wide as if they were my disciples rather than people who resent the fact that I'm treated as special. As I stand like Christ over Rio, one techie drops a small black oblong box into my right trouser pocket, loops a thin length of wire up my back and over my shoulder and presses a springy plastic mould of my aural canals into my right ear.

Our earpieces are made from a wax model by a Harley Street hearing doctor. It's strange in the waiting room when you go for the mould: a few people in their sixties and seventies looking worried, thinking their life is more or less over, and a couple of thirty- or forty-year-olds looking smug, thinking that they're finally getting to where they wanted to be. The conversations involve replying to a shouted, 'Haven't I seen you somewhere?' with a spoken and then yelled, 'Perhaps.'

As my deaf-aid goes in, the second techie is threading a wire through the lowest front button of my shirt, pulling it out again around the breastbone, where he clips a small microphone to my tie. Then he screws the lower end of that wire into a metal box like a cigarette case, which he drops into my other pocket. As he finishes, his colleague at my ear is hiding the tubing behind a wing of hair.

During these moments of helplessness, I feel like an astronaut or racing driver, dressed by expert hands, or a monarch or Pope, robed by servants to glorify my importance.

Now Toby – my dresser, the old theatrical term still surviving in this high-tech world – approaches from behind holding my freshly pressed suit jacket. I lower my arms from Messiah position to plane taking off and he slides the coat on, smoothing down the dark blue cloth. King-like until now, I bow down in serfdom as Fiona comes towards me with her powder puff, allowing her to reinforce the cover on my peeping scalp.

'*I can see his worm*,' says a voice in my ear. It's Lucy. One of the techies presses my deaf-aid further in. I can't see Lucy. She's sitting in the gallery high at the back of the studio, hunched over panels of switches and screens, like an air traffic control centre with no lives at stake and the staff paid twice as much.

'*Testing talk-back to Richard*,' she says.

'Bit louder,' I answer.

A sound man twists a button in my pocket.

'*Better?*' she says, more crisply.

I nod.

'Luce, did you ask Autocue to change millenn . . . millennium to Year 2000?'

'*It's done.*'

All broadcasters have trip-syllables, letters or combinations of them in which the tongue suddenly betrays the tension of the effort to seem calm, like the twitching eye of a shellshock victim. My misfortune – for a broadcaster who came to prominence during the late 1990s – was that mine was 'millennium'.

For some reason of brain or tongue, the word always left my mouth as 'manyum' or 'mullunum'. Only by separating the syllables and over-stressing the first – '*mill*-any-um' – could I sometimes produce a sound which the listener might recognize. The problem with having this downfall-noun – apart from the fact that I had thirty TV shows and 220 radio programmes to host during 1999 – was that there was no recognized synonym apart from The Year 2000. I also struggle, for example, with 'visitors', but you can always make that callers, guests or tourists.

Through my earpiece, the production gallery can speak to me in two ways. For 'switch talkback' they click a button on and off, like children playing walkie-talkies. 'Open talkback' means that you can hear everything said in the gallery at all times. I have switch. I don't want to risk overhearing something rude about me.

Viewers now are used to the little flash of plastic from he presenter's head. No host gets letters lamenting the loss of hearing in one so young. But, when I first watched television, the presenter had a telephone on the desk. The producer rang through if there was anything to be said. There was a famous day when the ringing started and the newscaster – like people now lunging for their trilling mobiles in coats or bags – couldn't see the phone. Eventually he found it in a drawer.

'Give us some level, Rich,' asks one of the sound guys.

It would be better for my reputation in the industry if I knew their names, but all techies look the same to me. My rival Peter Pennington would not only know his Freds from his Teds but doubtless send out cards on their birthdays as well.

'What did you have for breakfast?' the anonymous technician follows up.

It's the traditional sound-check but nobody understands what a problematic question it is for me. I lift my chin, nervous about my breath – that the mints won't be enough – as they stand in close.

'This is the BBC from London,' I say in 1939 tones, my preferred test sentence for level.

'Bit more, Rich.'

'I have to tell you now that no such undertaking . . .'

'Happiness.'

One of the sound guys for some reason always expresses pleasure as a noun rather than an adjective. Flowers for my mum and dad.

'*Clear your throat a bit, Richard.*'

They've been saying that for months now. A couple of Sundays before, a TV critic referred to Richard Fleming bravely struggling with a winter cold. But soon it would be spring and my throat would still be raw.

When switch talkback is deactivated, you have in your ear not silence but a distant fizzing like tinnitus. Under it I listen for my pulse. Not bad. Unexpected sex or a penalty shoot-out can both create a faster rate. I concentrate on my breathing. Images of Isabelle and Sophie being born. Forget them. Think of something else. Live broadcasting offers oblivion of outside distress as reliably as alcohol. You don't get to choose what you think about.

'*Coming*,' says Lucy.

My stomach tightens and I want to fart. But my intestines feel liquid and I daren't risk it. Live television gets you in your heart and bowels, and the terror of the presenter is that one of them will give out on air.

The fizzing and pulsing in my ear are replaced by words again. The PA Helen now: 'Running opening titles in ten, nine, eight . . .'

The floor manager nudges me in the back. The band begins the full-scale version of the tune my mobile plays, based on a saxophone riff around the sounds 'R' and 'F' and composed by a musician so rich from inventing singing kettles for a kitchen commercial that he now lives in Tahiti. The AFM brings his hands together above his head – encouraging the audience to applaud – and I walk down the ramp towards the waiting chairs.

'*Good luck. Your intro's on 2, downstage centre.*'

My eyes find the Autocue, one or two large words to a line, like a reading primer.

HELLO
MY GUESTS
TONIGHT

The scrolling prose is matched to the speed of my speaking voice by a bored-looking, middle-aged woman tapping her foot on a pedal like a seamstress with a sewing machine. Sometimes she knits or does puzzle books during the interviews.

INCLUDE TWO
PERFORMERS
WHO HAVE BEEN
SEEN AT
DIFFERENT TIMES
AS SEX OBJECTS –

The best thing about Autocue, I often think during

rehearsal, is that whatever rubbish you write comes up looking like poetry. But there are two traps in reading the receding green lines: blinking and staring. The trick is to imagine a person on the other side of the glass, not an actual member of the audience but an idealized receiver, sitting across from you, to whom you telegraph your message with the facial changes of ordinary conversation.

AND A
CONTROVERSIAL
CHURCHMAN WHO
HAS BEEN ACCUSED
OF <u>OBJECTING</u>
TO <u>SEX</u> (TURN TO 5)

I swivelled left to find Camera 5. As television becomes jittery about holding the attention of viewers, it's unusual to be allowed to speak a whole sentence in the same position. The tension in my lips had made me say 'objetting' but it was not bad enough for the shame of a retake. I focused on the audience. Television was frightening enough without the fear of a stalker sitting among the ranks of breathing scenery. But this crowd felt easy, desperate for enjoyment.

With an Oscar-winner and a rock star on the show, there were two groupie whoops during the intro, even though I was telling them what they already knew. Alice Jackett was a young English actress who had won an Academy Award for her performance as Anne Hathaway in the movie *Mrs Shakespeare*. Martin Stark was singer-songwriter of the platinum-selling 1980s band Time of Death and his latest solo album, *In Your Head with You*, was number one.

BUT MY
<u>FIRST</u> GUEST
TONIGHT –

Was a rare example of a clergyman recognized even by millions of people who had never been to church. In his first two months as Archbishop of Canterbury, Dr Peter Stirling had forced the government to include prayers at the opening ceremony of the Dome it was building for the Year 2000. As a moral crusader, he was credited with turning the Church of England from 'don't know' to 'don't do'. He had warned that Britain was facing a 'marital Armageddon' in which the 'nuclear family' might become extinct. Ladies and gentlemen, would you please put your hands together – and not in prayer – for the Archbishop of Canterbury.

Grudging applause – the audience was mainly Stark and Jackett fans – overlapped with the band's jokey jamming of 'When the Saints'. When cartoonists drew Stirling, they emphasized his height, beakish nose and swept-back greying mane, so that he was usually depicted looming sternly over politicians, single mothers or, during his rise as the Church's defender of tradition, the short, round, grinning figure of his indecisive liberal predecessor.

Stirling gave me a wintry smile as he reached the paired chairs. His handshake tingled my fingers. I airily indicated that he should sit, with one of those gestures stretching back to the American grandaddies of the chat show in the 1950s. Lucy and I had decided I should start light.

'I feel I should ask you to say grace or something.' I smiled.

The line had worked superbly at rehearsal, with a nineteen-stone props man sitting in as the leader of the Anglican Communion. Big Dave had grinned and grandly blessed the camera crew. The actual Archbishop didn't.

'Well, thank you. I will,' he replied, unsmiling.

'I was just . . .'

I glanced at the Autocue, where prompts for questions had just clicked into place.

IS THERE A GOD?
IS SEX WRONG?
WHEN WILL
THE WORLD END?

'No, this interests me,' the prelate went on. 'Mr Stark doesn't have to apologize for singing later. He's a singer.' He waited for the shriek from the Time of Death admirers to subside. 'So why should it be thought amusing that I might invoke God's grace? It's my job . . .'

'*Christ Almighty*,' Lucy breathed in my ear. '*Is there a God?*'

But it's a matter of pride for a presenter to ignore a producer's suggestions. I gambled that the answer was not a pass-back to the goalkeeper but a through ball: defence into attack.

'Well, isn't the difference, Your Grace' – some of the younger members of the audience wolf-whistled ironically at the formal title – 'that people believe in Martin Stark, have faith in rock music? They laugh at the idea of you saying prayers because it's just a man in a frock shouting poems . . .'

'*Steady. You answer the letters.*'

Dr Stirling grasped the crucifix which hung against the purple shirt which marked his rank and I wondered for a moment if he might wave his saviour at me like a priest in a vampire movie. But he merely said, 'Are you a believer, Mr Fleming?'

Jesus fuck, I thought, beam me up, Scotty. I said, 'I ask the questions.'

'But that's the one that everyone must answer.'

'*Is sex wrong?*'

'On the subject of sex, you've controversially—'

'I read that you were raised a Catholic, Mr Fleming—'

'*Armageddon! Armageddon!*'

'But you don't believe it any more . . .'

'You've said very strikingly, Archbishop, that, er, the nuclear family is, perhaps appropriately being nuclear, facing Armageddon.' Fuck, I was doing that tug on the left ear that one of the Sunday critics had just mugged me for. 'If so who, as it were, is firing the missiles?'

'The media. The teachers. The government.' Born in Derry – Londonderry, he would have said – but schooled expensively in England, Stirling still had a slight Irish lilt, which had eased his rise by giving a distracting charm to what were frequently inflammatory remarks. 'They all either actively promote, or at the very least tolerate, a culture obsessed with sexual opportunity.'

'Can you really blame the break-up of marriages on movies, schools, politicians?'

'Well, there you have the advantage of me, Mr Fleming. Perhaps you could share with us the reasons for the break-up of your first family?'

Beam me up. This troublesome priest. How *dare* he? For decades people had realized that presenters were the tribunes of the people. We were merely conduits, like Mary carrying the son of God, although the Blessed Virgin probably lacked the self-importance of the average television host.

The audience understood that we were purely objective questioners. But there'd been a bad moment on Radio 4 recently when Bruce Todd was sarkily asking a junior minister why he'd voted for an MP's pay rise and the bastard had said, 'Well, how much do you earn?' Who the fuck did these people think they were? I'd never talked about my first marriage – I'd removed it from *Who's Who* – but Stirling's people had found a reference somewhere.

'I ask the questions,' I told the Archbishop.

'Ah, come now, Mr Fleming, but this is an area in which you have some expertise.'

'There are other people involved,' I said. 'Private people.'

I couldn't see another road out which wouldn't give Bannoch and the tabloids somewhere to park their tanks. But it sounded prissy and the Archbishop grinned. 'I pray you were always so protective of their feelings.'

The audience – sick about having to sit through a heaven-seller before they got the singer and the actress – was now enjoying this. They booed and hissed like a pantomime crowd.

'Poor you. But it's fucking top TV.'

In the days when the screen in the corner seemed a miracle, viewers would have backed the presenter against the guest. But not now. They know how much we're paid. They've seen our houses in *Hello!* magazine, although I've remained sane enough at least to say no to that. I had to get this back. Humility. I had to act humility.

'You're right,' I said. It was the voice I'd used in marital rows and, before that, in the confessional, long ago. 'Like a lot of people out there, I need to understand this. So, with respect for *your* expertise, why do you think so many marriages end?'

'Because people expect happiness.'

Laughter and applause are the sounds you want from the studio viewers. Silence – awed or bored – is what you sometimes get. In the game within the audience over which of us to support, he had just scored an equalizer for me, deflecting the ball into his own net.

'Let me explain,' said the churchman, who was enough

of an actor and politician to sense and resent that he had lost the crowd. 'When I was growing up, there was a phrase the priests and grown-ups had. From the Bible. Vale of tears. Life was a vale of tears.'

I'd read in the research notes that the gay wing of the church mocked Stirling's rhetorical style by calling him the Reverend Jessie Jackass, but he truly had the incantatory rhythms of an American preacher.

'It sounds grim now, but it told you not to expect to be smiling every minute. Now. Now we've created a culture of instant gratification. If a child wants a video-game, let them have it. If a person wants a new lover, never mind the cost of that either.'

Only an occasional cough broke the silence, but you couldn't tell yet if the hush was resentful or attentive.

'*Half-way with him. Four minutes.*'

'And why has that culture developed?'

'I think it's a drawback of peace-time. The—'

A boy from Derry, my mind said.

'*He's fucking Irish.*'

'Can there be,' I translated these inspirations, 'I'm sorry to interrupt – but you were born in Ireland of all places – can there be drawbacks to peace?'

'I meant, of course, post-Second World War. Yes, I think there can be drawbacks. If a culture of rationing and community thinking gives way to a culture of excess and individual pleasure, yes.'

Are you beginning to suspect my perfect recall? I should explain that I'm using a transcript of the video. The BBC has a team of people (well, women, in fact, still) who type up the audio-tapes of interviews done for documentaries or transcribe the videos of shows which later prove to be controversial. They're given no guidance except their own ears so I appear as INT, *as if they don't know who I am*, and, if they're uncertain about a word, they put a question mark in brackets. There are no queries in the Stirling transcript. His meaning was all too clear.

Of all the regrets I now have about this edition, the first is that I pulled the Archbishop down from his pulpit. But we have come to fear seriousness in television. I was a journalist but I was permanently looking for feed-lines. I saw a possible 1–2.

'You're not seriously saying bring back rationing?'

'I think sexual rationing might actually be a good idea.'

Not only had he just lost anyone in the audience here or at home who had sentient genitals but he had, ho ho ho, shown me an opening. 'What? So people would present a coupon to their partner at the end of the week? And, if you were desperate, you might swap one with the farmer's wife for nylons . . .'

It was my first big laugh of the night: what Cornelius Raven – when he was on the show – called a 'woofer'. I was turning the audience towards me again. But then the Archbishop dared to quieten them with a raised hand. And – this was the really galling thing – they obeyed.

'No. Well, have your jokes. But this is my point. Waiting to come on here now – in what you call your Green Room – we heard the comedian that was on before you quipping' – he made that verb sound like a sexual perversion – 'that people here tonight with someone they shouldn't be should lean away from the cameras. But what kind of a culture is it in which people joke about adultery?'

Oh, my beautiful stooge. 'Yes,' I said. 'I understand that before talk shows in Iran, the warm-up man tells the audience that people there with anyone they shouldn't be will have their hands cut off . . .'

Another woofer. Lucy pressed talkback but all I could hear was laughter in the gallery. She clicked it off again but, in the fizzing silence, another talkback was activated in my head. OK, God's little skirt-wearer, declaring the most ludicrous beliefs as if they were certainties, and daring to humiliate me. 'Do you *like* sex?'

'What?'

'You're a married man. You're allowed to have sex, unlike your Catholic counterparts . . .' I saw for a moment an opening about RC priests and little boys but closed it. This is why live broadcasting is so frightening. I can only present it on the page as a series of decisions, but in reality references and censorships are made in brain-flashes. 'Do you enjoy it?'

'*Christ. Why not just ask him if Mrs Canterbury takes it up the arse?*'

It did not feel entirely like me. I had never been a shock-jock. No mention had ever been made of my penis or my piles on air, although so far I had only been in possession of the former. But perhaps Tony Andrews kept a doll of me in his bed-sit, aiming pins with shaking hands.

'How relevant is this?' questioned the prelate.

'It's important to establish – isn't it? – whether you're pro-marriage or simply anti-sex?'

'Let me put it this way. I've given several sermons against pre-marital sex. I've never preached one against the *post*-marital variety. And nor would I . . .'

A good answer, the bastard. He got from the audience what Cornelius Raven called a 'woofette'. They liked him. It was terrifyingly possible that they liked him more than me. At the edge of my vision, I saw the Stirling question-prompts slide from the Autocue:

WHEN WILL
THE WORLD END?

As if in response, it was replaced with the first line of the next link:

YOU'LL FIND OUT

So I knew the segment was near the end even before Lucy spoke:
'*Cut-throat. Cut-throat.*'
The pirate's cry which means that time is up in broadcasting.
'Archbishop Stirling, for the moment, thank you.'
'Thank you.'

YOU'LL FIND OUT
LATER TONIGHT
WHAT THE ACTRESS
SAID TO THE
ARCHBISHOP . . .

My own woofette. One-all. On the far corner of the platform, beyond the band, I could see figures moving in the shadows.

BUT FIRST LADIES
AND GENTLEMEN
MARTIN STARK

A cross-fade put Dr Stirling and me into gloom while illuminating Stark and his backing group. The singer performed the title ballad from his new album:

> I'm in your head with you
> I'm in your bed with you
> I'll be dead with you . . .

> When you smile I know
> When you sigh I know
> When you lie I'll know . . .

Stretching back, in the darkness of my part of the stage, I tried to score the previous conversation like a boxing judge. I'd lost control of the opening moments, and there were TV critics who would see and relish that. The bigger concern was whether Stirling had put my private life into the tabloid domain: TV's Mr Talk Called Marriage-Wrecker. Switch talkback clicked.

'Another minute thirty on this. That was great stuff. You got it back on track really well.'

Doreen on Autocue put down her puzzle book and tapped into position the trigger words for the interview with the rock star:

SEX?
DRUGS?
AGEING?

Martin Stark – sweat starting to darken his intricately arranged blond tresses – followed a driving guitar riff into the final verse:

> It's me on your phone
> It's me in your home
> When you smile I know . . .

During the song, a second chair had been placed alongside the Archbishop's. Stark, acknowledging the cheers with a hand shining from a swipe across his glossy brow, walked over and flopped into it, breaking the beams of the waiting spotlight. He lackadaisically slapped hands with me – his main career strategy was pretending to be a black American

– and nodded curtly at Dr Stirling, who extended a hand which hung unshaken.

Stark was a middle-class boy from Hertfordshire. A journalist on a local newspaper when Time of Death secured their first recording contract in the 1970s, he had gradually dismantled his manners and his accent in the cause of musical credibility.

'That was great,' I said with impeccable insincerity. ' "In Your Head with You". Now that's a love song but quite a creepy one . . .'

'Yeah. Well, that's because it's not about love as such but stalking. I wrote it about that guy in the papers that stood outside the house of a girl who'd chucked him for a year and then stabbed her new bloke through the heart next Valentine's.'

'Presumably, someone like yourself, in the world you're in, you must have stalkers?'

Stark hesitated. 'Well, stalkers are like Swiss bank accounts or a big dick. Only trouble can come from admitting you've got one . . .'

'*And we're supposed to conclude he has all three?*'

'And we're supposed to conclude you have all three?'

The producer-presenter equivalent of simultaneous orgasm.

'No comment, mate. No comment.'

On the transcript of programme 211, Stark's genital reference appears as 'd***'. The secretaries in the Transcription Unit are decorous.

'Of course, in the rock world it's sometimes hard to tell stalkers from groupies. You don't know until you wake up either with a smile on your face or dead.'

'*Bring in the Bish.*'

In the early days of television, talk shows had aimed to

bring together celebrities with common interests. Now, if Cheese agrees to appear, you phone Chalk's agent right away. Interest value is defined as conflict.

'Enjoy the song, Archbishop?'

'Well, I won't be having it scored for the Canterbury organ . . .'

'Do you have a *big* organ, Rev?' asked Stark. A woofer.

Stirling blanked him and carried on: 'But I am interested in stalking. Now this, it seems to me, is a phenomenon which results purely from promiscuity—'

'Oh, come on,' I said, following up with the slight involuntary head butt which was the main thing the impressionists turned against me, apart from my traffic-light ties and few rogue Bolton vowels. I still half-rhyme bath with dash and school comes out as sku-ell.

'I'm serious, Mr Fleming. Stalking – I'm not talking about celebrity stalking, which is a separate matter and speaks more to the sin of idolatry, but about the kind described in that song – is usually a refusal to accept sexual rejection. In lifelong monogamy with one partner, that can't happen.'

'Is that right, Rev?' Stark asked before I could. 'I thought most stalkers were people who'd been turned down for a shag in the first place.'

'That's a good point, isn't it?' I followed up, keen to have my show back. 'A lot of these poor women are hounded or even killed because they're refusing to sleep with someone. The strategy you recommend—'

As with Stark's riches, dick and would-be killers, only trouble can come from admitting this, but my first thought after the explosion was that I wouldn't get much space on the obituary pages if Stark and the Archbishop were laid out on the same day. I'd be basement at best – no picture, which might be a blessing – or even held over until the following morning.

My second reflection after the bang was that it sounded just like a rifle in the movies. The third was the surprising absence of pain. When I heard the noise, I had instinctively pushed back against the chair, twisting to one side with my hands raised in front of my face. Turning my head, I saw that Stark was slumped forward, almost on the floor. The Archbishop seemed scarcely to have flinched except to move his hands together apparently in prayer. The bastard didn't even have the grace to be a hypocrite.

My final – and lasting – reaction was embarrassment as, past my lowering hands, I watched Barry skip calmly on to the set and say in his finest airline pilot's voice, 'Ladies and gentlemen, little technical problem there. In television, we use big, hot lights – like the ones you can see above your heads – and one of them just exploded. It happens sometimes in winter, like your pipes at home. If anyone feels they need treatment for injury or shock, please raise your hands or, if you are unable to do so, ask someone near you to alert us. Good, good. It looks as if the glass fell on the set over there. We'll restart the programme in a moment.'

*

Adrenalin is like a tapeworm and – first to the Green Room afterwards – I had eaten eight of the sandwiches when a pudgy, ruddy-faced man in a clerical collar appeared at my side.

'ABC is furious.'

'What?'

'Asking him about his sex life on television. The DG is lunching at Lambeth in April, and ABC will certainly raise it. It's beyond me how the BBC can go on denying dumbing down.'

As he angrily exited, I suddenly understood ABC. How DG and MD.BRO would envy the Archbishop of Canterbury, possessor of this alpha among alpabetical labels.

I turned back to the sandwiches.

'Bastard, you've had all the smoked salmon . . .'

As I spun back round, Lucy was leaning up to kiss me. I met her half-way, her lips touching my cheek at the very edge of my mouth so that the red of her lipstick was flecked orange from the powder on my face. Fiona had rubbed with the babywipes but there would usually be pancake on the pillows for two days after a show. It was a very thick mask we wore.

'Top show,' Lucy said. 'It's post-watershed so I won't refer "dick" upwards. As it were.' She giggled, and I tried not to think about what she would be like to sleep with. 'Who was that angry little man?'

'The Archbishop of Canterbury's aide-de-camp, apparently. Who, if you ask me, should be more worried about his boss's views on gay priests. The ABC – as they apparently call him, making him sound like a cinema to someone of my generation – is furious about my asking whether he has Mrs Stirling howling like St Teresa in ecstasy. Who'd think you'd ever get into trouble for asking a C of E clergyman if he does it with a woman?'

The Green Room – which witnessed each day a cycle from fear to release, both fuelled by snacks and alcohol – resembled the lobby of a motorway motel, though gloomier because placed in a windowless basement. Worn olive-green banquettes which prickled your hands with static were arranged in a square at one end. The rest of the space held a fridge and tables on which stood silver-painted plastic platters of sandwiches, pastries and cakes. Framed behind glass on the walls, comics and frontmen now decades dead flashed black-and-white grins in frozen scenes from television's innocence.

In one corner, Martin Stark's swigged beer bottle came dangerously close in its arc to Alice Jackett's sipped plastic beaker of cheap red. In another, technicians, moustachioed with pastry crumbs, huddled in groups, mocking their bosses: 'Please God his leaving party's not a piss-up in a brewery!' / 'Yeah. And the party game's not point to an arse and an elbow.'

We moved away in case they reached their views of us. Lucy tilted the bottle of Australian Cabernet towards my glass.

'No. No, thanks. I've got the car.'

'We'd drive you in and out. You do know that?'

'No. There'd be a *driver*. I know this will make you think I'm even worse than you already think I am, but I find it harder and harder to talk to . . . that phrase "ordinary people" is awful, isn't it?'

'Oooh, Richard, spook-eee,' laughed Lucy. She dropped her voice. 'Did you see that thing in the Stark cuttings about the days when he was still doing coke and he rang down to the bellman at the Paris Ritz and told them he wanted it to stop raining? You'll be sending me memos about the weather soon . . .'

'Fuck off.'

My parents' generation would never have believed that it was possible to say this to someone in an affectionate way. But did Lucy think I did coke? There was no time to ask because she teased, 'You're not like that government minister who wouldn't have a driver because he said he disapproved of privilege, but then it turned out it was so he could go cruising?'

'No, I'm . . .' But her teasing about secrets touched off a worry I'd forgotten. 'Luce, that stuff from Stirling about my first marriage . . .'

'Yeah. I keep seeing it being played at awards ceremonies. Hey, have you ever noticed that men at award ceremonies always button up their DJ jackets as they go up to the stage?'

'Luce, I've never talked about it. It would snip out easily. A minute in post-prod . . .'

'But it's . . . well, it's not the best bit, but the programme would be thinner without it . . . It shows you're not pompous.'

'You think I'm pompous?'

'No – Christ, I forget how paranoid presenters are. This would convince any notional possible doubters out there that you're not pompous.'

'I'd be happier without it, Luce . . .'

'I'll look at it in the edit. We were ninety seconds over.' She whispered again, 'But I was planning to lose that from Alice Jackett. Earth to Planet Luvvy or what?'

'I know,' I murmured back. 'The single thing to choose between the many great directors she's worked with is their precise degree of genius. She was in a fucking clinic for three months after working with Garibaldi on *Roadkill*.'

'I know, Rich. And all she said was he was a blast. I mean, like the fucking IRA is a blast.'

'And the bit where she said she identified with Anne Hathaway because her boyfriend was trying to become a screenwriter . . .'

Lucy – who was leaning into me and standing with her back to the room – looked startled as I suddenly raised my voice to say, 'Alice, that was great. Thank you very much for coming on.'

My producer – turning with a blush which the actress would hopefully take as a nobody's discomfort in her presence – added her own tribute: 'That was just what we wanted, Alice. Especially the Garibaldi anecdotes. I hope his biographer will be watching. And you looked great. We already knew the camera loved you, but we were about to go to a magistrate for a restraining order on Camera 4.'

I knew Lucy well enough to understand that her insincerity took the form of exaggerated metaphors. Alice Jackett, though, looked as if she might weep again as she had when accepting her Oscar.

'Thank you, Lucy, it was a real blast.' The speech of this former head girl from Surrey was already becoming drawled for American ears. 'And, Richard, my General Studies teacher always told us to read your column and so, when I hear you're the interviewer, I'm, like, get outta here!'

It was ten years since I'd written a column. The cow had clearly never seen me on TV. And, as for radio, she probably listened to pop music stations.

'Thank you,' I said. 'And good luck with that remake of *Arsenic and Old Lace* you mentioned' – in a self-serving and seemingly interminable anecdote – 'on the show.'

'Right, Richard. I just wish I'd had time to mention my *Duchess of Malfi*. In the West End? It's, like, so scary but the thing about darling Oscar is that he gives you the oxygen to head for the peaks. Movies are movies but theatre is, like, theatre.'

With this confirmation of the accuracy of English vocabulary as it applied to entertainment forms, Alice Jackett, with a wave consisting of a slight bending of the fingers, left the room. Martin Stark soon followed her, dwarfed, even on his platforms, by the shaven-headed heavies of his nutter-buffer. As he passed, he shouted over, 'When that lamp went, man, I thought there was some fucker out there, been reading *Catcher in the Rye*.'

When he'd gone, Lucy said, 'Can you imagine what it must be like to worry all the time that there's someone trying to kill you?'

'Yeah. I read a book once about Tom Riley. When he was first running for president, a kid popped a crisp packet on an aeroplane. Riley's head hit the seat in front so hard they had to stitch him.'

Lucy gestured with the wine bottle towards the sofas. I grabbed a can of Diet Coke and followed. On one side, the lighting director was continuing his attempt to seduce the vision mixer, a project now pursued through two series.

'Luce, did you *see* Peter Pennington on Saturday?' I asked as we sat down opposite the stumbling seduction. 'With Felicity Hatch? He not only asked, "What's your book about?", but "Why did you write it?" as well. If I ever use either of those, you'll know I'm dead.'

'Yeah, Rich. We're the best. We're Microsoft. We're Marks & Spencer . . .'

'But for how long? The future of television is millions of digital channels with Cornelius Raven doing jokes about taking it up the arse . . .'

Lucy swilled her wine in the glass and stared at it suspiciously, like a pathologist with a body fluid.

'What have you heard?' she asked.

'What?'

No non-paranoiac can understand the thrill of worst fears being confirmed.

'Rich, I don't know quite how to say this. But there may be some changes round here.'

There were no clever follow-ups from the chat-show host off-air, only, 'Why? What?'

'It's just a feeling. You may remember that last year's memo was that ratings don't matter . . .'

'Yeah. We liked that.'

'Didn't we? Well, this year's is that they do. Ogg's fretting about our overnights last Friday.'

'He rang me. He blamed the weather.'

'I know, I know. Flaming February. The first beach parties of late winter. But if we're down this week as well, he's going to be wanting soap stars and slimmers of the year and so on. They're suddenly obsessed with audience share.'

'I know. We've had seven different start-times this run. But they'd never blame that. Have you heard this expression "share positive"?'

'I've heard *of* it. I tend to actually hear "share negative". Which is what my shows are said to be . . .'

'Fucking hell, Luce. Alice Jackett was about as low as I'd go.'

'I know. But my view is that the only good thing about them changing their minds so often is that the kites don't stay in the air very long. Working for *decisive* idiots is far more frightening.' Lucy ran another test on the Cabernet. 'Quiet weekend?'

'I've got voice-overs tomorrow morning. And a pilot Sunday.'

'You're fucking mad. Have some time off.'

'I can't.'

'I know. I think I can throw stones? It's being here all the time that's done for me and David.'

'Is it bad?'

'Share negative. And we've stopped counting the overnights.'

In our world, bad-marriage anecdotes were offered with a kind of pride. There was an unspoken assumption that anyone who loved their partner and saw their kids could not be working hard enough.

We looked away towards a photograph of Morecambe and Wise. Thirty years before, I'd been allowed to stay up late to see their Christmas show. The stress of television had killed Eric and there were only two channels when they started. I was competing with two hundred.

'How are you and Rachel?' Lucy asked.

'Even if Ogg's nightmare comes true and everyone goes to bed instead of watching television, we'd still be there in front of the tube. Not speaking. I sometimes think I'd be more use to the industry as a *viewer*.'

The lecture I'd really like to give to the Royal Television Society would concern the key relationship between television and divorce. There is a simple manifestation – the marriages of those in the industry fail fast because of colleagues working long hours with surges of adrenalin and alcohol – and a complex one – the rising divorce rate increases the number of households, as homes break into two, and therefore the quantity of televisions. Couples hating each other is good for ratings. We need sad people sitting at home.

'Rachel must hate the hours you work,' fished Lucy, a battle victim asking to compare scars.

'She says it's like those saints who were in two places at once. Bilocation. Except I'm in the same place twice. Work when I'm at work. Work when I'm at home. Which reminds me. Rachel said she'd stay up for me tonight. I'd better . . .'

This was spin. My phraseology was supposed to make Lucy think I'd be having sex with Rachel that night – was even Richard Fleming vain enough to think she might be envious? – although it was highly improbable that we would unless the United Nations had been working on some kind of peace deal quite secretly in Geneva.

As I stood to go, Helen the PA came over with a brown envelope.

'Gerry Armstrong left this for you.'

'Oh, right. Typical BBC, isn't it? Security leaving unexplained packages around the place?'

The envelope was thin, suggesting papers, except for a lump, which indicated that a stiff, cylindrical object had dropped to the bottom.

'I suppose, if I were really paranoid, I should wonder if it wasn't someone pretending to be the Head of Security.'

'Sorry?'

It was a sign of ageing that my grammar and vocabulary often made me incomprehensible to young people such as Helen. They frequently looked frightened when I spoke. Helen gaped like someone in a horror movie.

'Why are security on to you?' asked Lucy, who had understood.

'Oh' – I tried to sound casual – 'one of the nuts out there has gone from peanut to, I don't know, walnut – are walnuts bigger? – at least in the letters he's – she's, whoever's – writing.'

'Rich, take care!'

'Yeah, well, that's what this is about.'

I brandished Armstrong's manila package.

'Christ, Rich, there was that woman in Leicester, wasn't there?' remembered my producer.

'Who thought I'd stopped her periods by some ectoplasmic intervention through the set. The phantom Mrs Fleming. We don't think it's her . . .'

'You hear more and more stories,' said Lucy. 'It does seem

to be getting worse. Molly Durie told me that when she did that spell reading the Nine on TV – summer relief – this bloke wrote in and asked her to slow down reading the links because she never gave him quite enough time to come.'

'Jesus. I see what you mean about summer relief.'

'Yeah. The next time she was on, she was, you know, speed-reading, imagining his fingers in a blur like Brendel in a scherzo . . .'

'I know. And we go to all these conferences and say that television has no effect on the viewers.'

I fingered the envelope, wondering what Armstrong had sent for my defence.

'Thank you for tonight,' said Lucy. 'I'm at home over the weekend if . . .'

This usually meant: if there's anything more than usually cruel about you in the newspapers. Tonight it implied: if one of our viewers is holding you hostage with a knife. We were exchanging television's traditional post-show kiss – mouths meeting but theoretically without sexual intent – when a young woman came towards us from one of the production-team rucks beside the food table.

'You don't know me but . . .'

'This is Abbi Pascoe.' Lucy introduced us with what seemed to be slight disapproval. 'She's just joined the researchers.'

'Is it OK if I call you Richard?' asked Abbi Pascoe, who was small, with an urchin perkiness. I would have put her at twenty-two. Exactly half my age; precisely Isabelle and Sophie's.

'I just want to say how thrilled I am to be working here?'

Our newest recruit had her generation's tendency to turn every sentence into a question.

'There aren't many intelligent programmes left on television?' she added.

'I know,' I said. 'And the circus van will be coming for us soon. I don't know if Lucy's explained. But, as a researcher, you don't give me questions, you give me facts. I do the questions.'

'That's cool?' said Abbi Pascoe.

*

The plain grey Formica of the BBC lavatory cubicle had been vividly pictorialized with graffiti. Cocks like space rockets soared towards circles of scribble resembling eagles' nests. Scrawled on the inside of the door was the question 'What's the difference between the BBC management and a documentary on female circumcision?' I guessed the answer before I found it, lower down, overlapping a limerick about the Head of News. 'The BBC management is full of complete cunts.'

After I'd been sick for the second time, I hauled myself up and sat reading these cathartic riddles. Then I opened the package from Armstrong. On a map of west London were marked, in different shades of felt pen, six different routes from my house to Television Centre, although, given the shortness of the journey, two were indistinguishable from becoming completely lost: Alzheimer's driving. A typed note from Armstrong advised:

There's an obvious temptation to use A-B-C-D and so on but this merely replaces one pattern with another. Be as varied as you can D-C-C-A-A-B. Or whatever.

I thought of my parents tapping out rhyme schemes on the desk to forty years of sullen students. Armstrong's suggested rotation would be Ezra Pound or another of the American crazies.

The rest of the letter warned me to look out for unfamiliar cars near my house and offered a twenty-four-hour security number. I shook out the distended envelope. A black plastic rectangle resembling a rape alarm hit once-white tiles discoloured by what I hoped was mud. As I switched it on and put it in my pocket, I caught sight of my watch.

Another of my rituals was that I needed to be home before my programme started. It was not that I wanted to tune in. I could no longer bear to see myself on the screen. But nor could I stand the evidence on the streets of the viewers who had chosen not to watch me.

Interviews 2: He's Shining

ROLL 3 – DEAD ON LIVE TV – INTERVIEW 22/11/99

Int: And on the subject of the 12 February programme, was there, uh, any sense at the, uh, time of quite how, uh, significant it would be?

LB: Well, yes and no . . .

Int: I'm not here, Lucy. I'm not here.

LB: What? Oh, yeah . . . the 12 February edition – in one sense – was just programme 211 in a long run. In the Green Room afterwards we were already thinking about 212. And you have to remember that it would be four months or so before everyone was suddenly ringing the tape library for that one. On the other hand, though, I suppose Richard was unusually nervous about it afterwards. But that was only because he thought that the stuff with the Archbishop might have opened up his family to the tabloids. What nobody understood at the time was that quite so much started that night. I mean . . .

Int: No. Sorry to interrupt you, Lucy . . . Could you give me a clean-out on 'started that night'? I'm just thinking I could use it as a teaser somewhere near the front. Then have you unpacking it later . . .

LB: Right . . . What nobody understood at the time was quite how much started that night.

Int: Great. Can I ask you now. When did Richard start seeming strange?

LB: *(Laughter.)*

Int: Sorry?

LB: Well, I mean it is rather perjerratiff (?). *(Laughter.)* It's the old wife-beating one. And you'll be asking if he did that in a minute.

Int: OK. Let me rephrase. Did Richard start to seem strange at any point in that period?

LB: I . . . well . . . I started to worry about him more. I suppose *(unclear)* . . . I'm sorry . . .

Int: Do you want a glass of water?

LB: Can we stop for a moment?

Int: We can let it run. We've just changed tape.

LB: You won't show me crying, will you?

Int: I, uh . . . As you know, Lucy, we usually make those decisions in the edit . . .

LB: Promise me you won't or I won't sign the release.

Int: OK, Lucy, I wasn't . . . It's just that people are sometimes silly about that, I think. Showing emotion is often a way of connecting with the viewer . . .

LB: *(Laughter.)*

Int: Sorry?

LB: You have to realize that I have rather mixed feelings now about connecting with the viewer.

ROLL 43 – *DEAD ON LIVE TV* – INTERVIEW 2/12/99

(Indistinct background chatter.)

Man's voice: Up to speed. And running . . .

Interviewer: Could you please give your name – spelling anything unclear – and how you would like to be described on screen?

Man's voice: Gerry – with a Y, I suppose you have to say

these days with that pop star – Armstrong. I'm BBC Head of Security.

Int: Before 1999, how seriously did you take the safety of on-screen talent?

GA: You'd expect me to say very. But it's true. A lot of what people wrote was that it was like the Garden of Eden and after. But that's wrong. We'd twice had people getting into the newsroom. Once they got on screen. I expect you'll be using those pictures of Timothy Ledhill sitting on that lesbian during the *Six O'Clock News*. And what's-his-name had to get a restraining order against that nun . . . Oh, who's that young comic? . . . Goes on about bottoms and that all the time . . .

Int: Oh, er . . .that probably doesn't narrow it down very much . . .

GA: Bird's name. Raven. Cornelius Raven . . .

Int: Oh, er, right. Bottoms as in A.N.L. (?) sex? I was thinking bottoms as in farting. Hey, maybe there's an arts doc on the buttock in culture. Can you do that bit again? After sitting on the lesbian. As it were.

GA: Oh, er . . . And the comedian Cornelius Raven had got a restraining order against a woman who'd been fol-lowing him. So it wasn't as if we thought everything was rosy in the garden. But we had this brilliant defence, you see. Or so we thought. Three words: 'This isn't America.' That's what we'd say whenever it got really heavy. 'This isn't America.'

Int: But it was?

GA: Well. Yes.

Int: Gerry, could you just say for me, 'But it *was* America.'

GA: That isn't what I said.

Int: I know that. But would you say it for me now?

GA: Listen, love, when I was a copper, they brought in a law to stop us doing that.

Int: What?

GA: Changing witness statements. There are mad, bad buggers out and eating Sunday lunch because we gave them a hand with what they wanted to say.

Int: I hear what you're saying. We can come back to that ... When did you first become aware of Matthew Harding (?)?

GA: Oh, er, late. Too late, you'd have to say. But you have to realize that his letters were very polite. Correspondence sent them on very happily to Mr Fleming.

Int: So BBC stars were always at risk from a *polite* psychopath?

GA: Oh, come on. You said it wouldn't be one of those interviews.

Man's voice: He's shining. Sorry. He's shining ...

Int: I'll rephrase, Mr Amstrong. And Fiona will just mop the top of your head a bit.

ROLL 56 – *DEAD ON LIVE TV* – INTERVIEW 4/12/99

Man's voice: Tom Ogg. O-G-G. I'm emdy (?) blow (?) ...

Int: Sorry. People may not get the abbreviation.

Man: What? Oh. I'm Managing Director of Broadcasting at the BBC. Incidentally, sorry to keep you waiting. I was having lunch with Tommy Rankin and Cornelius Raven.

Int: That's fine. Mr Ogg, how responsible do you feel as an executive for what happens on screen?

TO: Oh, very. I mean, if you're making the point I think you're making, the DG and I are both on the Memorial Fund Committee. Look, what you have to understand is this. Television is about being friendly. You get ratings because people think you're their mate. A good presenter is at some level seductive. The old cliché – about hosts being invited into people's homes – it still has something in it. That glass screen looks like a window, but it needs to be a door. You want people to let you come into their lives. The problem comes when they try to push the door the other way . . .

3. THE PAEDOPHILIA DONUT

That Monday – after the first Jackett / Stark show – my morning bath looked even more like a suicide scene than usual. Two of the Sundays had picked up on the thing with the Archbishop, which Lucy left in. She had to. Professionally, she had to.

Luckily a plane had gone down off California in the night, killing 390 people, which made us page-three basement rather than the bottom front we might have been on a slow-news Saturday. Both publications, though, used a photograph and it was the one I dislike most.

I am caught laughing at the pre-drinks do before the ceremony at which Peter Pennington – from a short list of four described as distinguished, one quarter of it particularly so – won the BAFTA for Best Chat Show. The bottom half of the picture is dominated by a huge flute of champagne. The top half – in which I am rocking back open-mouthed with the comedy of something Rachel has said – is all chins and fillings. Apart from being a reminder of the time when we still made each other laugh, the picture defines me to the reader as privileged but ugly.

This reminder of my appearance made me unable to face myself even in the steamed-up tiles. Shaving entirely blind, I watched the water redden: blood on the bubbles of unguent, like a scene from a documentary on the clubbing of seals. I distracted myself by trying to breathe the steam deep towards my larynx. Obsession with my face had now been joined by paranoia about my voice. The sound guys would soon notice that the frog was default.

When I started in broadcasting, I thought that vocal protection was pretension. My real job was in newspapers; an occasional croakiness showed that I wasn't taking this too seriously. Then, beginning to face microphones almost daily, I developed an opera singer's obsessiveness. I inhaled steam in the morning and drank honey and lemon at night. I learned that, tempting as hot drinks may be for colds, they loosen phlegm; icy water is better for the throat.

Although there were many other reasons for celibacy now, even our currently sexless marriage – it was three months since a sullen Friday night coupling in which neither of us came, a rare case in lovemaking, I hope, of simultaneous non-orgasm – had started as a broadcaster's precaution. Marriage is among other things a germ circuit and we had been swapping a nasty cough back and forth for a fortnight. I had suggested a quarantine week – with irritatingly little resistance – and it had somehow stretched.

As these pages will now definitely never be a memoir to be promoted on chat shows, I can admit that come followed blood on to the water: a squalid mix of vital liquids. And, at the risk of being expelled from the talk-show host's union for improper usage of a guest, it was Alice Jackett I imagined astride me as I whipped my fist up and down. It was a satisfactory fantasy as long as one tuned out before the talking afterwards.

I reached the breakfast room at seven forty-five. Paula and Tash were watching Tommy Rankin hiding inside a mail box to frighten passers-by on a breakfast show I privately called *Egos and Bacon*. But he was the kind of TV star they would have loved me to be.

'Do you know what, Richard?' Tash asked, without her

eyes leaving the screen. 'Tommy stuck his hand out of the box when this very old lady was posting a letter.'

It sounded to me like the beginnings of the second hospitalization to result from one of his stunts – a student was currently on a nutritional drip after taking up Tommy's ad-libbed challenge to live entirely on sherbet dips for a year – but I said, 'That sounds very funny.'

'He's actually done it before,' said Paula, tempering the enthusiasm of her six-year-old sister with the worldliness of a girl of eight. Represented in two under-tens, we had the blessedly undemanding mainstream television viewer and the sickeningly unimpressible TV critic.

I piled up cornflakes – the kind with honey and nuts, which ridiculously always feel healthier – in such a hill that the dish became almost spherical.

'Richard's being a big fat pig,' trilled Tash. Even the very young have a sense of where to hurt someone.

I flapped with false casualness through a newspaper – President Riley had denied the latest rape charges, Terry Perry had been dropped by England after admitting to taking cocaine, Alice Jackett had failed to wear a bra when attending a première where she was also without her screenwriter boyfriend, a train crash in Salvador had killed 1,000 – but thankfully found nothing about me.

Beside the cereal packets on the breakfast bar six other titles were stacked, food for the journalist's neurotic habit of comparison. But, unfortunately for someone in my profession, on most days now I was either bored or frightened by the news. There were also – in a neat, reproachful pile – eight editions of the previous week's *Big Issue*. Such was my guilt at the cash to be made from mere chattering that I bought a copy every time a seller caught my eye. It was particularly difficult if they recognized my face. By giving income and stability to the homeless, the *Big Issue* had created an entirely fresh hazard for stars: beggars with televisions.

I flicked the newspaper Rachel wrote for towards her without looking up – we hadn't yet spoken that morning – and opened a research brief for the radio show. I was due to interview Samantha Gravure Sebastian, a Manhattan psychologist who had written *Seven Brides for Seven Husbands*, a book which argued that romantic attraction inevitably fled after eight years and so the end of a relationship should no more be seen as a failure than changing car or moving house. She argued – at least according to Sunil, who was one of the team who read the books for me – that it would become normal in the twenty-first century to meet octogenarians who had walked down the aisle seven times, a statistic which inspired her cutesy title.

'Is it good for the girls to see you reading at the table?'

During the first crisis in our marriage – two years earlier – we had come to an arrangement that we would discuss how things were done in the house rather than making dogmatic statements. Questions were theoretically less threatening.

'Will they even notice if they're watching British television's most talentless and egotistical presenter at the same time?'

'Wouldn't he have a lot of competition for that position?'

Ms (Mrs? Mrs × 7?) Gravure's book was not the right reading matter for distraction. Although we had been married for less than six years, our relationship had so far lasted eight. We had been lovers during the final two years of her first marriage and I sometimes wondered if Tasha might be mine, but Rachel insisted it had, been a late, rare burst of husbandly spunk. There were days when she seemed to have my eyes. But husbands and lovers are sustained by the same delusion. A child will look like you if you want it to.

The only thing to be said for the bickering was that it was better than the silence, which was our main programme now. Live radio shows are set up so that if a switched-on microphone picks up no sound for a set length of time – such silences are called 'dead air' – the studio closes down and a continuity announcer takes over. The more reflective speech stations are allowed around fifteen seconds of dead air – the gap might merely be a philosopher thinking – while the pop music networks tolerate as few as three seconds without babble. This is a precaution against a broadcaster becoming unconscious at the microphone, or terrorists seizing the studio.

Any time I spent with Rachel now contained hours of dead air. Either we had nothing left to say or we were saving our thoughts and stories for broadcast to a different listener. But there were no rules for how much silence a marriage could contain before continuity – *dis*continuity – stepped in.

'Can you take them to school?'

'Didn't I tell you that I've got a voice-over at eight thirty?'

'For what?'

'Would it matter?'

'Are you incapable of saying no to work?'

'Am I?'

Our preference for questions over declarations had begun with another book by an American therapist I had read for a drive-time interview. But we had soon proved that queries could be just as fierce as the forbidden statements. And I spent all day at work asking questions. It was too much to be sitting at a kitchen table with invisible clipboards. Now – faced with a pantomime sequence of echoing responses – Rachel chose dead air again.

'Do you know what, Richard?'

'What, Tash?'

'Tommy just said bum!'

'That doesn't altogether surprise me, Tash.'

I don't think it's merely my profession which leads me to see marriage as a chat show. Both are conversations which wind down from curiosity into silence. You begin by wanting to know everything about the other person, willing their replies to be likeable and funny. At the start, you probably laugh more than their jokes deserve. But gradually the anecdotes become repetitive. You think: not that one again about the Oscar / schooldays / meeting Princess Di / irritable bowel syndrome / charity work / mother. I could do the fucking punchline myself. And soon there's someone in your ear shouting at you to wrap and move on.

It would be wrong to say that it was the girls I felt most sorry for because I always kept the greater share of pity for myself. But I *also* felt sorry for them. I loved Natasha and Paula. (We use the word love so loosely. What I probably mean is that I was grateful to them for letting me sleep with their mother and for rarely mentioning the shadowy Anthony, their father.) I genuinely believed that I had not made them substitutes for my twins. And I had only once asked Rachel if the sex had been good on the nights they were conceived and that was after too much Australian red at an awards dinner.

But Archbishop Stirling had been correct in one of his warnings against relay matrimony. Genes are the seal that really matters. When a first marriage collapses, the children benefit from cleverly selfish biology which ensures that they remind you of yourself. When a second marriage begins to fail, the stepchildren remind you only of their mother.

'Anything good on the show today?' asked Rachel.

'I won't really know until I get there.'

A lazy lie. I already knew what roughly ninety of the 180 minutes would be in any event except a royal death. The book for the day's big interview was on the table in front of me. But it was less tact than tactics that persuaded me not to tell Rachel about Dr Gravure Sebastian and her theories of cyclical indifference. One of the ways in which my coldness towards her showed was the withholding of information, like those guests who come on chat shows and demonstrate their independence with surly one-word answers: the great American author Jacob Goldman, for example, whose constipated responses so famously made Peter Pennington look like the sweaty fraud he is.

Only a few pages after my insistence that these words are private, I find myself imagining them again in a glossy oblong sarcophagus on a shelf. An unread memoir is strip-tease in an empty room. In as much as I understand myself – and I am now finally being helped to do so – central to my temperament has been this tension between disguise and display. I want to be known; I want to be alone.

Viewers always laugh at the idea that those appearing on television might be shy, but the schedules are full of people who would never have had the nerve to go on stage. Broadcasting is the most private performing medium. With the exception of studio audiences – their generosity boosted by free tickets, free booze and someone to remind them precisely how to bring their hands together – you don't have to be there when people see or hear you. It's the only viable kind of celebrity for the sensitive, apart from posthumous fame.

In the same way, at a social level, fame is the perfect cure for shyness. You never again have to begin a conversation (except at home, which is perhaps the problem), or continue one if you don't want to. You never have to explain who

you are or what you do. The introductions have been pain-
lessly done.

'Are you back at the normal time?'

'Yes.' My diary synapse fired. 'Er, no. I'm doing an interview. I mean, with me on the other side of the mike.'

'For who?'

'*Vogue.*'

'Oh. Who are they sending?'

I was being the nightmare chat-show guest, making
each admission dependent on a supplementary. But Rachel's
interest was now professional rather than personal.

'Lizzie De Mare,' I admitted.

'Jesus. Ask the old bat if it's true she had a face-lift in
Miami.'

'Jesus died for us,' testified Natasha in the staccato
soprano of a six-year-old. A couple comprising a lapsed
Catholic and a longtime agnostic, we had sent Rachel's girls
to a Church state school while we held out for as long as
possible against pay-as-you-learn. The head teacher had
turned out to be on the Church of England's more certain
wing. There were nights when you were scared to bath Tash
in case she ducked your head under the bubbles and called
down the Holy Spirit.

'I won't be cooking tonight,' said Rachel, reverting,
against our domestic rescue plan, to statements. 'It's my
column day.'

'Fine. I'll pick up some stuff at the deli on the Avenue.'

I thought of asking what her column would be about.
But the question was unnecessary. For several weeks now
the theme of her Tuesday articles had been the clues to a
ruined marriage. The character of 'Bloke' – as the columnist's
husband was identified – had begun as lovably chaotic and

incompetent, but he was now increasingly the villain of the pieces.

*

I had used the car four times over the weekend, choosing routes F-A-D-C from the Security Unit list. Now I added E to this modernist verse scheme. As I walked down the drive, the frightened part of my mind I was trying to ignore prompted me to glance around for a lunatic viewer with a blade between the pages of an autograph book. But after one half-turn of the head, I felt as self-conscious as if the camera were on me. What greater egotism could there be than the fear of assassination?

It was a slow drive to Soho. Some of Armstrong's runs were so circuitous, or favoured lorry-clotted A-roads over sassy switchbacks, that they seemed likely to induce a seizure, overturning their life-extending intentions.

Arriving long before nine, I still had to cruise five floors of the car park to find a space. So many people now drove in early to spare their blood pressure from the rush hour. In a decade, the start of the London working day had pushed forward two hours. Thirty years ago, futurologists had predicted that people in the year 2000 would work for a few hours a week, spending the rest of the week on yachts. But the opposite phenomenon suited me. Like an alcoholic in Ireland, the workaholic had a good chance of passing for normal.

As I buzzed the door at SoundScape, it pulled back and Cornelius Raven came out. 'Man,' he said, flashing high five fingers which I uneasily pressed. Like Marty Stark, he wore social black-face.

'We had good feedback on the show,' I said. In fact, there had been fifteen complaints to the duty log about the routine in which his girlfriend farted as she took it up the arse. But Lucy and I had been relieved. In the stage version of the gag, his date defecated.

'Wicked,' Raven approved.

'Voice-over?'

'Yeah. Some drink that makes kids' teeth drop out. You?'

'Mobile phone thing. Super lightweight . . .'

'Which is why they booked you, then, mate.'

'Yeah.'

I forced my face into a look which made me seem to take this sportingly. As a clear liquid jetted from his nostrils, Raven tipped back his head and pulled a wodge of shredding tissue from his pocket.

'Christ, man. What's good in a pussy ain't so nice in a nose.'

'The curse of the age,' I said.

'What?'

The scared tone of Raven's response was so out of step with what had been said that I worried my croaky throat was now affecting my sense. I clarified for him what I had meant: 'Winter bugs are getting tougher. Too many antibiotics.'

'Right, man.'

I thought of asking him about his stalker – the showbiz equivalent of quizzing local parents about the schools – but you never knew with Raven what he might use in a routine. There was a shtick he did about how fame changed your brain.

In the sound-booth, the green baize on the table was still darkened in several places from Raven's nasal cascade. In the regulation funeral dress, a too-smiley blonde from the agency placed the script on the lectern in front of me. Pouring

me a glass of water from a flask, she spilled some, enlarging
one patch of the comedian's secretions.

UNTIL YOU PICK UP A FEATHER 141 (PAUSE) YOU REALLY
HAVEN'T LEARNED TO TALK YET.

The sentence contained none of my trip-words. I had been
lucky to be hired by one of the few advertisers not trying to
invoke the spirit of the millennium.

'Bit of level, Richard, please?' asked a crackly-calm
Mission Control voice in my padded-leather headphones.

'The President of Nigeria's wife and I have never been in
a room alone together,' I said in cod-American. It was the
headline phrase from the rape-scandal press conference at
the White House the previous day, with the difference that
it was true when I said it.

'Do you want to just clear your throat a bit, Richard?'

Oh, God. 'Sorry. I'm a bit . . .'

'Yeah, do what you can. Everyone's got something.
Cornelius Raven was just in here with nostrils like a pissing
contest.'

The director of the commercial – a deliberate-baldy in his
forties, also dressed for the crematorium – pressed his own
earth-to-orbit switch and said in a light and reedy voice
which was the precise opposite of the one he would need to
coax from me, 'OK, should we think about going for one?
Think lightness, Richard. Babies – you'll see this on the
screen – but babies holding telephones is the idea. Show how
small and light the Feather 141 is. Warmly ironic is what
we're looking for. But ironically warm would do.'

On the monitor, a pack of grinning infants – two of them
black, this social range the main change during my ten-year
career in commercials – crawled across a floor strewn with
white feathers. The mobiles in their hands were so small that

you really saw them only when the camera went in close for the money-shot.

The babies reversed across the floor ten times, as the tape was repositioned for another intonation. I did four takes which successively increased the stress on 'feather'.

'Whoah, Richard. Let's try soft-pedalling "feather". Make the word *float*.'

By the sixth variation, they were happy with the weight given to the trade-name. The next four attempts concentrated on achieving the correct ironic warmth or warm irony for the pay-off about learning how to talk. In the end, they preferred the first. They always do. The retakes are part of the constant struggle in show business to make a simple instinct feel like work.

Soon my endorsement of tiny mobiles would take its place in the ad gaps alongside my other current enthusiams: for breadcrumbed chicken dinosaurs, an anti-bacterial lavatory cleaner and low-cost home insurance. None of us summoned to these cells to read a single phrase at boxer's pay really understands why, in the minds of advertisers, one voice is bleach and another beans. The trick is the ability to achieve a kind of simpering conviction, a sale which sounds like a gift. There is at least a surface logic in mobile phones being hawked by a talk-show host. Only I knew that the Great Communicator they were paying had a raw throat and a speechless marriage.

'Nice one, Richard,' said the director. 'The cold didn't show.'

My parents would have taught for a term to make the money I'd earned – or would be paid – for twenty minutes in that cell.

*

There was a surprised half-smile on the young Hispanic's face as he asked, 'Skinny piccolo mocha no whip, was it?'

Even Londoners who had failed French and German at school have a second language now. Everyone speaks fluent coffee, educated by the new refreshment bars with their rich lingo of drinks.

'Er, yeah. Assuming piccolo's the small size.'

'Sorry? No, piccolo's the middle one. Maybe you want a lento or a forte?'

'Piccolo's fine.'

'Can I get you anything to eat with that?'

Hating this primitive sales trick, I always want to say, 'I'd have asked if I did,' but I'd guessed that he had recognized me so said, 'No thanks.'

'Hey, Richard, I hope I can answer your questions!'

As fan-taps go, it is nicely done, avoiding the idiot reverential ('Excuse me, but are you really . . . ?'), the ignorant aggressive ('Haven't I seen you somewhere?') and the specifically hostile ('You think you're fucking smart, don't you?'). We all say in interviews that we hate being recognized in the street, but the truth is that we crave a certain kind of recognition: discreet adoration. Skinny piccolo worship no whip. No, make that forte.

'OK if I ask *you* a question, Rich?'

'Sure.'

'What's Cornelius Raven really like?'

Go back to Hispania, you little fucker. 'Oh, Con's a really funny guy. In at least two senses.'

I thought my server was going to need urgent treatment at the Laughter Injuries Clinic. Billy Connolly – a talk-show dream: ask him a question and he'll busk you an hour – once said that the Queen must think everywhere smells of fresh paint. Celebrities come to believe that everything they say is amusing.

'Hey, Richard, not being funny or anything but, if you could interview anyone in the world, who would it be?'

'Oh, the Pope, I suppose, is what I usually say.'

My phrasing gave him just a hint of how tediously repetitive these conversations with The People were.

'Really? Why him, then, Rich?'

'Because no one's done him.'

'Except for a few nuns and altar boys!'

My own laugh would not have caused admission to the clinic. I'd be lucky even to be seen by the practice nurse. The Hispanic handed over my coffee with a small card. Assuming it to be my loyalty wallet – drink ten coffees, get one free – I was surprised to see a name beside the logo of a laughing face in red.

'Richard, if you ever need some gags for your show.' Fucker: they were supposed to think I wrote my own, although I didn't. 'And I'm at the Comedy Store Fridays and Saturdays, although a busy guy like you . . .'

It used to be that everyone wanted to have their own show. Now everybody has one. Your cleaning lady probably fronts some home improvement series on a distant cable channel. I pulled a crisp new twenty from a fat stack in my pocket: carrying so much put me in danger from muggers but made me feel safer from failure. The cappuccino comedian waved it away.

'This one's on me, Rich.'

'But I earn' – twenty, thirty times what you do, no, they can only hate you if you say it – 'I mean, doesn't it mean the till won't . . .'

'I'll put it in, Rich.'

'No. No, really, you . . .'

'I'm serious. You've given me so many nights of pleasure. And you must be good at that, with having had so many wives and that.'

It was only two. Headteachers and police make the same complaint. They cheek you back now; there is no mystique. But I beamed benignly as I left with my free drink.

Even dissatisfying adulation is better than hostility or ignorance. It's like celebrity lightning: that moment at a movie première or charity gala when you walk through the electrical storm of camera flashes. The first few times you attend – a C-list marginal, only there because someone has cancelled – the air is dry as you pass, but you feel the hot rain just behind you for someone else. On the day when it breaks over your head, you start to live. After that, if the lightning ever fails to strike, you know you're dead.

When I reached the radio office, the swearing and plotting which generally took much of the staff's energy were intensified because we were under investigation by the BBC Complaints Unit. A Beaconsfield pensioner claimed to have heard the word 'fucking' during our 26 January edition. Anna – my main producer, a sociopathic Australian transferred to the show because of my reputation for difficulty and her own as a horse-whisperer for broadcasters – threw a cassette at me as I walked in.

'Richard, can you listen to that and see if you can find what the fuck the cunt's on about? I've fucking listened through twice and we're as clean as choirboys. Some fucking deaf grey-head wasting our time.'

As usual – through a combination of the antique BBC lifts and the journalist's religion of the last-minute – I reached the radio studio less than a minute before the Greenwich Time Signal. Anna was in my cans as soon as they were on my ears. They were damp. Dominic Kingsley, who hosted the lunchtime news show, was a nervous broadcaster – he just can't do live – who dripped sweat even during cold snaps. I took out a handkerchief and swabbed the padded muffs as Anna ranted.

'Welcome, Fleming. We were just about to phone Peter Pennington. Listen – that dumb cunt has forgotten to book the fucking radio car so the middle's about to fall out of the cancer donut. Fuck, here we go . . .'

The last bleep of the four p.m. time code was followed by the two words, 'Richard Fleming!', crooned a cappella on a rising intonation by a tenor session singer. Only four groups of people ever get to hear their names sung on occasions other than their birthdays: Popes, monarchs, sports stars and radio presenters.

The light which showed the microphone was live was set in a varnished wooden cone, like the craft in which spacemen splash down in the sea. Now the dull bulb glowed bright lime. *Gatsby believed in the green light*, I thought.

'Hello', I said, in a voice both crisper and friendlier than the one I used to those who loved me. 'It's Monday. Four o'clock. I'm Richard Fleming and this is *UK Today*. In the next hour . . . Hate after Eight: an American author explains why you might be cutting seven wedding cakes in your lifetime . . . *Clicking* with someone: the couple who found love through the Internet . . . The Magic Fruit: the secret gay codes supposedly hidden in Mozart's operas . . . And our phone-in today: would *you* ever smack your children? . . . But, first, the news headlines from Ruthia Hortenwurst.'

When Ruthia started, she had several times read the same news story twice. We called her Déjà Roo, which would have been better if she were French not German, but office jokes are a rough science. And no newcomer to the team would see the humour: she was becoming distressingly fluent. When the bulletin was under way, Anna was back in both ears: '*You can't say Magic fucking Fruit. You answer the letters.*'

I reversed the intercom, Eagle to Houston: 'Count yourself lucky. I could have said Bugger of Seville and don't even think about Cosi Fan Tutti.'

'*Fuck you, Fleming. By the way, the cancer donut's fine. But the Satanic Package depends on whether they can de-um it in time.*'

De-umming – once done with razor blades, now achieved through computer deletion – is the process of cutting hesitations and stumbles from recorded tape. While most editing tricks in broadcasting are mischievous, this one is kind: making speakers more fluent than they are.

'*Coming in thirty. You'd better clear your throat.*'

The feed from the newsroom next door was played into my cans – 'And this news just in. A thirty-three-year-old man has been jailed in California for breaching a court order preventing him from harassing the Oscar-winning actress Lindsay Lennox' – and the pushy little trust-fund Kraut, fast-tracked for stardom according to department rumour, finished the bulletin, pitch perfect in the camp familiarity at which the station now aimed: 'Richard?'

'Thanks, Ruthia. You're looking tanned. Been somewhere nice?'

She was four floors above. I'd seen her earlier in the canteen.

'Seychelles.'

The ad-lib cortex of my brain offered the play-yard answer, 'Shells', but a critic had twitted me for 'inanity' the week before and so, experimenting with an aggressiveness which I envied in the younger generation of presenters, I said, 'We must be paying you too much. Next scheduled headlines at four thirty.'

'*Poor Ruthia. Wouldn't she fuck you?*'

Anna's voice was so loud that some of the talkback spilled out of the cans and was heard in the more attentive homes. A listener once rang to complain that a foul-mouthed mad-woman was trying to break into the studio during the show.

I swung an extravagant V-sign towards Anna through the glass of the observation window, where she and the studio managers glared like the prison governor and the victims' families in a movie execution scene.

I leaned closer to the microphone, pitching my voice slightly higher to reduce the risk of scratchiness. Imagine you're talking to one person only. If the programme's ratings continue on their current path, perhaps you soon will be.

'How much trouble did you go to to find the person you love?'

I knew long before I reached 'love' that I was in trouble. There was a high-pitched whistling in my ears and, as I spoke each word, a reverberating echo created a back-up version of the sentence one beat behind. Howl-round. All you could do was keep going, forcing through the rhythm of your original sounds like someone singing counterpoint.

'Meals? Phone calls?' I had gained all my major relation-ships through a war of adoration, a fusillade of compliments and gifts. 'Flowers? Letters?'

The white-noise torture was continuing; every example I gave had its parroting shadow. In the cubicle, Anna and the SMs were on their feet, flicking at switches on the flight desk. Then the techie with the droopy eye – I really must ask the secretary for a list of their names – gave the thumbs-up. My voice sounded right to me again, like the moment in the airport arrivals hall when atmosphere-ears clear.

'Well, my next guest went further. At the age of forty, he hired private detectives to trace the childhood sweetheart with whom he'd lost touch. He finally found her, and they're getting married next month. Jeff Tims and Angela Shipley join me now from our Leeds studio. Jeff – what made you decide to get back in touch?'

'To be honest, Richard, I realized what I were missing. Me first marriage had ended and when me mates were clearing us stuff out of house, like, I found this big box of photos and that of Angie. There were even ticket stubs from films us went to . . . I got to thinking . . .'

I was only half-listening to Jeff's romantic nostalgia, the rest of my attention on Anna in my cans: '*Sorry about fucking howl-round. Two faders on the same circuit. You did OK, though. You've got six on this.*'

'. . . first lass I'd ever felt serious about, Richard, to be honest . . .'

'OK, Jeff, I think we need to fear from' – Fuck you, Revd Spooner – 'hear from your future wife. Angela, why had you split up originally?'

'We was very young, Richard. I mebbes felt he were getting a bit serious. The break-up were a bit, you know . . . and I found it easier not to hear from him in end . . . You know how it is.' I knew how it was. 'But he's forgiven me for that now . . .'

Even then – when they were just another six minutes in another three hours on a day when I was thinking of other things – that sentence unsettled me. What disturbed me was the subservience. There was a clattering sound from the Leeds studio. I guessed that the couple had just clasped hands and bumped the microphone. Anna seemed to have reached the same conclusion. Through the glass, she stabbed a finger between her open lips in the mime for sick-making.

'So, Jeff, how did you go about finding her?'

'Well, at first, it were like they say – needle in haystack . . .

though our Angie's bigger than a needle . . .' There was a giggle and an off-mike sound louder than before, which I took to be a playful slap. 'I rang all the numbers I'd ever had for her, but you could tell it had been a while because they were all longer. I was always adding sixes and fives and that. Finally I got her Auntie Sadie, but she said Angie were married and that it wouldn't be right . . .'

'*Would you pay a private dick to find her? I'd pay a contract killer to ice her?*'

I'd heard enough by now of Anna's contrapuntal mono-logues to smile rather than laugh. Interviewees never knew about this stream of someone else's consciousness in your head. It was like the times when, away from Rachel in the early days of our relationship, I'd turn our calls into phone sex without her knowing.

'So then, Jeff, you hired private detectives?'

'Yeah. I'd seen a thing on telly about missing persons and that.'

'*Three minutes on this.*'

'And they reported back to you?'

'Yeah. They said they'd never have found her without the Internet, Richard. They told me she were living with a bloke and two kiddies in Norwich.'

'What did you think?'

'To be honest, Richard, me first thought were crap foot-ball team.'

The louder off-mike sound again. 'But, seriously, I thought she'll not be wanting me then . . . But I rang her on the number they gave me.'

'And, Angela, how did you feel when he called?'

'I were surprised, Richard, to be honest . . . but I'd just realized I were in an abusive relationship.' All those sob shows on morning television have changed the way the

English speak; a once-reticent people now spout American emotionalese. 'It felt like it were meant . . .'

'*But did he tell her how he found her?*'

Sometimes Anna had a good idea, fuck her. 'But how did you feel when . . .' Bugger, reviewers always kneecap you for 'How do you feel?', a question which reveals you as a sentimental imbecile. 'I mean, some people might think that it was a bit creepy, hiring private detectives and so on, creeping around . . .' Fuck, repetition of creeping, echo-words weren't as serious in speech as on the page but they knitting-needled the ear. 'I mean, I know it's turned out fine, but it was almost like a . . .' God, I'd gone into monologue, which only Irish, Scottish or Welsh presenters can get away with, because of some odd English historical tolerance of Celtic verbosity. 'Like a, er, stalker . . .'

'*Last answer.*'

'To be honest, Richard, I thought it were romantic . . . It were like he were looking out for me . . .'

'*Cut-throat.*'

'Angela and Jeff, we wish you luck. News and sport from the BBC. It's time for the latest sports news from Barry Accrington.'

'Richard, thanks. There's no hiding place for the England manager,' began a laddish Lancastrian voice in my cans.

The cue into Jeff and Angela was on the desk in front of me. I therapeutically rolled a foolscap snowball, spun it into the battered tin bin in the corner of the studio and forgot about them.

*

In the second hour of the programme there was the worst possible combination: straight out of a down-the-line live into a link in which the M-word was unavoidable.

UK Today – With Richard Fleming – Monday 15 February

Second Hour – Draft Running Order

17.00 – GTS – Jingle – Menu
17.01 – News Headlines (Ruthia Hortenwurst)
17.05 – Pres Rape – Washington Live 2 / Way (Clem
          Sadley)
17.10 – Millennium Tape Package (Robin Nicholas)
17.17 – Sports Desk (Barry Accrington)
17.19 – Travel (Lavinia Eldersbury)
17.20 – Live 1 + 1 – with Samantha Gravure Sebastian on
          her book *Seven Brides for Seven Husbands*
17.25 – Cancer Donut (details tba)

On the printed script, I scratched out my nemesis-expression with a BBC felt-tip and scribbled above it mill-any-um. Only by splitting the word into three sections and over-stressing the first could I hope to make it recognizable.

'*Coming in thirty.*'

Anna's smoker's Australian was replaced by the bouncy sound of the newsroom's own Eva Braun: 'And, finally, spokespersons' – she gave the word a little tremolo of distress at gender-inclusive language – 'for the rock star Marty Stark and the Oscar-winning actress Alice Jackett are refusing to comment on tabloid reports that they spent the weekend together at top London hotel Overnights. Stark's third wife – the supermodel Jennifer Jeffs – told a newspaper this morning that the singer had left her for the star of *Mrs Shakespeare* and *Roadkill . . .*'

The story had been written by Gordon Bannoch. I hoped it didn't mean that he was closing in on me.

'Apparently, Richard, if the reports are to be believed, they met on your television programme . . .'

'Yeah. Apparently . . .'

'So should I call you Cupid?'

'Or Pandarus . . .'

'Er . . .'

I sensed the panic in her voice and knew that she had heard it as 'pander us'. Whichever Düsseldorf Roedean had educated her had favoured Goethe over Chaucer or Shakespeare.

'Er, yes.'

Though mystified, she produced a perfect knowing laugh, and I knew in that moment that she was going to be a star in this business, so disliked her even more.

'OK, Ruthia. See you at five thirty.'

'If you're gonna wave your willy, give out microscopes first.'

Jabbing a finger at Anna through the glass in the European fuck-you, I continued to read in the sweet, clear tones of a likeable and open-minded man: 'This is *UK Today* with Richard Fleming. As you may have heard there in the news bulletin, just when it seemed as if things were looking better for President Riley – after the settlement last week of the lawsuit brought by the Northern New Hampshire Mother's Union – more dirty linen has spilled out of his closet. Despite strenuous denials by both sides, a well-respected Washington website is quoting new evidence from a highly placed medical source that Mr Riley attempted to rape the wife of the Nigerian President after a state dinner at the White House last month. Live now to our Washington correspondent, Clem Sadley. Clem, how seriously is this being taken in Washington?'

'Richard, I believed in Tom Riley when I first met him. Like a lot of the White House press, I saw him as a new kind of politician. I liked what I saw. Today I have to say that I am coming to terms with how wrong I was . . .'

Sadley's measured tones, gentrified Welsh, were under-scored by soft hissing. Transatlantic lines, fittingly, produce the sound of waves.

'Among my friends on the circuit here are some of the biggest names in American journalism and, as I called them up this morning, they were saying that, like me, it was a case of admitting: I was wrong . . .'

'*Yeeeeeeeeeeeeeeeeeeeees!*'

Startled by Anna's orgasmic roar in my ear, it took me a moment to understand that she must have won the usual sweepstake in the booth on how often the first-person pronoun would appear in Sadley's report. Indeed, so loud was her shout that she had probably also cleaned up in the side-bet on the appearances of 'me'.

Sadley was the dean of a new breed of reporters who always brought the story back to their own presence and response. An unexceptional fireman in the news pool, he had become a darling of the middle classes after a radio programme in which he delivered a sobbing monologue to his aged parents, both Alzheimer's victims, as they sat uncomprehending in their rest home. He later padded out the transcripts into a best-selling book and couldn't under-stand why colleagues laughed when they heard his chosen title: *Do You Know Who I Am?*

These may seem strange complaints to make in a memoir but this manuscript is not for publication. Unless I rip it up, it will lie in my file in some cabinet here until I die.

'If you ask me,' Sadley was saying, 'I think what I would predict is, as I say, a slip in President Riley's approval ratings. I wouldn't like to be him . . .'

'This is being denied from both Washington and Lagos,

Clem. What evidence is the website, er' – fuck, I couldn't think of a verb: giving, adducing – 'producing for this story?'

'My sources are telling me, Richard, that the Nigerian First Lady was treated at an emergency room in Washington in the early hours of 11 January, that there was evidence of sexual assault and that she made an accusation against President Riley – subsequently withdrawn. I can tell you that the medical records appear to show . . .'

'*He can't say vagina before seven p.m. And make this the final question.*'

'I won't go into clinical detail, I think . . .'

'*Yeeeeeeeeeeeeeeeeeeeeeeeeeeeeeeeeeeeeees!*'

Anna must have won the weekly accumulator as well. Fuck her on the final question then.

'I suppose the question is, Clem, why would the Nigerians deny this if it was true?'

Served me right. If it *were* true. If one of the wrinkly radio critics was listening – were listening? – there would be some stuffy paragraph in the next column about the lost delight of the subjunctive.

'As I say, I really wouldn't like to be him,' concluded the Washington egomaniac.

'Thank you to Clem Sadley in Washington. I'm sure we'll be hearing more on that story. It's ten minutes past five. Coming up: Hate after Eight – why ninth wedding anniversaries may soon be as rare as a Pope's wedding . . . and bucket dot com: the window cleaner who became an Internet millionaire . . . But, first, it's just over ten months to the manyum' – fuck, shit, concentrating on the two-way with Sadley, I'd forgotten it was there, tricked into complacency by managing 'millionaire' – 'and countries around the world are getting ready to celebrate this once-in-fifteen generations calendar jackpot. In Britain, there's been much controversy over the Mullunum' – double fuck – 'Dome. But, in the second of his special reports for *UK Today* looking at whether other countries are spending as much time and money on their celebrations, Robin Nicholas reports from Russia, where the red-letter date has brought conflict between Church and state . . .'

The chanting of Russian Orthodox liturgy began the report. I pressed the switch that linked me to the booth: 'I'm sorry. I can't fucking say men-manyum.'

'*We were just laughing about it in here.*'

'Oh, thanks.'

This wasn't right. A presenter's insecure or self-deprecating remarks were supposed to be followed by lavish compliments from the producer, suggesting that such worries were unfounded. Indeed, self-criticism from a presenter is only ever an investment on the compliments Stock Market.

'No. *It's just the station have got you on the short list to do the 31 December overnight. It's like asking someone with a lisp to present the greatest hits of Yes.*'

'You're very supportive today.'

'*Why were you such a cunt to Ruthia?*'

Occasional visitors to the studio – work-experience students, journalists writing profiles of me, network executives – were always surprised by the obscenity of the off-air exchanges. The puritanical attribute the profanity to machismo, but I think it's the pressure of decorum in broadcasting. Tongues are so constrained in front of microphones – even a stray 'God' or 'Christ!' will result in letters from vicars which the BBC insist on taking seriously – that there is an over-reaction in release.

'What the fucking fuck are you on about?' I snapped at Anna, glaring at her through the glass which separated me

from Mission Control, my finger stinging because I had
pressed down the reverse talkback switch so hard.

'*That fucking Panda thing? Ruthie coped brilliantly
but . . .*'

'She's had her life on a plate. Her career can't be second
helpings. How long on this tape?'

'*Another six fifteen.*'

'I'm going for a piss.'

'*Another one? I'm going to put in to Resources for a
commode.*'

There's always unease when a presenter leaves the studio
during a live broadcast. Over at the pop stations – where a
urination break is frequently a euphemism for the taking
of drugs – there are stories of broadcasters failing to return
and a six-record segue being played while the slumped DJ is
revived with cold water and black coffee.

Here at the speech end of radio, an allergic reaction to
camomile tea was the most they had to fear, but it's a
superstition among live presenters never to risk defeca-
tion in a toilet break because there's always a risk of the visit
becoming extended. Such is the terror of dead air that, even
for this mere pee, I ran to the Gents and rapidly splash-
washed my hands and mouth afterwards before sprinting
back to the rectangle of settees outside the studio where
the next guests sipped polystyrene beakers of a generalized
brown beverage.

Two women were waiting now. Both, I guessed, were in
their early forties but had nothing else in common, resembling the two sides of the page of a cosmetics commercial in
advertising's pre-ironic days. The woman on the left was tall
with blonde hair cut short above a tanned face in which the
sparkle of the eyes suggested contact lenses or extreme good
health; her neighbour on the sofa was smaller with a bleached

complexion offset by hot-spots on the cheek and forehead. A tangle of auburn hair seemed imposed rather than grown, suggesting a wig.

I instinctively offered my hand to the healthy and attractive woman first. Darwin would have laughed.

'Hi. I'm Richard Fleming.'

'Hi, Richard! Samantha Gravure Sebastian.'

'Oh, yes. I found your book very interesting.'

'You read it?'

No.

'Yes.'

'Of course, what I fear is interviewers who've been happily married for thirty years.'

'You needn't fear me.'

Thirty years. She had taken me for at least five years older than I was. But American medicine and nutrition had confused evolution. No English person could stand beside a Californian without looking like Dorian Gray's portrait.

The sound-proofed door of the production hutch flapped back and Anna shouted, 'Three forty-five on this tape.'

On the inside of the door was a poster showing in pictures the techniques of emergency resuscitation. A studio – the place where friendly voices come from – holds odd intimations of danger. Apart from the mouth-to-mouth graphics, there was a sealed yellow bucket marked SHARPS ONLY, for the razor blades used to edit tape. In a locked case at Anna's feet were obituary tapes for the Queen Mother and the Queen. But what seemed to outsiders the most sinister sign – DEAD BATS FOR RECYCLING – referred not to witchcraft but to spent batteries from recording machines.

The woman I had been ignoring now held out her hand. Aware of her frailty, I scarcely brushed it with mine.

'Diane Labone,' she said. 'SPAT. Staffordshire Patients Action Team.'

'Ah, yes.'

'Who have you got against me?'

Although my nerves were better then than later, I guiltily, subliminally, heard it as '*What* have you got against me?' before recovering to say, 'Oh, one of the doctors, I think.'

'It's not Carson, is it?' she said intensely. 'He was the consultant who started all this.'

'I don't really know. I'll tell you before we start. Dr Gravure Sebastian . . .'

'Samantha, please . . .'

'We'd better go through. We're on next.'

Anna was ranting even as I rearranged myself in the pilot's seat: '*OK, you've got about five on your 1 + 1 with the divorce queen, but if she doesn't deliver, ship out and we'll give another minute to the cancer donut. This package ends on the words "A hundred years after the Revolution is the only date I'll celebrate", spoken by an old commie. Back-anno it but maybe you should say Year 2000. The out words on the sports tape are "fair play to them, they dominated the game", aren't they fucking ever? Another minute on this tape.*'

The prophet of marital misery, who was reading sideways a copy of the running order which had been knocked across the desk, asked, 'So donuts are carcinogenic now, is that right?'

'What?' I grabbed the sheet of paper from her. 'Oh, fuck, I don't want that poor woman seeing that. No, a "donut" is this term we have in radio for an item in which you hand over live to a reporter in the middle. The reporter is the filling, as it were? Hence "cancer donut". Although we've also had an "incontinence donut" and a "paedophilia donut" . . . We're kind of like this Quentin Tarantino version of Dunkin' Donuts.'

She didn't smile. If we fear the way Americans look, they are frightened of the way we sound.

'My second husband has a tumour right now,' Dr Gravure Sebastian said, and I took it from her calmness that she had reached at least her third.

'*Forty . . .*'

I checked my guest's name on the running order: 'Er, Samantha, we'll be able to have a quick chat in a minute. I just have to hand over to the travel.'

'*Ten on this and you need to clear your throat . . .*'

I coughed and prepared to summon my public voice. Anna's grizzled Sydney was followed by a heavy Russian accent complicated by asthma: 'Why would we celebrate two thousand years of Christ, I ask you? A hundred years after the Revolution is the only date I'll celebrate!'

The green light glowed. 'An old Russian general – more interested in Lenin than the' – separate the syllables, stress the first – '*Mill*-any-um' – yeeeeeeeeeeeeeeeeeeees! – 'concluding that report from Robin Nicholas on' – take the purse, don't fight a rematch – 'the Year 2000 celebrations in Russia. Tomorrow, in the last of his reports, he'll be in California, where the date is being marked with characteristic extravagance. This is *UK Today* with Richard Fleming. It's just coming up to seventeen minutes past five. Time for travel with Lavinia Eldersbury . . .'

'Yes, Richard. You don't see too many people walking around wearing T-shirts saying "I Love the Hanger Lane Gyratory System" and tonight there's another reminder of why . . .'

Samantha Gravure Sebastian was very good. Broadcasting courses teach that the best interviewees have the gift of spontaneity but the most successful guests are those who can deliver carefully prepared material in a credibly extempore manner. The only problem was that this speaker seemed to be improvising an obituary for my relationship with Rachel.

'But silver weddings used to be the norm,' I challenged her. 'Why suddenly now would there be this eight-year cut-off?'

'Oh, excellent question, Richard. Listen, the math has always been there. But, in the past, people – women especially – were too frightened or too poor or too religious to write the final line of the equation. What's happened now is that society has come into line with psychology . . .'

'*Cut-throat.*'

'We're going to have to leave it there. Thank you very much to Dr Samantha Gravure Sebastian. Her book, *Seven Brides for Seven Husbands: Serial Love in the Twenty-first Century*, is published in hardback by Quinney.'

'*Programme ident.*'

The session singers sang my name in a euphoric chorus – again that heady moment of knowing what it might be like to be a dictator – intercut with an ego-reel of jauntily taunting moments from past interviews – 'Another word for it would be cock-up, Prime Minister . . .', 'Pity you can't reincarnate the 1966 World Cup-winning team . . .', 'So the bank did know about the loan?' – subliminally instructing the listener that Richard Fleming was a man by whom very famous people liked to be patronized.

I shook Dr Samantha Gravure Sebastian's hand, then waved vaguely towards the studio door, which was opening to reveal the SPAT woman walking in with the heaviness of someone dragging across soft sand. The woman who hoped to have four more husbands and the woman who prayed for perhaps four more months passed each other, symbolizing the uneasy balance between the tragic and the trivial as broadcasting tried to satisfy the dreams of both its founders and its accountants.

'*Be ready to blather to fill. The cancer chick may be NVR.*'

NVR – not vocally reliable – was engineer-speak for contributors whose delivery showed wide variations of volume or pitch.

'There are no easy answers with Richard Fleming,' boomed a semi-American voice at the end of the ego-reel. As the woman in the wig carefully sat down, the cue-light glowed green.

'We can all imagine the joy,' I began, 'of the letter from the hospital which says the test was negative: the lump was nothing, the shadow was a thumbprint on the X-ray.'

In order to avoid accusations of insensitivity, a broadcaster needs two voices: a would-you-believe-it aria for the light items and a there-but-for-the-grace recitativo for death, disaster and the passing of monarchs. The first is tenor and pacy, the second stately and bass. The cancer donut called for the latter: 'We can also imagine all too horribly the second letter from the hospital, which says: please disregard the first. That – tragically – is what happened to a group of Staffordshire woman, who got the all-clear from their smear tests in 1995 . . .'

*

The cancer woman hadn't liked me, I was sure of that. She had winced angrily when we reached the fakely apologetic, 'I'm sorry, that's all we've got time for.' She had seen my guilty glances downwards to check her name at both ends of the segment. That had been a mistake. I usually taught myself who they were before they came through the door.

Successful broadcasting is all about pretending to know people: your listeners and your guests.

'Carson was given much more time than me,' she complained, as I led her from the studio. The extended news and sport on the half-hour gave me seven minutes' grace. 'And you cut me off before I could go back at him on God-like consultants . . .'

'Our time is limited,' I said, then realized the tactlessness of this remark when addressed to someone nearly dead. 'The problem with a don . . . with an OB, an outside broadcast, is that they tend to overrun because the guests can't see the body language telling them to stop . . .'

Christ. Illness undermined every word. Her body's language was furiously gesticulating for a finish.

'The fact is, you gave more time to some drivel about Californians all getting divorced than to thirty-five women whose cancer went undiagnosed for two years!'

Don't say it, I thought, don't say dumbing down. What profession were you in – are you in? Whatever it is, don't you find it tougher to keep customers than it used to be? We're not stupid; we're desperate. Show me one area of commerce where seriousness sells any more. Look along the high street. Even sandwiches and coffee are ironic products now.

'The BBC is dumbing down,' complained the cancer woman.

'There are the lifts.' I pointed down the corridor. 'We were happy with your contribution, even if you weren't.'

The disgruntled contributor, I noted, would be further irritated by a long wait for the lifts. The floor indicators above the doors all showed paired red Xs, meaning that the cars had been taken out of general service. This was a precaution by the security staff to avoid the possibility of the

Director General, an unpopular reformer, meeting any of his staff as he came and went.

I turned back towards my studio. On the hospitality sofas outside, experimentally dribbling the cooling coffee into cups, sat two men with beards so long and lavish that they resembled diners in a meat restaurant where the pelts of the animals were turned into bibs.

I was about to shove open the heavy studio door when the parallel entrance to the production booth sprang back and a tall man dressed entirely in black stooped through.

'Richard. Hi, hi, hi.'

'Oh, Ol, hello. OK?'

Oliver Mendip was the programme's editor. In a newspaper, this title implied total control; in broadcasting, it was almost honorific. Mendip supervised several different series and was involved only through a process called 'referral upwards', in which items including swearwords, interviews with convicted criminals or derogatory references to the BBC itself were offered to him for veto.

Mendip visited the studios usually only on Christmas Eve, bearing a tray of twice-microwaved mincepies uneaten at the executive lunch and looking resentful at the failure of paper-hat makers to fashion one in black to match his habitual inky suit and polo-neck. It could not be good that he was here now.

'Richard, I was holding you up at a conference the other day as a wholly successful example of bimediality.'

I had heard that somewhere very recently. Where? *Ogg.* Executives here swapped opinions like addicts passed round needles.

'Oh. Well, I'm glad to be bi . . . I've always said.'

'Are you dashing off after the programme?'

'Well. I, er . . . I'm doing an interview – giving an interview – for some magazine . . . I could maybe be ten minutes late. More than that and she'll come on like the War Crimes Tribunal in the piece . . . Why?'

'Oh, just something seems to have gone wrong with drinks cabinet provision and I've actually been sent a decent red. Arf, arf.' One of Mendip's peculiarities was that he spoke out his laughs, like a character in a cartoon strip. 'Should I have two glasses out at seven?'

'Yes. I suppose . . .'

'Smashing. Christ . . .' He lowered his voice. 'Are they rabbis or what?'

'Where?'

'In the pig pen,' he whispered, nodding towards the guest hospitality seats, where the two hirsute men were trying to sip coffee without soaking their bristly bibs.

'They're for some item in the fourth half-hour,' I murmured back. 'But I don't remember the Amish or anything coming up at conference. Shit, are you . . .'

Mendip had been knocked forward by the force of Anna slamming open the door of the production hutch into his back. Her physical energies matched her verbal aggression. Regulars on the programme always stood in the middle of a room.

'Christ!' said Mendip.

'Sorry, Ol,' said Anna. 'Less than ten on this, Fleming.'

I ran across the studio but was off-mike when I said, 'Thanks, Ruthia . . .'

*

If the BBC lifts had been fruit machines, I could have won the jackpot and retired. All three indicators showed XX. The Director General must be going home.

'Good show today.'

Anna was beside me. We stood watching the unchanging display like passengers at a fog-bound airport.

'It was OK.'

'Are you off to see Mendip?'

'Yeah. How did . . .'

'He asked me whether I knew if you were dashing off.'

'Right.'

'Richard, I know I get on your case all the time, but I do think you're a' – she waggled her fingers in the air to make quotation marks – ' "a really good broadcaster" and all that.'

I understood what the compliment must have cost – her working style depending so much on sarcasm – and so there was genuine warmth in my nod. I considered how much spin to put on the return. 'I have this theory that the best programmes are the ones where the production team hate each other.'

'Well, this must be the best fucking show in history, then.'

The pay-out line of XX-XX-XX still glowed red. Perhaps the DG had been seized in his carriage by a hit squad of those he had sacked.

When I finally opened Mendip's door – late for him, later for the interview with Lizzie De Mare – he began to pour red wine into the second of two glasses waiting on the table.

'Ah, Richard, come in. Imagine my surprise when the box from the Hospitality Unit contains one stray bottle of Pommard among the flasks of Chilean Pisspot with which we're normally expected to raise morale. Strictly, I should fill in a misassignment report, but I think the Corporation owes us this one. Arf, arf.'

Accepting the brimming glass, I sat down beside Mendip on the dark green sofa where we'd shared warm champagne two years before when the deal for the radio series had been signed.

'That piece on the department store that has banned facial hair was top, I thought,' said my editor. 'Of course, strictly those guys with these great hessian scarves hanging from their lower lips would have made better television. But you could actually hear this kind of swishing as they spoke. I think the more sophisticated listener will have appreciated that.'

Mendip was in his late forties. He had begun in television in the 1970s, making reverential documentaries about novelists who wrote whole books without vowels or artists who painted single-coloured squares. Most of his colleagues from that time were now showing their experimental video installations at seaside art festivals, but Mendip had reacted to television's shifts in taste and finance by turning up to work one morning as a breezy populist, his briefcase (replacing the previously familiar satchel) containing proposals for series on thriller writers and amateur poets.

When those programmes were judged to contain too many cheeky camera angles and educated allusions, Mendip had convinced his superiors that his experience might now be useful in management. After irritating the reformers there with too much reference to a BBC past which was by implication glorious, he had written a paper which argued, counter-intuitively, that the true future of broadcasting was radio.

His lips reddened by wine, he asked me, 'Did I tell you that we held you up as a wholly successful example of biomediality?'

'Yes.'

'Well, you are. But there's just a bit of a blipette on the radio side of the equation.'

'But Ogg threw a party for us just before Christmas because we were something or other – 4 per cent, was it? – up in the last quarter.'

'Mmm. Mmm,' Mendip was acknowledging even before I had finished. 'Actually, 3.7 per cent. Yes. MD.BRO was right on the headline figures. But people like me are paid to see the underlying. You're rather more male than you absolutely should be at four p.m.'

'Excuse me?'

Open talkback. What was happening? In the fifteen years of my rise, I had smiled knowingly with others among the young on reading in a press release or newspaper that some middle-aged journalist or broadcaster was 'leaving to pursue other projects'. Would it now be me telling an interviewer with chirpy perjury that I had decided to concentrate on television, until that went too and another hack was summoned to hear my smiling lie that newspapers had always been my main love? I had worked with men who had lied to the press that their wives had cancer to reduce the stigma of dismissal.

'Your audience splits 62–38 male–female,' Mendip explained. 'Even allowing for a majority male car-user base in your time-slot, you're dressing too far to one side. MD.BRO agrees absolutely. We need to make you more female . . .'

The final words were spoken with no quiver of silliness. Mendip wore the expression of a man offering a solemn business proposition.

'So what are we talking, Ol?' I asked. 'A training course? Or hormone therapy?'

'What? No. MD.BRO and I think you need to go buddy-buddy. Just over 81 per cent of drive-time shows on speech stations internationally are co-hosted . . .'

'Co-hosted?' Joy at my survival in this job was soon overtaken by irritation at the division of the limelight. 'Is this theoretical or have you got someone?'

'We've had an eye on someone for some time. It came to a head when she was offered something elsewhere.'

I mentally catalogued the young presenters who had moved me to envious resentment in the car. Molly Durie, who had lured listeners and critics to late-nights; Kirsty McGregor, who had taken over weekend breakfasts with worrying aplomb; Agnes Kerr, who had merely been skeleton cover (appropriately as it turned out) in the newsroom on the holiday weekend when Diana died but had won a Sony for her firm but sensitive hosting of a rolling seven-hour phone-in, *The Nation Remembers*.

'It's going to be a Scot,' I predicted.

'Why?'

'It always is. There's this terror of English accents now in British broadcasting. It's because the audience can guess what class you are. So they use Scots because somehow they're supposed to be classless. But the joke is that half of them are the offspring of baronets, brought up in castles.'

'It's not a Scot. In fact, we thought of Agnes Kerr, but she's probably too big for a co-pilot's seat now.'

'Oh.'

'Closer to home . . . it's Ruthia.'

'Ruthia!'

'We think she's a real talent.'

'Are you going to give me a rope to get her back down?'

'What? I . . .'

'She's so far up herself . . .'

'Oh. I see. Actually, I'd been meaning to mention this, Richard. Your metaphors sometimes on-air are a little . . . The point is that most of the audience are coping with contraflows or temporary traffic lights at the time. I don't expect them to know *Troilus and Cressida*.'

I knew that I could refuse to speak further without my agent present: the creative's equivalent of a suspect's insistence on a solicitor. I was, though, familiar enough with my contract to stall Mendip now. 'But I have "favoured nation"—'

My editor pushed his hands out in front of him like a goalkeeper in a one-on-one. 'Sure, sure. We're aware of your deal. The formula for billings – and any other publicity, of course – would be: "Richard Fleming's *UK Today* – with Ruthia Hortenwurst". So you still have favoured nation. In salary as well.'

There's a French saying: 'The cemeteries are full of indispensable men.' It's equally true that local radio is staffed by former star broadcasters whose tactical resignations were accepted. I had to be aware of the possibility that Mendip was trying to remove me from the show.

'Isn't Ruthia – I don't mean this nastily at all – more of a man's woman? You say it's women listeners we're trying to attract . . .'

'Well, we've focus-grouped her, when she holiday-reliefed for Agnes Kerr.' The key to executive success in the BBC now seemed to be turning nouns into verbs. 'Asked to describe Ruthia in three adjectives, ABC1 women predominantly said: professional, confident, independent. They identify with her as a woman who has made her own way.'

'She's heiress to some Kraut tool factory, isn't she?'

'Ah, now, Richard, you know you wouldn't make that kind of crack about your black colleagues . . .'

'Ogg gave me the TV bollocks, but am I focus-grouped' – the verb hurt me as I said it – 'here too?'

'Sure. It's on-going. In TV, they're responding to your

face.' I flinched. 'Listeners build up a picture of their own to fit the voice.'

'What were my adjectives?'

'Er . . . clever – this is without the file in front of me – and authoritative . . . I momentarily forget the third.'

'Are you sure we'll work as a double-act?'

'I'll tell you something strange about radio.' Mendip refilled my glass. 'And this is the experience of speech networks right around the world. Lunchtime is solo: a voice in your ear. So is late-night. But breakfast and drive-time are about couples. All morning and afternoon shows these days are going boy–girl. My personal theory is that it's when listeners are thinking about their relationships. They're at the breakfast table. They're driving home to their significant other. So the dynamic of these shows is: are they / aren't they?'

'Are they / aren't they what?'

'Shagging.'

'Did you do Latin at school?'

'What?'

'There was this construction: question expecting the answer no. I think that would cover it with me and Ruthia on the sexual-tension front.'

'Oh, come on. Ruthia? I think it would be a lucky man who did.'

So the water-cooler rumours were true.

'Are you fucking her, Ol?'

In any other corporation, such cheek from twelve-month scum to a pensioned executive would have ended my career. But the management dynamics in show business are unusual. Bosses are often frightened of their employees, at least for as long as the latter seem to have the public's love.

'You have just suggested, Richard, that Ruthia Hortenwurst owes her promotion to a sexual relationship with the editor of the strand.' This strangely formal statement of the implication contained in my remark made me wonder if Mendip kept a secret recording system in his office, as the really mad executives were rumoured to do. 'What is it with you and women, Richard? You'd already made a racist remark about your colleague. You've now added to that a sexist allegation. Are you going to suggest now we try to stop her voting? Or ask her to guarantee she has no intention of becoming a priest?'

'Don't be ridiculous.'

'I think you've just stolen my line.'

'My producers – in radio and television – have mainly been women.'

'Yes. Well, I think we know why that is, don't we?'

'What? How fucking dare you?'

'Well, you started it!'

'Christ, listen to us. We need teacher to blow the whistle for end of break. Look . . .'

'I agree. Look, Richard, between mates, do you remember what the England manager said about Terry Perry? That he had a refuelling problem . . .'

Open talkback. What was this? What did Mendip know? Were they trying to trigger the professional disrepute clause?

'I don't know what you're getting at.'

Mendip tapped the side of his nose, in the code for knowingness. No, on closer inspection, he was pointing towards a nostril.

'Jesus, you're trying to say I take cocaine?'

'All I'm saying is I've heard the stories.'

'What stories?'

'About the frequency of your trips to the john before and even during a programme.'

If it had not been for the need to sustain an expression of disapproval on my face, I might have giggled. They thought that my – admittedly frequent – toilet breaks were recreational.

'And when would she start, my little Bavarian co-pilot?'

'MD.BRO and I thought July. Give Promotions time to work up a campaign. Sides of buses and so on. They're kicking about the idea of some R & R in the afternoon. Ruth and Richard. By which I mean, Richard and Ruth, of course . . .'

Standing up to make a disdainfully dramatic exit, I accidentally tipped my resentfully left wine over a pile of papers. From upbringing rather than conviction, I dabbed at the expensive puddle with a handkerchief, soaking a script for a series called *The Cooking Vet Mysteries*.

'Oh, fuck it,' I said, worsening the mess with a flap of the hankie. 'You're going to have to do all this through agents.'

My fury as I left was not just at the loss of professional power represented by Ruthia's rise, but at the way in which these people tried to soften treachery with sentimental gestures. Anna's unexpected compliment at the lifts was now revealed as apologetic diplomacy. She had known about the co-hosting. And Mendip had believed that he could heal my ego with a sip of decent Burgundy.

On the way out, my shoulder caught two of his award statuettes from the 1970s and knocked them from the filing cabinet to the floor. I let them lie.

'Easygoing,' I heard Mendip say. I turned back.

'What?'

' "Easygoing" was the third word. From the focus group.'

*

The taxi driver recognized me and praised my chat show ('Is that Terry Perry mental or what?') which healed my ego slightly, although a part of me seethed at his failure to acknowledge my radio work, which was mathematically the greater part of my career.

I was already fifteen minutes late for Lizzie De Mare, who had chosen the American Bar of the Savoy for our interview. Nervously calculating the relationship between subject's tardiness and profiler's nastiness, I opened my radio post.

A man in Wellingborough wanted to know what the England football manager was really like; an Inverness woman complained that I had confused 'who' and 'whom'; a throat cancer charity wanted me to be become a patron; and –

> This letter has been passed to the BBC Security Unit, who will be in touch if further action is considered necessary.

There were two empty envelopes containing such slips – postmarked Exeter and north London.

'You must get a lot of fan letters, do you?' crackled the cabbie, through his profession's version of switch talkback. I was suddenly troubled that he had been watching me in his mirror.

*

Lizzie De Mare – stout and greying – looked old enough to be the mother of the steeply cheekboned beauty whose photograph still topped her columns and interviews. One of her favourite charges against her subjects was vanity.

'What do you use?' I asked.

Cold, suspicious eyes suggested that she had taken me to mean narcotics or contraception.

'Tape recorder? Notebook?' I prompted.

Producing one of each from her bag, she explained, 'I take a good note. The one advantage for those of us who could only get into the profession as secretaries.'

Cornelius Raven – one of those she had previously monstered – had warned that if I got into trouble I should encourage her to talk about herself. Journalism, once a biographical form, was now essentially memoir. Reporters, taught to observe the external, now interrogated themselves.

'And then – do you type it out yourself or use a transcription firm or . . .'

'I use a firm that my husband – who's a barrister – put me on to. It comes back looking like a will: all curly writing and parchment paper.'

We once did a murder squad detective's autobiography on the radio show. Policemen (my research notes told me) denote a fellow copper as being 'job' or 'ex-job'. These questions of technique to De Mare were to establish that I was job, but also to cause delay. I was never at ease answering the questions.

'Which issue is this for?'

'July,' she said.

Four months until it reached the bookstalls. There was a sudden picture in my head of our double bed with its unstained sheets; the incipient dip in the middle no longer a problem because we crabbed towards the separate edges. Relationships are so unstable in entertainment business that many have been embarrassed by the length of magazine lead-times. You walked to the divorce courts past headlines advertising your happiness.

The magazine interviewer played out a long fuse. Would I light it? For the first time, I had an image of my interviewees, being driven away from the studio, thinking: what did I say? At least for them, the echo came back quickly.

*

Going home – route E – I encountered a driving hazard of which the Highway Code makes no mention. Stuck at a four-way, my car waited beside a vast picture of my own face, placed beside the Westway to plead for potential viewers, looming over drivers like a giant hitchhiker.

Perhaps – by now – it won't surprise you that my favourite novel is *The Great Gatsby*: the story of an apparently glamorous man with terrible secrets. The huge eyes – spookily only the eyes – of Dr T. J. Eckleburg, oculist, stare out over Queens in an early version of the celebrity advertisement. Fitzgerald – one of the first writers to become truly famous – foresaw a world in which your own great, glossy face might be a traffic hazard.

It's possible that Dr Eckleburg was able to look himself in the eyes as he drove by. I couldn't. Turning my face away from its huckstering double, I missed the sequence of the lights and jumped at the squall of punched horns.

Interviews 3: Half (?), Half (?), Half (?)

ROLL 38 – DEAD ON LIVE TV – INTERVIEW 03/02/00

Interviewee: Oliver Mendip – M-E-N-D-I-P . . . I'm an editor in Radio News Features. I was for two years editor of *UK Today* with Richard Fleming. Which subsequently became, of course, *UK Today* with Richard Fleming and Ruthia Horton-Worst (?) . . .

Int: Er, yeah, sure. Was the decision to make Ruthia a co-presenter an attempt to downgrade Richard Fleming's importance?

OM: Not at all. MD.BRO and I, as you know, Agnes . . .

Int: Sorry. I'm not here, remember, and jargon . . .

OM: Sorry. Alphabeti Spaghetti is the special every day in the BBC executive dining room, I'm afraid. Half (?), half (?), half (?). I'll start again . . . When the Managing Director of Broadcasting and I decided in February 1999 to expand Ruthia's role in the drive-time show, it was in no way a diminution of Richard Fleming's position. Right around the world, drive-time shows had shared-air formats . . .

Int: And how did he seem to take it?

OM: Well, frankly, at first there was a bit of handbags, as they say in football . . .

Int: Er, I'm not here.

OM: Bugger. I must say every time I actually have to look down the big glass eye, it increases my respect for those who do it for a living. Not that it will affect me in contract negotiations, Agnes. Half (?), half (?), half (?) . . .

TRANSCRIPT OF INTERVIEW BETWEEN ELIZABETH DE MARE (EDM) AND RICHARD FLEMING (RF) – RECORDED 15/2/99 AT SAVOY HOTEL

Legal responsibility for the material transcribed does not rest with Typescript plc

EDM: Let me start, this may seem . . . but you and I we're both questioners by profession . . . do you think people tell the truth in interviews?

RF: Christ, it's like that . . . Did you ever cover one of those juvenile murder cases? The Kenny Cole thing or . . .

EDM: I did the Kenny Cole case, yes. Three weeks in some ghastly motel outside Nottingham with retard staff who thought haute cuisine was pizza . . .

RF: No, just that moment just before they gave evidence when the judge asked the Ealham sisters if they understood the difference between lying and telling the truth . . . your question reminded me of that . . .

EDM: And a barrister would ask it again. Do you think people tell the truth in interviews?

RF: I think . . . the interview – the media interview, as we know it in broadcasting and newspapers – is like a first date. You tell your funniest stories, present your most attractive side. If they say how much they hate fish, you're probably not going to order prawns off the menu, even if you want them. Sometimes the deceit goes further. You might – metaphorically – slip off your wedding ring while you're dressing, although – in fact – in an interview you're more likely to wave your wedding ring around, especially if you're a politician . . .

(Interruption.)

RF: Thank you very much.

EDM: There's a distinct lipstick mark on that glass. Could you take it back and bring another one?

RF: You really do drink champagne a lot? It's not just your persona as a columnist?

EDM: It would be cheaper if it was.

(Laughter.)

EDM: The interview as first date you were saying . . .

RF: Yes, I was . . . *(Indistinct. Coughing.)* Sorry, those peanuts sometimes just get you . . . What I was saying is that an interview is like deliberately not farting in bed when you first spend the night with someone . . .

EDM: Did you have a happy childhood?

RF: Well, I, er . . . when someone asks you the standard questions, you realize how complicated they are, don't you? I grew up in Bolton. Some viewers and listeners still write to the BBC about my 'rogue northern vowels'. Although, actually, I was sent for 'elocution lessons', as they were known, when I was seven. Quite deliberately to get rid of my northern accent. Ironically, as it turned out, the elocution teacher – Sister Bernard – used to go on about 'BBC English' . . .

EDM: Why did your parents want you to lose the accent?

RF: My mum and dad were both English teachers . . .

(Interruption.)

EDM: That's better. Tell Anton I won't expect to be charged for it. Sorry . . . private or state?

RF: State. Grammar.

EDM: Were they happily married?

RF: I . . . how can you tell? It lasted. But marriages and

restaurants – you can easily be fooled by how they look from the outside.

EDM: Can I talk to them for this piece?

RF: Not even someone with your tenacity, Liz. My dad was dead by sixty-six. My mum at sixty-eight. I have terrible genes.

EDM: You use a lot of food imagery.

RF: Ah, the clever non sequitur. Do I? Er . . . it's probably because I'd be at home having supper if I wasn't talking to you . . .

EDM: Is home important to you?

RF: I . . . er . . . I'd hoped the press bloke had explained. The family stuff . . . they've rather put a cross on the coupon for no publicity . . . as it were . . . I'm not sure you can still do that since the Lottery, but . . .

EDM: Why do you think your first marriage failed, Richard?

RF: Again . . . it was actually part of the settlement that I wouldn't talk about it . . . I'm not stonewalling you . . .

EDM: Said the line of bricks. How painful is it for you that you don't see your daughters from your first marriage?

RF: Look, as an interviewer myself, I know how frustrating this is, but there was more or less a court order . . .

EDM: Court order? Or agreement between solicitors?

RF: Whatever . . .

EDM: Come off it, Rick, you asked the Archbishop of *(deleted)* Canterbury on live television if he *(deleted)* his wife . . .

RF: Well, he's telling people how to live their lives. I've never preached to anyone . . .

EDM: All right, more generally . . . do children enrich a life? *(Laughter.)*

RF: Liz, you're good at this but I know too much about

interviewing to fall . . . It's like trying to saw off a surgeon's leg without him noticing . . .

EDM: Richard – generally speaking – does a man who works long hours have to close his heart to some degree to his children?

(Laughter.)

RF: You don't give in, do you? . . . Look, I'll tell you this . . . the really great thing about having children around is that you get to park closer to the doors in most supermarkets these days. Parent and child parking bays are God's way of keeping the world populated if you ask me . . .

(Laughter.)

EDM: Yes . . . I'm afraid I'm one of those dreadful people who uses them anyway and I haven't changed a nappy for twenty years . . .

RF: Shocking. Does your editor know that?

(Laughter.)

EDM: OK, I give in. Let's try another line of questioning . . . Do you accept that you're a workaholic?

RF: Well, no I . . . not really . . .

EDM: But you're on air every day with voice-overs, pilots, charity stuff at weekends . . .

RF: I don't think a teacher – say – or anyone running their own business would find my hours exceptional. I think the media world's idea of a week's work is maybe . . .

EDM: Workaholics are often said by psychologists to be hiding from something . . . death, insecurity, relationships . . .

RF: But I haven't admitted to being a workaholic.

EDM: Has either of your wives – or any of your children – ever complained that you work too hard?

RF: Does your husband ever complain that you won't take no for an answer?

(Laughter.)

RF: Actually, this won't hold as an exclusive till July but you're the first person I've told. A daily three-hour radio show was getting a little too much. So I suggested that I should have a co-host. From July, Ruthia *(Indistinct)* . . . Do I need to spell it?

EDM: I've heard her. Name like she ought to be Hitler's mistress, voice like the Duchess of Devonshire. I'll get it from *Radio Times* . . . You personally suggested her?

RF: Er, yes . . .

EDM: It didn't worry you that some people might see that as an abuse of your position?

RF: What? Oh, look, it's not at all a personal thing . . . *(Extended pause.)* I just, er, admire her broadcasting . . .

EDM: You're enviably thin for a man in middle age . . .

RF: I'd hardly say I was that.

EDM: What? Middle-aged or thin?

RF: Either.

(Laughter.)

RF: No. Thin.

EDM: Do you diet?

RF: I go to the gym. Less than I should . . .

EDM: Being in the public eye, how do you feel about people coming up to you in the street and so on?

RF: Well, Liz, people probably recognize you from your picture byline and . . .

EDM: Actually, you know, not really . . .

RF: My mum and dad used to come home from parents' nights sometimes, raging at some of the complete cretins they'd dealt with. But they knew they wouldn't have a job without those parents. That's in the end how I feel about it.

EDM: That some of your viewers and listeners are complete cretins?

RF: You said that. I didn't.

EDM: Do you have stalkers?

RF: Oh, no. This isn't America.

EDM: I think I wouldn't mind another one of these . . .

(Interruption.)

ROLL 42 – *DEAD ON LIVE TV* – INTERVIEW 05/12/99

(General indistinct chatter.)

Interviewer: If you could just give your name – spelling any parts which may be unclear . . .

Interviewee: Oh, er, Tanya – T-A-N-Y-A – Griffiths.

Int: But that wasn't in fact the name you used when you applied for a job at the BBC.

TG: I'm not sure exactly what I can . . .

Int: But that wasn't in fact the name you used when you applied for a job at the BBC.

TG: Er . . . no.

Int: What name did you use?

PART TWO

ARE THEY THE SAME AT HOME?

The celebrity interview is, in fact, fairly new ... In the mid-twenties ... there appeared a collection of interviews by, of all improbable pioneers, Beverly Nichols. I remember the ones he did with George Gershwin and Al Capone in which, for the first time in my experience, anyway, an attempt was made to recognize the double image of the private and the public man or to watch them merge into focus. The aim was explicit in the title: *Are They the Same At Home?*

Alistair Cooke, 'The Art of Interviewing'

4. CUT-THROAT

A jump-cut, as we say in broadcasting, to July. Or a caption (which we call an Aston): Four Months Later.

We were coming to the end of the sports news when I guessed that the Queen was dead.

'Any prospect of play at Lord's, Barry?'

'If I tell you, Richard, that I've just seen a man with a long white beard leading animals into a big wooden ship two by two, you'll know that England have a good chance of getting away with a draw . . .'

Barry Accrington's metaphors had become a feature of the sports news – there were days now when he put so much effort into his exotic comparisons that he actually forgot to give the scores – and I could hear laughter in the background when Anna hit the switch.

'*Buckingham Palace is about to announce a death. Not Supergran. Repeat not Supergran. This is news.*'

The BBC had been rehearsing the Queen Mother's death at least twice a year since the 1970s, which had also been hers. 'As old as the century' was one of the sentences you carried in your head in case she croaked during your programme and you had to fill without a script. But the *mill*-any-um now threatened us with finding new platitudes. At least 'The Nation's Grandmother' would remain usable even if she drew level with Methuselah.

Ruthia had been talkbacked simultaneously and she gave me the double thumbs-up. I could bad-mouth her for callousness – it's my memoir and I'll lie if I want to – but she was just being open about what we all thought. We'd got the big one. Everyone in the profession had read the autobiographies and heard the Television Hall of Fame induction speeches. All seriously great careers in broadcasting had included a war or a royal death.

During one of those excited fortnights of potential rationality in Ireland – when rumours of a dis-arming handshake reached our studio – a producer (Anna's even more aggressive predecessor) had hissed in my ear during a tape, '*You do realize, Richard, this could be peace in our time.*' I reversed the switch and demurred at this dim pick-up phrase from history. '*No, I mean peace in our time-slot.*'

Royal death in our time-slot now. Clem Sadley and Agnes Kerr – two of the contemporaries we most resented – had been hauled to fame behind Diana's hearse.

'*Finish sport. Then into showbiz. I'll come through then.*'

'Thanks, Barry, whose Noah news is bad news for New Zealand.'

'Ouch, you're worse than me, mate.'

'Back to Lord's in half an hour. Now it's four twenty-six and here with the latest showbusiness news is Jonquil Mason-Lee. Jonquil?'

'Richard, thanks. Later . . . top comic Cornelius Raven on his raunchy new video, *A Trip Up Brown Street* . . . and no more Mr Bad Guy – why Arnold Schwarzenegger is giving up villains to play Jesus – but first I've just come off of the phone from talking to the representatives of the Oscar-winning actress Alice Jackett who have confirmed newspaper reports that she *is* pregnant. She's been seeing top rock star Marty Stark for the last three months . . .'

The techies faded down Jonquil's breathy irrelevancies on

the speakers as Anna banged into the studio, flapping a sheet of agency copy.

'Which one is it?' squealed Ruthia. The liveliness death brings is one of the media's most terrible tendencies.

'It's still just coming in,' explained Anna. 'At the end of the showbiz we go to name and programme idents. Special bad-news voices please. The copy will come up on the screens. Read as fucking written. No flourishes. Then Richard hands over live to Julian Hudson at Buck House, who will have the statement.'

'Questions?' asked Ruthia.

'Wing it, honey.'

The SM crackled through that Jonquil had thirty to go. Anna ran out. I glanced at Ruthia across the table and liked it that she looked so frightened.

'The Queen?' she mouthed, worried that they had already faded us up. I made back the shape of 'I guess.' The showbiz news returned at full projection. Arnold Schwarzenegger was saying that he saw Jesus as the kind of guy who worked out most days – 'Hell, he survived on that cross for hours, some pecs' – so the physique needn't be a problem.

'John Woo's *Christ Help Us* opens in Britain next Friday. I'll be back with your personal map of the West End and Broadway tomorrow afternoon. Richard?'

'Jonquil, thank you. Now, I'm afraid, a rather abrupt change of mood.' Pausing to put an air exclusion zone around the fatuities of the luvvy stuff we'd just heard, I tried mentally to swap my slacks and sports shirt for a dinner jacket and the bright red spongy lollipop mike in front of me for a Bakelite shoe-shape. 'This is the BBC in London – *UK Today* with Richard Fleming . . .'

'And Ruthia Hortenwurst . . .'

The lines rolled on to the screen. They would have to be

read cold. I just hoped that, whichever royal had gone, they had not collapsed while receiving British visitors in connection with the millennium.

'It is with great regret,' I read, 'that the BBC announces the death of His Royal Highness Prince Philip, the Duke of Edinburgh . . .'

Opposite me, Ruthia looked liked someone expecting her lover who opens the door to find a charity collector there instead. 'Boor-ring,' she goldfished.

'He was seventy-eight,' I continued. 'The BBC's royal correspondent, Julian Hudson, is outside Buckingham Palace. Julian – we saw the Duke looking pretty chipper on TV as recently as the weekend, when he and the Queen received President Castro on his state visit. So clearly this news has been something of a shock?'

'Yes, Richard. The Duke had been in good health. In fact, his medical condition would not necessarily be relevant to what has happened, because he did not die from illness. I stress that details are still sketchy but Buckingham Palace has just confirmed that the Duke died from gunshot wounds at Balmoral, the Queen's Scottish estate, where the royal family was on holiday.'

'A shooting accident?' I prompted.

Ruthia, who had become visibly more enthusiastic at the mention of violent death, now perked up further as she cheerfully noted my stupid breaking of journalism school rules about the causes of a death.

'Richard, all we're able to say at the moment is that the cause of death was gunshot wounds. We'll bring further news as we get it.'

'*Out of this and hand to Ruthia.*'

'Thank you for the moment to Julian Hudson outside Buckingham Palace. This is the BBC and – in case you're just joining us – to repeat that we are reporting the sad and sudden death of His Royal Highness Prince Philip, the Duke of Edinburgh, apparently from gunshot wounds at the Balmoral estate in Scotland. I'm Richard Fleming and with me is Ruthia Hortenwurst. Ruthia . . .'

'Thank you, Richard. On this very grave and solemn day for everyone in the United Kingdom . . .' This was sickbag stuff, an unknown announcer coming on like a head of state, but this, I feared, was what the bosses wanted and she would go far. 'Our thoughts are obviously with Her Majesty the Queen, the Prince of Wales and the rest of the royal family. Joining me now on the line from his house in Shropshire is the best-selling author and charity fund-raiser Lord Haydon of Hitchin, who knew the Duke well. Lord Haydon, this must be a deep personal blow for all who knew him.'

'Very much so, Ruthia. You know, ill-wishers used to say that the Duke didn't have a proper job. But his job was to make the monarchy possible. And he did it splendidly . . .'

When we went off-piste with rolling news, the rule was open talkback in all cans, and so I heard Anna object, '*He was a racist, sexist pighead, love.*'

'But it has to be admitted, Lord Haydon, that he wasn't a man who suffered fools gladly . . .'

'Oh, well, Ruthia, with the Duke, what you saw was what you got. It's true that he called a spade a spade – he certainly didn't take any prisoners – but, at the end of the day, his bark was worse than his bite . . .'

Five dead expressions laid end to end. I was close to the resignation letter of laughing aloud during an obituary broadcast. Ruthia and Lord Haydon were both so devoted to cliché that a conversation between them began to resemble a daring stylistic exercise: like a poem written backwards.

'But some would say, Lord Haydon, thinking of the kind

of remarks he used to make abroad, that he was his own worst enemy . . .'

'Yes, he was a man who spoke as he found. But that meant, Ruthia' – this was Haydon's extra-pompous voice, which declared that he was about to pass off as his own a remark which had been through several thousand more mouths even than was usual with him – 'that he could always see the wood for the trees. He had that special gift . . .'

'Police sources are unofficially suggesting suicide. Cover us.'

Jesus fuck, beam me up, Scotty. Beam *her* up. Initially resentful that Anna had given her girl the most important interview, I was now happy to rubber-neck the car crash towards which Lord Hard-On and the Kraut heiress were accelerating. Ruthia fluster-blushed, and two decades were shaved from her age: she was back at school, with a question the swot couldn't handle.

'Er, Lord Haydon, had, er, this may seem odd, but had, er, had the Duke been entirely himself recently?'

'Fit as a fiddle, Ruthia. Fit as a flea. Which only makes this tragedy more tragic . . .'

'Had he, well, had he, um, seemed depressed or down at all?'

'Huhhh!' He sounded like a young actor asked to do a snort at a drama school audition. It was a pecularity of Lord Haydon, on which the judge at his fraud trial had commented, that the more he tried to appear sincere, the falser he seemed. 'Ruthia, I think one thing all the Duke's friends knew was that you didn't turn up to dinner feeling a bit sorry for yourself. I remember once going a little gently at the pheasant because of toothache and the Duke said, "For God's bloody sake, man, I was making small-talk at a hospital this morning with a girl with no bloody arms and legs." He absolutely couldn't stand people making mountains out of molehills.'

'*A coroner's office source is saying suicide. Press him.*'

Ruthia's face reddened to a level which suggested fever.

'Lord Haydon, it's been a bad time for the royal family in recent years – what with the divorces and Diana and that kind of thing. Had the Duke ever, er, talked about maybe seeing someone, um, I don't mean, er, romantically of course but in the sense of therapy or, er . . .'

'Huhhhh!' RADA would have rejected the applicant. 'The Duke's biggest bugbear was counselling. He just couldn't understand these police and firemen who had to go and see a shrink after doing the job they were paid for. I remember him saying once, "Did we get bloody counselling when we were dragged from that bloody torpedo boat after strangling a hundred Hun submariners with our bare hands?" He was a man who believed that, if you couldn't stand the heat, you should get out of the kitchen.'

Ruthia looked at me and spread her hands wide in a gesture of helplessness. I held up one thumb to encourage her.

'But Lord Haydon, is it at all possible that the Duke of Edinburgh did decide to get out of the kitchen using, as it were, the fire escape which we should only ever use in emergencies? In the end we never know what is in the souls of our friends, and might there not be some of those who know – who *knew* – him who, hearing that vague – that necessarily vague – police phrase about gunshot wounds, might not just fear that, no longer able to stand the heat, he turned, as it were, the extinguisher on himself?'

There was an understandable pause while Lord Haydon, sometimes confused by even the merest trickle of a tangent in an interview, fought for his footing in this sudden flood of metaphor. At last he raised his head and spluttered: 'Even for the bloody BBC, girl. Even for the bloody BBC. Have you really just suggested that the beloved husband of Her Majesty the Queen bloody shot himself?'

Over the termination burring of the telephone, Anna snapped, '*Richard, pick up and fill,*' but I was already saying, 'Lord Haydon of Hitchin – one of many friends showing his shock at the news the BBC is now reporting – the death of His Royal Highness Prince Philip, the Duke of Edinburgh, from gunshot wounds at the Queen's Balmoral estate in Scotland . . .'

There is a death tone in broadcasting, and also a royal tone, and when they come together you sound like a recording played back at the wrong speed of someone who had already been suffering laryngitis when afflicted by a stroke.

'*Downing Street. PM's statement. Moody.*'

'Live now to 10 Downing Street and political correspondent Rachel Moody. Rachel – first reaction from the Prime Minister?'

'Yes, Richard. Lawrence Castle has described Prince Philip as the Duke of Hazard . . .' Again, I managed to stall a guffaw. An increasingly demented populist, Lawrence Castle (or, in truth, his press secretary) would have seen nothing odd in marking a royal death with a pun on a late-1970s American television comedy. 'Mr Castle said that the Duke spoke his mind always but his devoted husbandry' – Christ, they made it sound as if he'd been a part-time vet – 'made it possible for the Queen to set her mind to ruling.'

'Rachel, can I just ask you . . .'

'*Cut-throat. Hudson. Buck House. Breaking news.*'

'Sorry, Rachel, we're going to have to leave it there

because our royal correspondent, Julian Hudson, who's outside Buckingham Palace, has important news. Julian?'

'Richard, Scottish police have just confirmed that a thirty-five-year-old man has been arrested on the Balmoral estate and charged with the murder of His Royal Highness Prince Philip . . .'

My first thought was of stalkers. Ruthia double-punched the air like an athlete breaking the tape.

'Julian, this had been assumed to be a tragic accident, but now . . .'

Now what? Bugger. Barristers were taught never to ask a question in court to which they didn't know the answer; broadcasters should never commence a question to which they don't know the ending. But Hudson caught the three dots I had thrown him. 'Yes, indeed, Richard. A family coming to terms with an apparently senseless event – and, moreover, under the relentless gaze of the world's media – now has to take in the even more shocking possibility of intent.'

Hudson, like me, was a pro. We could talk total bollocks in a tone of complete authority for hours if necessary. It was a dubious art but it had bought us houses bigger than most people would ever own.

'*Sky News is reporting Prince Edward arrested.*'

Scotty. The scriptwriters were overdoing it now.

'Julian, do we know anything about the identity of the man under arrest?'

'Richard, we're obviously restricted in what we can say at this stage. We understand, though, that he was not a member of staff but a guest at the estate and that he had been known to the victim for some time.'

'*Sky News says Countess of Wessex being treated for shock in hospital.*'

I saw a way in. 'Julian, are the royal family gathering at Balmoral following the news?'

'They were mainly there already, Richard, for the holiday. The Prince of Wales is here, the Duke of York is here. They're said to be comforting their mother. The Earl of Wessex – Prince Edward – was here until a short while ago, when he was driven away by police . . .'

'*Smooth fucking bastards.*'

We'd planted the clue for the sharper listener without being monstered by Editorial Policy. I flipped Anna a V-sign more affectionate than many.

'*Richard, cut-throat. Ruthia cue next insert.*'

'Thank you for the moment to Julian Hudson outside Buckingham Palace. Reporting the news of the death of the Duke of Edinburgh from gunshot wounds at Balmoral – a thirty-five-year-old man, a guest at the estate, is under arrest – this is *UK Today* from the BBC with Richard Fleming and Ruthia Hortenwurst. Ruthia . . .'

'Richard, thank you. As the nation adjusts to this sudden and terrible news, in a moment we'll be hearing extracts from speeches made during his lifetime by the Duke of Edinburgh on one of his favourite causes – the preservation of wildlife . . .'

In the hope of putting her off, I silently mimed a double-barrelled hunter's gun blowing birds out of the sky, but Ruthia had her head down in a trance of ambition.

'But – first – I want to say something on a personal note. Reporters and broadcasters are asked to be objective at a time like this . . .'

She had turned away from her computer screen, which showed a simple two-line cue into a pre-rec on the World Wildlife Fund.

'My dad was an industrialist – a big shot – and that gave

us privileges. It got us into places. We met people. One of the people we met was the Duke of Edinburgh, Prince Philip – I'm not quite sure what I'm supposed to call him, he was just "Uncle Phil" to us – who died so horribly today . . .'

I produced a bemused little *moue* and tried to make her see it but Ruthia had gone EVA. It's a term that broadcasters took from astronauts. Extra-vehicular activity: their term for space walks. Ruthia was floating weightless on a wire somewhere, entranced by the curve of the earth.

'I said just now I didn't know what to call him. Well, all sorts of other people did know what to call him. Parasite, anachronism, bigot, racist, adulterer, appendage . . .'

I waited for Ruthia's green light to extinguish and mine to ignite, as the SMs used the mike-override they keep for strokes and sieges. But, when I looked through the glass, Anna was smiling and rocking her head in contentment as though listening to a favourite album on her Walkman.

'Well, call him those things. Call him them now he's dead. But when I think of all the people who play it safe, who watch what they say all the time and permanently watch their backs' – and here, for the first time, she briefly looked up and across the table at me – 'I respect a man who didn't – a man who thought spin was a sin and second thoughts were second best. We'll miss him. I'll miss him.'

Ruthia had to stop now because it was hard to both speak and conduct the scale of mopping up which her eyes demanded from her handkerchief. People will often say of those they dislike: nothing X did would surprise me. We mean that we have their personality worked out. I had said it to my wives at the times when our conversations involved insulting outsiders rather than each other. But watching Ruthia now was like the last ten minutes of a thriller when you've just realized that the Greek CIA man is really the Turkish FBI woman. The plot was all twist.

'Goodnight, sweet prince . . . rest in peace, Uncle Phil,' my co-presenter was able to splutter, and then, 'Sorry, Richard, could I ask you to read the next link?'

'Oh, er . . .' Ruthia had done my legs. It was an expression we had imported from gangster movies, meaning kneecapping. 'This is *UK Today* with Ruthia Hortenwurst' – a self-indulgent, unprofessional little cunt, I wish I could tell you listeners – 'and Richard Fleming. Let's hear now about one of the great passions in the late Duke of Edinburgh's life – the protection of wildlife. Suki Appleton reports on the British royal family's very own St Francis of Assisi . . .'

She'd reloaded and shot my shins as well, by forcing me to read her brown-nose intro. As soon as the tape was playing – Lord Haydon of Hitchin with some awe-struck story about the Duke nursing a cancer-stricken sparrow back to life at Sandringham – Anna slammed into the studio. I assumed she would shout Ruthia out with her most supernaturally wounding Australian expletives, and when she lunged towards my co-presenter's chair, I thought for a dizzy minute that she might actually punch her. But I should have guessed it would be a hug.

'Fucking bonzer, darling. You're a star.'

'Did you actually know him, Ruthia?' I asked.

'Fuck you, Fleming,' interjected Anna protectively. Her protégée looked as smug and confident as Peter Pennington drooling at his Autocue as she said, 'You know why they call what we do *broad*casting? Because it's about the broad sweep, not nit-picking detail.'

Heading for the Gents, I was intercepted by Cornelius Raven coming into the studio, blowing his nose with elaborate delicacy.

'That was a blast,' he said.

'Your Lord Haydon of Hitchin is great,' I complimented him. 'Almost indistinguishable from the false thing.'

'You think? You're a brother. The bugger of it is I didn't get to do my Lawrence Castle. "Look, he was, you know, the Duke of Hazard" . . .'

Raven's impression of the Prime Minister's clenched sincerity was a vocal clone. Show-business convention is that you are nice to impersonators in public: that English requirement to seem 'a sport'. In private, Raven's isolation of my verbal perversions – the half-choked northern vowels, the tenor swoops when excited, the mid-word pauses for thought – had made me cry and plot consequences which he seemed helpfully to be achieving for himself with cocaine.

'You two were wicked. Christ, you take it seriously, though. There were times I thought you believed it was real . . .'

'I know.' I indicated Ruthia with a slide of my eyes. 'What's Hecuba to her etc? They expect you to take it seriously. These rehearsals are the casting couch. They hand out the best jobs in the future on the basis of how well you fake it. Richard Rennie got his break after impressing them in a practice for a jumbo-jet crashing in the Thames. It's never happened, but *he* did. I fear Ruthia's arranged her coronation today.'

On the tape in the background, former prime minister Richard Anscombe – another perfect piece of speech-deceit by Raven – was nervously explaining how a love of wildlife was compatible with a passion for hunting.

*

Oliver Mendip moved so smoothly that we only knew he was in the studio when he spoke.

'MD.BRO and I are very happy bunnies. Absolutely ecstatic rabbits in fact,' he said, then walked across to take Ruthia's hand and kiss it. 'That moved me more than anything since Clem Sadley's series on his first wife's miscarriage. Richard, well done too. And Con's voices are spot on as ever. Let's just hope you get to be on`air when any of them really dies.'

But that would be my last rehearsal for a death.

'I need to talk to you about that complaint, Anna,' said Mendip. 'They're getting heavy.'

'I've listened to the tape three times, Ol. Nobody says the word "fucking". She's hearing swearwords where there aren't any. Tell the silly cunt to go and rim her sister.'

She's a customer,' said Mendip. 'We take our customers seriously.'

*

The Duke wasn't dead but, later that day, in the world conventionally described as real, I was due to interview the Prime Minister. I was in Dressing Room 107 at Television Centre when I received a death threat from myself. With the brown paper protecting me from my reflection in the mirror, I opened my electronic letter-box. But, before fear, there was pleasure:

From: lucy.brooks@bbc.co.uk
To: rgfleming@newtalk.com
Subject: Luck
Time: Friday 17:18:41

Its going to be a wonderful show tonight. Again. I will be whispering sour nothings in your ear soon but see you in the Green Room afterwards to celebrate another ratings tiumph.
Good Luck. Lots of love, L XXXX

The message was identical every week. It failed to acknowledge, for example, that our ratings were now falling. One of the sweet things about Lucy was that – though she could have simply forwarded the file from sent messages each Friday after the first – she typed a fresh copy each week. As live. This week's typos were a missing apostrophe in 'It's' and an 'r' omitted from 'triumph'.

About to click the second message open, I paused, confused by the fact that my name seemed to be in the sender's box. Curiosity overcame my fear of a virus: the old rule of sex applying newly to computers.

From: rgfleming@freetalk.net
To: rgfleming@newtalk.com
.Subject: Who's Who
Time: Friday 17:35:22

People are going to find out, Richard. People are going to know. That you're not who you say you are. With me live in the studio. No, Richard. Dead in the studio. People are going to find out, Richard.

Both my names are common in England, separately and in combination. When I was first on television, there'd be jokey letters from sales reps and schoolboys saying, 'I'm you.' It was perfectly possible that my message came from one of the seventeen other entries under Fleming, R. in the London phone book. But I was experienced enough in hate-mail now – in the last four months, they had begun to arrive in a politician's torrent – to feel that the parents of this writer had called him something else. He had adopted the name, making me an impostor.

I had just given Anna a cutting for a possible discussion on the radio show. There was an American cosmetic surgeon who operated to give you the face of a famous person of your choice. You could shave President Riley's face every morning. You could suck off your boyfriend with Alice Jackett's lips. It sounded spooky, but the Internet already let you assume any identity you wanted. Years ago, setting up e-mail addresses for Rachel, I had sent her a message from herself: some lover's pun about how nice it was to be inside her. There was nothing to stop me from registering myself with an e-mail provider as Lawrence Castle and sending the leader of the opposition a message confessing that I'd just fucked seven Girl Guides in Number 10. Nor was it surprising that this other rgfleming had been able to find my sign-on. There were websites which listed celebrity addresses, electronic and brick. It seemed to me they should simply call such services stalker.com.

I selected Reply To Sender and asked, 'Who are you?'

My mobile phone rang on the dressing-room table. In a film, it would have been my namesake, but reality brought Gerry Armstrong.

'Yeah?'

'Mr Fleming, I shall be knocking three times on your dressing-room door in one minute.'

Since the volume and hostility of the letters had increased, I was told by phone when I should open my door. It was like being Secretary of State for Northern Ireland in every respect except that there were thousands of people who wanted my job.

It had briefly seemed an unreal way to live, but there was now little concrete in my life to measure it against. In the corridors and canteen of Television Centre, I had kept checking people's faces for their reaction to the sensational slaying at Balmoral before remembering that we had invented it.

The first time Terry Perry was on my programme, he said that no footballer should ever miss a penalty deliberately, even when shooting for charity against six-year-old goalies, because the mind remembered the wrong coordinates. Well, that's my language. Perry said that your head might do it proper, like, next time. Perhaps journalists should have the same superstition about speaking false facts.

Three knocks on the door. I knew by now that part of Armstrong's professional manner was an emotional flipover in which, the worse things were for you, the perkier he seemed. I opened the door to find him grinning like a Lottery winner.

'Christ, sir. It's like a leaving party at Scotland Yard out there. I keep bumping into people I haven't seen since stake-outs at IRA dosshouses at Kilburn in the 1970s.'

'I know. I sort of hope that the ones here to stop the PM being shot might accidentally protect me. You can tell that I'm trying to stay cheerful about these things, Gerry.'

There were now so many people who hated me that I was using Armstrong's first name. But he still granted me the police's victim honorific.

'That's the way, sir.'

He sat heavily on the sofa-bed, trapping under his buttocks one arm of my television shirt, which Toby would now have to iron again.

'Have you interviewed the Prime Minister before, sir?'

'Not since he was elected. I did him once before they attached the strings to his back.'

'Yeah.' There was a folder in his hand: the letters. 'Have you had any bother this week, sir?'

'I hadn't . . . until . . .'

I gestured at the laptop. Armstrong came across and read

the message from my impersonator or namesake in cyber-space.

'Is this the first time, sir?'

'Yeah. I sent one back . . .'

'You did? Saying?'

'Ditto. Who are you?'

'Any reply?'

'I don't know. I was just going to . . .'

'Can we?'

I played the mailman. The envelope icon broke open to show, 'I am Richard Fleming.'

'Well, I think we'll leave it there,' said Armstrong, almost chuckling. His breezy and beaming demeanour made clear how much this development had unsettled him. 'Any reply and we'd get into that pantomime thing: oh no you're not . . . Do you mind if I?'

He forwarded the messages to his own log-on.

'You can theoretically trace these things,' he said. 'But needle in a haystack doesn't even . . . pin in a cornfield. At least with postmarks . . .'

He understandably failed to complete a sentence which could only really have concluded: at least with postmarks, you knew the two broad geographical areas from which escalatingly aggressive letters were now arriving almost daily. It did not, however, mean that you could do anything to stop them.

'How are the letters, Gerry?'

'North London is definitely worse than Exeter, sir.' I felt like a king in Shakespeare, threatened by geographically named barons. 'In content, that is. But they're both writing most days.'

'And saying the same kind of things?'

Every few weeks, I had exercised my right to see the contents of the empty envelopes.

'I'd say yes to that, sir. Exeter goes on more about your private life, is the way I'd put it. North London has this thing about how rich you are.'

'Has either of them actually threatened to kill me, Gerry?'

Armstrong looked now as if he'd just been told the funniest joke of his life. Not vocally reliable.

'It's never as simple as that, sir, is it?'

'Isn't it? And do we have any more idea of who they are?'

'It's early days, sir.'

But it already felt very late to me.

'Can I see the new letters?'

'You know we advise against that.'

'Yeah. And I'm going to go against the advice.'

Opening his folder, Armstrong shuffled the contents: a connoisseur of hostility. After twice changing his mind – so that I knew there must be letters more threatening than the ones I was to be shown – he handed over one from each postcode.

My lord (or lady) Exeter had clipped from a *TV Times* profile a sentence describing me as a 'loving and dedicated stepfather'. This had not been my phrase but the sentimental invention of a journalist irritated by my usual refusal to speak about home. The four words had been scissored round and the cutout cloud shape stuck to a blank postcard in the classic graphics of blackmail. Circling the glossy strip of magazine paper were exclamation marks like the hair of a frightened person in a cartoon. There were three words in a large looping script: 'Yeah fucking right.'

The tone was pretty standard non-fan sardonic – although it was usually your studio persona they were rude about –

and was not particularly frightening in isolation. But I knew that Armstrong had chosen from the sweet end of the menu.

'Are you a stepfather, sir?'

'Yeah. But it definitely isn't their handwriting. And Tash can barely use scissors.'

Armstrong looked flustered. 'I wasn't suggesting it came from them, sir. I was ascertaining if the phrase applied to you.'

North London used a word processor and his (or her) style had the tenor of a postgraduate essay:

> The central paradox of television involves distance given the illusion of intimacy. The most successful presenters imply that they are just like the viewers at home. But the enormous rewards for achieving this deception systematically strip away any resemblance between the two groups of people. Layers of money and protection ensure that the presenter must never meet those whose friends he pretends to be.

There was – cheeringly – nothing here that you might not read in a Sunday supplement from an embryonic essayist just down from Oxford. But then the tone became – though very obliquely – lethal:

> Video-tape confers the illusion of immortality. The family camcorder means we are the first generation whose descendants will routinely see us living and breathing (on screens) after our death. How much more so, then, for television presenters. They live for ever as video ghosts. Whole retro networks on cable are presented by the dead. The living dead. The television celebrity never dies. But the television celebrity does die. The television celebrity will die.

Our childhoods mould us just as much as DNA. The son of English teachers paused to be impressed by how well-written his death threat was.

But north London, I guessed, was a prisoner of his upbringing as well. For some reason – illness, friendlessness – he had watched too much television when young. Presenters had become his friends and then later – whether because of unemployment, celibacy, a humiliation on some game or dating show – his enemies. I imagined a long-bearded postgrad in an N7 flat with ancient wallpaper. Baked beans and video-tapes would be what the detectives noted. The jury would be told that he had once appeared – with terrible and blushing unsuccess – on *Fifteen to One* or *Family Fortunes*. But why me? I had never hosted a quiz show.

'I did tell you not to read them, sir. It's the last thing you need two hours before you go on.'

'No. I'm glad I saw them. I imagined worse.'

'We're searching them at the door, sir. From tonight's show. We're searching them at the door.'

'Good. That's good, isn't it? I mean, it would be better if you didn't have to, but . . .'

'Sir, this may seem a strange thing to ask. But could you sit down some time quietly and make a list of . . . well, of anyone who might benefit from you being dead?'

'What?' I was cultivating a robust chuckle which showed my calmness as a death target. 'Every television presenter under forty, for a start.'

'Not seriously?'

'Semi-seriously. I mean, they'd walk quite jauntily to the memorial service. But this is someone I've never seen, isn't it? Who's seen me on the screen?'

'There are always the two possibilities in these cases, sir.'

As he left, Armstrong took a manila envelope from within

the folder. All my BBC post was now being checked by the Security Unit. This was the harmless residue.

Huntington's Chorea, Late Onset Diabetes, Dyslexia and Severe Head Trauma. Mainly from guilt at instinctively checking the dyslexics' letter for misspellings, I agreed to become a campaigner against word-blindness, rejecting the other three. A man from Nottingham felt I had given away my New Labour views in the interview with the Leader of the Opposition. A woman from Buckingham accused me of playing down Terry Perry's history of domestic violence.

And there was another letter from my most regular correspondent – the unemployed Midlands accountant. After my initial rejection of Pardon's letters, he had written several times a week until, though making clear that there was no chance of a job, I allowed him occasional gracious replies signed by a secretary:

Dear Mr Fleming,

I hope you realize how much I (and the other sacked workers!) appreciate your tolerance of my many letters. And if it ever becomes too much, you must say so!

The reason I'm writing again is that, on 12 September, we're planning to organize a benefit evening – quizzes, acts etc. – to raise money for the families of the sacked Plasco workers.

Knowing that we're 'pen-pals', the committee insisted that I asked you if there were any chance you might 'present' it? Otherwise it's muggins here with the microphone and you, quite frankly, are a bigger 'draw'!

We can only too easily imagine what your 'schedule' must be like. But I said I would ask.

Incidentally, that story about the horse farting you

got out of the Princess Royal on last week's show had us crying with laughter here.

Yours in admiration and gratitude as ever,
Matthew Pardon

If only Exeter and north London could be more like Solihull. But – in retrospect – I may have been seeking to refute north London's allegations about the false friendship of the presenter and viewer when I scrawled on the letter that I would meet Mr Pardon on 19 July for an early lunch (twelve noon) at Afters in order to discuss his proposal, adding that Jenny should find a tactful way of indicating that I would pay.

The rapping at the door had not been heralded by telephone. My daily dilemma at this time was how paranoid to be. I risked admission.

'Hello, buggerlugs, I thought I'd catch you before you put on your other face.'

This was no stranger. But being stabbed to death by a crazed fan suddenly seemed preferable to a conversation with Nick Percival. Almost forty years before, we had started at the same Bolton primary school and been classmates – though never friends – until eighteen, when I went to university and he joined the local newspaper.

We'd met again in the 1980s at the BBC, where Percival became a sports reporter, before leaving to serve as press officer to Lawrence Castle, then an Americanesque young politician trying to make the Labour Party palatable to the middle classes. Now he had a desk in Number 10 from which he strained to manipulate the news to benefit his employer.

'Have you put the plums in yet, our Ricky? I tell you, folk'd fall over at the idea we once spoke the same.'

But, even without elocution lessons and the weight of BBC English on my tongue, our childhood accents wouldn't have matched. In symbolic rejection of the élitism he perceived in the media and politics, Percival had maximized the Lancastrian in his voice. He now talked stage northern.

'I don't suppose you're here to reminisce about sports day in '66, Nick. Make it quick. You've got a country to run.'

'About the interview, buggerlugs. I can't stop you talking out of your arse but I can spray some scent on what comes out. It's my opinion that, if the voters hear cne more word about the NHS, they'll all be needing fucking treatment for boredom. Tonight is about Lawrence Castle as father, husband and churchgoer. The PM specifically didn't want me to tell you this but, driving here from Chequers tonight, we passed a car on the M40, weaving towards the hard shoulder. You could tell at once there was summat wrong. The driver was a diabetic about to go into a coma. The PM fed him the chocolate he always carries in his pocket in case he gets sleepy when the Leader of the Opposition's speaking in the House. When the guy comes round and finds Lawrence Castle cramming fruit and nut in his gob, he thinks he's hallucinating in a diabetic coma. Which is of course the opposite of what the situation is!'

'Yes, well, thank you for helpfully pointing out the moral of the story, Nick. He's going to try to drop this heroic anecdote in at some point, is he?'

'You're not listening, buggerlugs. I told you he wants no mention. This is deep background, as the – in my view, far superior – press of America say. I thought I just read in *Vogue* that you like to know all you possibly can about a guest.'

Percival rotated the ragged stack of periodicals and folders under his arm to show the latest edition of *Vogue*.

I had been trying to forget that it was published that week. The Number 10 press secretary showed me the cover lines, which included:

NO-TALK SHOW:
WHAT RICHARD FLEMING
WON'T SAY
by Elizabeth De Mare

Percival pulled the magazine away from my reaching hand.

'What's it like?'

I remembered him smirking in the same way when, at the age of fourteen, he had emerged from a bedroom at a party and offered us sexual laggards his finger to sniff.

'I think she's got you, mate. She's really got you.'

When there was knocking at the door again minutes after Percival left, I assumed he was returning with another quip.

'Richard, hi. Is this an incredibly bad time?'

'No. No, of course . . .'

'Cool?'

The next guest Abbi Pascoe was researching – Tommy Rankin, clown of kids' TV – was not due to appear for two weeks.

'Can I talk to you now?'

The interrogative inflections of the young made no concession for sentences which were genuinely questions.

'Yeah.'

'Look, Richard, we're both grown-ups and it's almost the twenty-first century? So, listen, I want to fuck you? We could do three months of ambiguous looks and sneaky lunches and does-she-mean? But it's simpler to just have it on the table?' She giggled. 'As it were. If you won't, no offence. If you will, cool?'

Some guests on the morning talk shows – with their wet-eyed tales of incest and bestiality in extended stepfamilies – had been exposed as actors, bringing many memos from executives which stressed the importance of labelling. The audience must be told if something was a reconstruction; actual news footage in plays must first be viewed by the characters through a television on the set.

But how could I label that day? I had spent the morning reporting the murder of the Duke of Edinburgh by his youngest son. Now a colleague half my age whom I had never met socially was apparently offering a no-hassle shag. I knew that the first event had been a fantasy that felt real. The second was apparently reality that felt like a fantasy.

'And don't worry? I don't want to be the third Mrs Fleming?'

That was the thing about sleeping with a researcher: they looked you up in *Who's Who* first.

'I know that it could probably just be once?'

Abbi Pascoe twirled her dark fringe around her fingers and flexed restlessly up and down on air-cushioned running shoes which extended her five-five.

In the previous six months, all my orgasms had been poured into bloodstained morning bathwater. It was three months since Rachel and I had even mentioned our marital celibacy, a conversation which had begun an argument so harsh that it ensured the drought continued. I was no moral philosopher – was likely to interest that discipline only as an admonitory example on exam papers – but it seemed to me that you could not sexually betray someone with whom you were not sleeping.

'Fuck,' I said.

Abbi Pascoe (I use both names because I knew her no better than that) giggled again: 'As it were.'

'Suppose we . . . I mean . . . presumably not here?'

'Don't think I'm kinky or anything? But, in my fantasy, it does actually happen here?'

I tried to check my watch but, gliding my eyes towards my wrist, saw also the straining cloth at my crotch. The body always voted first, and early.

'You've got an hour before you go to make-up?' she said.

'Right. I suppose the point about the old conventions of going out for meals or to see a film or whatever is that they build up slowly to what may or may not happen. In this case, it's a bit like going on without rehearsal.'

Abbi Pascoe walked across and, like a hairdresser or dentist, used her hands gently to steady my head. She moved her tongue in a slow and steady rhythm between my lips: a preview of the movement and sensation open to me lower later. It is the most difficult of kisses to resist, and I didn't.

As we tried to stand, entwined, she saw the papered mirror.

'Oh, why's that?'

'It's a thing I have . . . I can't stand seeing my face.'

'I can.'

Her tongue underlined her declaration. Our fingers moved downwards and scrabbled across their targets like a drunk trying to open a door. One reason that sex is better at the beginning of a relationship than at the end is zips. Being easily naked together can never match the glee of feeling and freeing unseen places. But trousers versus the uniform black dress of the TV female was an unfair contest, and my fingers won. Abbi leaned back against the wall, winded and distracted. She began to bend and, guessing that she was trying to kneel in front of me, I caught her by the shoulders and ducked down myself.

'That old dilemma,' she joked. 'Your face or mine?'

In the colour code of underwear, black means you've just met; grey that you are married. I licked her through the inky gusset until the fabric taste gave way to bouillabaisse, then pulled the black cloth down. Cricket pitch or jungle, we used to say at school. Abbi was jungle. I kissed her twice there and then lapped again. When she came, she fell across me in a fireman's lift.

My intention is still not to publish this, though I'm increasingly prone to the consoling fantasy of the manuscript being found among my papers after my death. So let me explain. These pages may be taken as pornography or boasting. But it matters in sex who did what to whom, and it's even more important when the man is twice the woman's age and she's on a short-term contract in his office.

It's an easy picture to have: the middle-aged man pressing down on the head of the sore-kneed employee the age of his daughters. Take President Riley. But, while female voters over fifty may have been shocked by the blow-jobs themselves, women under forty were more appalled that he didn't reciprocate. The point is that Abbi Pascoe's story of what happened in that room is only one version.

As she pulled at my trousers, I reached for her breasts. She pushed my hand away.

'That would be lovely but I've got these, like, really sore boobs? It's nearly my period?'

This news reassuringly reduced the risk of pregnancy, but I had done at least twenty radio discussions about Aids. 'I, er, don't have anything,' I said. How strange that the phrase which warns we might be at risk of a disease is identical to the one which would declare us free of it. This was a linguistic oddity which my parents would have enjoyed if they a) were still alive and b) had been less puritanical about sex.

'Don't worry,' said Abbi. 'I have a clever little inside pocket.'

'I'm sure,' I said, tremblingly.

Laughing, she reached for her discarded pants and showed me the little flap inside them – above the sodden crotch – from which she pulled a foil square. It was printed with a picture of a banana. These young women.

'The knicker industry liberates women from the handbag.' She smiled.

When she pulled off my shirt, she gently touched the plaster on my right arm.

'What's that?'

'Oh, some Celebrity Blood Donor thing last week. We bleed to encourage the ordinary people.'

Abbi lay back on the camp-bed, her black dress bunched around her waist. Both of my wives and my various other entanglements had made love with their eyes shut and with little sound except, on a good night, for the closing yodelling. But Abbi watched me all the time and spoke urgently in my ear like a director. Open talkback.

'Say, "I'm going to fill your hot wet cunt with my come"?'

I compromised with, 'Oh, Abbi . . .'

'Richard, say it . . . "I'm a big, powerful man and I'm going to fill your hot wet cunt with my come"?'

I stopped.

'As you've probably heard my producers complaining, I don't like speaking other people's words.'

'It's just it's a big turn-on for me?'

'Actions speak louder than words,' I insisted, moving inside her.

'Say, "I'm going to make your hot wet cunt drip"?'

Switch talkback. It's a problem for my generation of men, conditioned to put female pleasure first, that ejaculation at almost any stage, even with fingers slippery and tongue furred from work, feels like a failure. But, if Abbi resented my dissolved solidity, my orgasm was met with cheers and whistles from the crowd outside.

The terrible fear that they had been listening through the window gave way to the realization, from their stampeding feet, that they were reacting to the opened studios. The feet stopped again. They were being searched tonight at the door for the first time.

Spent, I kept moving for Abbi's benefit. Whatever she has said, those final moments were like rodeo.

'Christ,' she said eventually, dreamily. 'When you fuck a girl, she stays fucked?'

My shirt for interviewing the Prime Minister – one arm creased earlier by Armstrong's weight – now looked as if it had been worn for a week. As Abbi's head rested on it, her eyes closed for the first time. In the larder-sized bathroom, I peeled off the sheath – the sweet banana smell now mixed with the fisherman whiff of sperm – and dropped it in the empty pedal bin in a thick twist of tissue to spare the cleaners.

When I came back into the dressing room, Abbi was reaching for her pants and – despite being due on air in ninety minutes – I felt regret at the impending enclosure. But she said, 'Let's see what else I have in my handy little pouch.'

'Er, look, you may not realize . . . with men of forty-four . . .'

'No. I . . .'

The plastic bag was the same size as a prophylactic wrapper but transparent, showing powdery white contents. Next Abbi extracted a short length of metal which looked like a nail or screw but which, as she folded it out to four times its length, proved to be a silver collapsible snorting straw. These young women.

'I had to send my credit cards back? But you'll . . . ?'

'No. No, go ahead. But I don't . . .'

Her face showed a momentary anger which had also been there when I'd declined to speak her erotic dialogue.

'Right? Not before a programme? You're a pro?'

'No, never actually. It's never been my thing . . .'

'You can tell Auntie Abbi? I know you have to be cautious? But everyone knows that almost no one in television uses nostrils for the official reason? It's like arseholes in San Francisco?'

'No, really. There'll be no stained-glass windows made of me – as you now know – but that's not my sin.'

She shrugged and rubbed the powder across her gums as she walked towards the bathroom.

'You're almost as good a fuck as Peter Pennington,' she said, waiting for my dismay before adding, 'Teasing? I'm far too old for him?'

Abbi left ('You can be fairly sure the PM hasn't prepared in the same way?'), the only evidence of her visit a dusting, like talcum spill, on the cheap green carpet. I picked up the powder with tissue but, when I dropped this new litter in the pedal bin, there was now no other waste to break its fall. Some words do two jobs. Abbi Pascoe had fucked me but had she also fucked me?

*

Critics and producers like to say that the best interviews have the shape of a conversation. It's a neat conceit, but the world would fall silent if ordinary talk took place under the same constraints as a broadcast encounter.

How many of those you chat to regard the exchange merely as a pretext for saying one particular thing? Well, new lovers and oncologists perhaps, and some civilians, it's true, 'plug' their children like books, or tell self-adoring anecdotes about their career, but you would rapidly limit contact with these people. And how common is it for you, beyond the occasional single-issue uncle or remorseless aunt, to spend a tête-à-tête desperate to stop someone addressing a particular topic? Finally, do you possess any friends or relatives who send someone ahead of them into the house to negotiate what they want to say and then to explain after-wards what they really meant?

Despite Lucy's insistence that he should watch from the hospitality room, Nick Percival placed a chair in the wings. When the floor manager warned him about my eyeline, he barked that it was my own business if I wore mascara. Three minutes into the interview, he was glaring at me as I said to Lawrence Castle, 'We've seen many examples recently of how exhausting politics is. Those *Time* magazine covers of President Riley . . .'

'Yeah, yeah . . .'

'At his first and second inaugurations, like the before and after photos in a hair-restorer ad but in reverse . . .'

'Yeah. Well, you know, Richard, I have to say that some of the things that made President Riley tired I certainly won't be getting up to!'

If not a conversation, then an interview is tennis and I'd just set up Castle for an unreturnable forehand pass and a victory jig around his own myth. Athletes abstain from sex before a race in case it drains their physical energy. In the case of broadcasters, I now realized, it leaves them too mellow and accepting. Castle was our first British leader from the American template – tan, teeth and anecdotes –

and he accepted the audience's applause for his uxorious credentials with an actor's bashful panache.

'But, er, that side of it, I mean do you get tired by it?'

'Sure, Richard, yes, your energy levels drop. In fact, now you mention it . . .'

'*Chocolate alert.*'

Warned about the Good Samaritan parable they wanted to drop in, Lucy had agreed to watch for any opening Castle might see. Looking out past Camera 4, I saw Percival nodding combatively.

'I've started carrying round a bar of fruit and nut in my pocket,' the Prime Minister confided. 'It's for those moments when I might feel myself nodding off. Like, you know, the Leader of the Opposition's speeches!'

Game and first set to Mr Castle. I needed to sit on my chair with a towel over my head and eat a banana. Christ, don't think of bananas.

'And, look, that chocolate may not be very good for my health but you know . . .'

When we look down from heights, we fight a sudden impulse to jump. On live television – OK, on as-live television – there's an instinct to say the unplanned. I fought a mad temptation to turn to Camera 2 and confess dressing-room sex with a twenty-two-year-old researcher to the 500 here and the 9 million (OK, 8.4 million last Friday) at home.

'There's at least one guy in Britain who's glad that his Prime Minister carries . . .'

'*Richard, waiting lists!*'

'You mention health, Prime Minister . . .'

'Yeah, if I could just . . .'

'You mention health, Prime Minister. You made promises about NHS waiting lists. When exactly will . . .'

'*Good boy.*'

'Well, I've always said, Richard, I won't make rash promises. Every prime minister would like to wave a cheque and find a cure for cancer. But I say let's see what we can do about serious but more easily treatable conditions. Take diabetes, for example . . .'

After the broadcast, I had several letters from insulin users, scandalized by my apparent callousness. But I was reacting in admiration of Castle's sheer shameless efficiency, when the vision-mixer cut to my single and I was seen to greet the mention of diabetes with a satisfied smile.

'*Chocolate alert.*'

'No, well, let's take cancer, because, while you may not be able to find a cure, survival rates in different parts of the country . . .'

'No, well, look, Richard, there's a story about diabetes which . . .'

'No disrespect to diabetics, obviously, but cancer is the test case, Prime Minister. Waiting lists and survival rates . . .'

Nick Percival – on his feet now and prevented only by prospective bad publicity from intervening – had the demeanour of a diabetic in an ice-cream parlour.

*

We got to the Green Room at nine p.m. and were still there two hours later. The celebration had a thematic flourish: Moët et Chandon and Fruit 'n' Nut. Lucy had dispatched Abbi for the bottles and bars as soon as Castle's detectives reopened the corridors after his departure, a snarling Percival dashing after him while flourishing his copy of the new *Vogue* in my direction like a gun.

'I'm a spin homeopath,' claimed Lucy tipsily.

'What do you mean?' I said.

'I got through without the spin doctors.'

Abbi Pascoe behaved like a junior researcher who had yet to meet me properly. There was no way of knowing if this was professional etiquette or because this afternoon was already the deep past. She stood and smoked with the junior staff whose names I didn't know, leaving me with Lucy.

At eleven fifteen, our theme tune bleated from her mobile. We were hoping for a hero call from Ogg, who was watching the transmission at home, but the show still had fifteen minutes to go.

'Probably the husband,' Lucy slurred as she took the call, 'moaning that the boys won't settle.'

But the look on her face could have been explained only by his admission that he had killed them both.

'Oh, fuck . . . fuckety fuck . . . Really? . . . What did they say?' Her last words were, 'Yeah. Keep me in touch.'

'What?' I said.

'That was Publicity. The *Daily News* have got a story about you.'

'What about?'

'They won't say. Only that it's about you and children.'

Isabelle or Sophie, then, or both – a reunion through newspapers.

*

Ignoring Armstrong's many lectures on driving variety, I left through the main gate. Being slaughtered by a stalker might at that moment have been a relief, although any potential killer would have been confused when I turned not right towards Holland Park but left to the Westway and the Euston Road.

The *Daily News* would already be printed, the first editions selling at the railway stations. On several occasions, many years ago, I had travelled to King's Cross or Euston as midnight approached on a journey which would go no further than a round trip from my home.

First, as a young journalist, I stood among the hookers, beggars and reluctantly parting couples, gazing at my own name above one of my first freelance pieces, delirious with egotism at the thought of those two words, Richard Fleming, lying scorched and glistening in their tray of type in a Fleet Street building where names which were now famous had been built up letter by letter by the same hands. I would walk a circuit of all the London termini – a lap of honour granted to myself – to buy at each of them another copy of the cherished edition.

Later – when the newspapers had moved to Docklands and from metal to computer sceens, and I had switched from print to television – I bought five or six copies of different titles from one stall. Sitting with a polystyrene cup of burger-bar coffee, deaf to the last-train warnings booming across the emptying concourse, I would read the first reviews of a new series. Once, after a consensus demolition of programme one of *Fleming Faces*, I had been unable to hold back tears. The last dashing passengers must have taken me for someone unlucky in love.

When I had enough viewers and listeners to survive journalistic wit, that night became a sanitized anecdote for family and friends ('On Euston Station, I sat down and wept . . .'). But now, I was again in search of a paper with tomorrow's date.

I wore a baseball cap in case there was a picture on the front page. But there were only words:

TOP TV STAR IN
CHILD JOKE STORM

If the content of the story warned that my career might be over, the wording taunted me that it had never quite begun. Every celebrity knows that, if they don't use your name in the headline, it's so that people will buy the paper thinking that it's someone *really* famous.

Interviews 4: Old-fashioned Nose Work

Man's voice: Gurra (?) Dunn (?) Bannoch. B-A-N-N-O-C-H. I'm chief reporter in the special investigations unit of the *Daily News*.

Interviewer: Who made the decision to target Richard Fleming?

GDB: Well, you say target. He said something bloody stupid in an interview and we reported it.

Int: Who drew your attention to the *Vogue* interview with Elizabeth De Mare?

GDB: I was the star reader in Miss Rennie's class, you know. I was on reading scheme C when most of the other bairns were staring dazed at A. I can read. I read it.

Int: You're a regular reader of *Vogue* magazine as a source for stories?

GDB: Aye, that and *Sporting Life*. I wouldn't be without them. It was old-fashioned nose work.

Int: You must know it's been said that the tip-off came from the press office at Number 10 Downing Street?

GDB: That's what was said by some of the pointy-heads in the unpopular press.

Int: And you never received a phone call from Nick Percival?

GDB: Who?

Int: Didn't the *News* – in that front-page story – make just a bit much of what was pretty obviously a jocular remark?

GDB: It was a shocking thing to say about your kids. And from a guy who presents himself as Mr School Run and Barbecue.

Int: In what way did Richard Fleming present himself as a family man?

GDB: Television's for the family. He was a guest in people's living rooms.

Int: Isn't it the case that what you were actually doing was deliberately setting up Richard Fleming's family life as an issue in order to justify running the next two stories? It was, in that sense, a classic tabloid sting.

GDB: Sting? What is this? It's all very flattering. But it's not the FBI, you know. We're just a bunch of guys with beer-guts and typewriters.

ROLL 2 – *DEAD ON LIVE TV* – INTERVIEW 22/11/99

Int: Lucy, do you think it was an organized attempt by the press to get Richard?

LB: No, er, not to get him personally. To get anyone in the public eye. To get them out. This thing had started – it still goes on – which I call assassination by quotation. The England football manager had just had to resign for saying – appearing to say, actually – that God had killed off the brother of Mexico's top scorer in a plane crash so that the striker would miss the match and England would get the goalless draw they needed. His enemies twisted that line around his neck. Most days there was a Cabinet Minister under pressure to resign over something he might have said to a school magazine . . .

Int: Well, I see what you're . . . but it's pretty clear now they were on to him even before the *Vogue* interview appeared . . .

LB: Yeah. My sister – who works for the *Indy* – says the word in newspapers is that it all began with this rumour – started doubtless by someone sacked in one of the BBC's many reorganizations – that Richard was always going to the loo. Which he was, of course. They were simply wrong to assume it meant he was a coke-head. This was just after the Terry Perry sting when he bought Charlie (?) from that African prince who turned out to one of Lucas Quinney's hacks. They just struck lucky with everything else they got.

ROLL 78 – *DEAD ON LIVE TV* – INTERVIEW 8/12/99

Man's voice: Nick Parsifal (?). I won't spell it because it's not about publicity for me. I'm chief press officer to the Prime Minister, Lawrence Castle.

Int: Did you tip off the *Daily News* about Richard Fleming's *Vogue* interview?

NP: Listen, b*gg*rlugs, I'm going to the match on Saturday with the Director General . . . Can we go off the record? Is that camera off? Look, we're sorry about what happened later and everything. I wish I could tell you about the letters the PM wrote afterwards to the families. But he hates that kind of thing being publicized . . .

ROLL 98 – *DEAD ON LIVE TV* – INTERVIEW 03/02/00

Int: Mr Mendip, the decision to suspend Richard Fleming . . .
OM: Yeah, yeah . . .

Int: How much pressure was put on the BBC by the government and the Church?

OM: Oh, don't be ridiculous. The only contact we've had with the Archbishop of Canterbury in the last year is to ask him to pray for better ratings. Half (?) . . . Half (?) . . . Half (?) . . .

ROLL 43 – *DEAD ON LIVE TV* – INTERVIEW 2/12/99

Int: Certainly by the July, Mr Armstrong, you were reading all of the letters sent to Richard Fleming at the BBC?

GA: Yeah. That's right.

Int: But wasn't having lunch with a viewer – with Matthew Harding(?) – an obvious security risk?

GA: Well, a monkey could win the Pools if you gave him the results in advance. But you have to realize we didn't know he'd done that.

Int: You didn't know?

GA: No. Because, um, Mr Fleming arranged it in an, um, outgoing letter. We didn't read those. Obviously, er, now we've changed our procedures.

Man's voice: He's shining.

BANNOCH / SPECIAL INVESTIGATIONS – TRANSCRIPT (14/7/99)

RF: Fuck.

AP: As it were.

RF: Suppose we . . . I mean . . . presumably not here?

AP: Don't think I'm kinky or anything. But, in my fantasy, it does actually happen here . . . *(Pause. Rustling.)* . . . You've got an hour before you go to make-up.

RF: Right. I suppose the point about the old conventions of going out for meals or to see a film or whatever is that they build up slowly to what may or may not happen.

5. THE CHILD-KILLER DISCO

In the weeks before edition 222 of *Fleming Faces* – the final programme – the key events were three meals: lunch with Matthew Pardon, breakfast with Lucy and dinner with my daughter. My off-air life had become, appropriately, a talk show, though with me always in the unaccustomed second chair. But, before that, the first in the series was not a meal or even a snack but still two people at a table: coffee at midnight with Rachel.

One of Armstrong's rules was that I should drive away from the house and call the police if there were strangers outside. But when I reached Holland Park that night – the *Daily News*, still officially an hour away from publication, folded on the passenger seat with the headline downwards – the path was flanked by a dishonour guard of seven or eight. Not all were strangers. I had sat with some of them on election buses and courtroom press benches.

'Richard! Richard! Do you regret what you said?' someone shouted as I blinked into the celebrity lightning.

'Sshhhhh!' I whispered. 'There are children asleep inside.'

'And you want them nice and fresh for the supermarket tomorrow,' joked Charlie Durrant of the *Mail*.

'Fuck off, Charlie.'

'Has the BBC been in touch with you yet?'

'This is a tsunami in a saucer,' I said, but the reporters looked bewildered and their shorthand halted. Richard

Fleming hadn't learned. Trying to be clever to the press had started this.

Rachel was waiting at the kitchen table. There was an inch left in the big cafetiere, but a crossword grid – the five-minuter – had only two short clues filled in. Over Rachel's defensively hunched shoulder, I saw a red 26 on the answer-phone call-counter.

'What the fuck have you done, Richard?'

But this was an expression of disgust rather than a request for information. She had her own copy of the *News*, its headline hiding against the pine.

'One of them pushed it through the door. I've worked with some of them.'

'So have I. But it won't mean they hold the dogs off for even a minute. Anyway, you might get a column out of it.'

'Richard, I won't get a fucking column out of it. In the kind of pieces I write – as you'd know if you weren't too wrapped up in your own career ever to read them – "Bloke" has a kind of generalized presence. An egotistical fuckwit who thinks dustbins empty themselves and probably has other women. Something my readers can identify with. There's a kind of tease in which it might be TV's Richard Fleming or it might not be. This is too specific . . .'

'I don't sleep with other women.'

'No?'

'I don't sleep with anyone. As you may have noticed.'

'It takes two not to . . .'

'It takes two to . . .'

Before we improvised a new Dr Seuss, I flicked the paper over.

'Rachel, I'm sorry about bringing the barbarians to the garden gate. Of course I am. But look at what I actually said. She was nosing after Isabelle and Sophie, so I made some joke about the only point of children being that you got to park closer to the supermarket doors. It was a deflection.'

'Yeah, well. When the BBC sacks you, I wouldn't go into business making bullet-proof vests.'

'It's an hysterical overreaction . . .'

'Of course it is, Richard. But do you know what the biggest single item left at lost property offices these days is? After umbrellas? A sense of proportion. People are losing them all over the place. We've all read those is-this-really-England pieces – Christ, I've written them – about the teacher or professor whose life is ruined by some stray remark. And the newspapers are always appalled. But journalists do the same thing to people all the time.'

'Oh. This will blow over.'

'Just before you got here, Charlie Durrant shouted through the letter box that the Archbishop of Canterbury has called for you to resign.'

Rachel left me in the kitchen, reading and eating. When I went up, she was still awake and I considered a conciliatory kiss but didn't trust the mints to hide the smell.

*

News perishes, like food. Reporters are refrigerators, extending the length: one-day, one-week, long-life. 'Are we taking this on?' the news editor will ask.

The *News* published TOP TV STAR IN CHILD JOKE STORM on a Saturday. Over the next few days, the other newspapers took me on. Most of the Sundays reported the Archbishop's demand that I should go. Nick Percival – calling himself 'senior government sources' – said that the Prime Minister had no view as a politician but that, as a father, he was horrified by my attitude.

Lucy – now operating, ironically, as my spin doctor –

warned reporters that both Archbishop Stirling and Lawrence Castle were disgruntled victims of my brilliant questioning. But news stories are cast like dramas. I was the villain in this, and so Lucy's charitable clarification was presented as the observation that 'the Prime Minister and the Archbishop suspected from personal experience that the broadcaster was spiralling out of control.'

Several of the newspapers ran extracts from Rachel's columns – the picnic, holiday and breakfast ones from early on – changing my designation from 'Bloke' to Richard in order to establish that I had fraudulently presented myself to the public as a loving stepfather.

In the tabloids, I was indentified by one of those three-word designations, like a Native American Chief, becoming CHILD JOKE STAR. Elizabeth De Mare – smartly catching in her weekly newspaper column the ball she had thrown in *Vogue* – argued that most men were Parking Pass Fathers in some way, interested only in the benefits their offspring brought.

My BBC mailbag was suddenly bloated with letters from mothers' groups and scribbled panegyrics to nappy-changing signed Proud Father. Some included condoms, urging me to use one next time I was worried about where to park my car. Of my potential murderers, north London made no reference to the events, continuing to send tightly argued paragraphs about celebrity's illusion of eternal life, but Exeter expressed vivid vindication. The more devastating sentences of the columns about my domestic dereliction were forwarded from Devon on postcards porcupined with exclamation marks.

The BBC, though, stayed firm or at least maintained a flaccidity which might have been mistaken for it. Ogg was cautiously supportive in a phone call, while Mendip – though he might have welcomed the excuse to fly Ruthia solo on the radio show – needed for career reasons to echo MD.BRO.

And then I had two days out of the papers. They seemed to have no other way of taking me on. On the Thursday night, Rachel and I made love for the first time in six months: hesitatingly and selfishly, the pleasures separate and the most giving acts omitted, but with no resentments at the end.

Heading for the en-suite to desheath as she slept, I heard cars pulling up and parking outside. The eleven p.m. sound in a city is vehicles receding as friends leave. This could only be enemies arriving. Nervous of the photograph which shows you peeping guiltily through a curtain slit, I risked only a confirming glimpse of cigarettes, notebooks and mobiles.

My own pocket phone was ringing in the study across the landing. Tash was a shallow sleeper and waking her up would ruin my truce with her mother. I sprint-tiptoed to it.

'Oh. You're there,' said Lucy. 'Publicity rang you on the home phone. The answerphone was . . .'

'Yeah. Early night . . .'

'Right. Why are you whispering?'

'The children. *Step*children.'

This redefinition turned out to be fitting.

'Richard,' Lucy told me. 'Gordon Bannoch has got Isabelle.'

*

My producer's phrase had made the transaction sound like a kidnapping and, when I saw the *Daily News* next morning, it was clear that blackmail was intended, though of the moral kind.

CHILD JOKE STAR'S FORGOTTEN DAUGHTER
'Chat show king never talks to me'

The pictures of Isabelle I owned stopped at six, the age at which, after a weekend in which the girls wept when they left their mother and howled continually with me, dealings with my family had been reduced to a monthly subtraction from my bank account. Distance was the official excuse – Imogen chose our weekend house in Somerset as her family home – but the true reason was ambition. The admiration of viewers and listeners was simpler to court than the love of two nervous little girls schooled to refuse me. In their teens – when I finally had time for others – I sent letters through my ex-wife's solicitor but there was no reply.

And now here was Isabelle at twenty-two, photographed with her head tilted on one shoulder in the pose which, in tabloid iconography, means decent and wronged. Rachel once said that your children are either mirror or photo-frame: they look like you or others in the family. Isabelle was mirror. I instinctively looked away because it was like seeing my own face, though deftly feminized. The text made no mention of her twin, which led me to hope that Sophie thought more kindly of me.

Bannoch's piece looped with graceless variations of the same phrases around a single irony: that a man who was famous for talking – fourteen hours of radio and one hour of TV each week – had maintained a sixteen-year silence to his own daughter. What was most irritating was that Bannoch thought he had spotted this paradox. But I had known it was a psychosis for years: the public talker who can't speak privately. The newspaper, however, presented it as hypocrisy because the agenda of journalism these days is largely to monitor contradictions.

The paradox of the clammed-up chat-show host was explored by most of the columnists who followed up the story. Few avoided the pun Daughtergate. I wrote to Isabelle at the paper's address, and Rachel posted the letter because, for the second weekend in succession, I was under house press arrest.

On the Monday morning, Lucy phoned to go through that week's guests. Tommy Rankin – spiky-haired daredevil of children's television – was appearing, and I had promised Tash and Paula the treat of meeting him.

'Oh,' said Lucy in closing. 'You may get the Rankin brief late. Minor staff crisis. I don't think you properly met Abbi. Little researcher? Cocky but competent. There was a message on my voice-mail saying she's left. Won't be coming in any more. Wants to try something else.'

The mobile was in my pocket as I left home for the radio show. But, on the drive, the signature tune struck up again beside my heart.

'Hello?'

'Mr Fleming?'

'Bannoch, why would I talk to you?'

'Because I'm holding a bucket of warm shit over your head and I'll drop it the moment you stop talking. I'm calling about your other little girl.'

Gurr-ull. 'Sophie?'

'I don't know about any Sophie. This is Abbi.'

'I don't know what you're talking about.'

'If you're going to deny this, I should say that – apart from the transcript we have – Abbi took precautions. Precautions which allowed the keeping of a sample. And don't think we can't match it. Guess who sponsored Celebrity Blood Donor Day?'

The paper had literally taken my blood. And my spunk. And Abbi had kept her dress on not because her breasts were sore but because her chest was wired. It was my proud claim as an interviewer that I knew when someone was lying, but I had been duped twice within a week, and robbed of my own body fluids.

I met Ogg in his office at eleven a.m. It felt solemn – like a Cold War summit – and indeed we both carried ancient and dignified titles: MD.BRO and CHILD JOKE STAR. Although, in fact, my own designation had now changed. Bannoch had faxed over the next day's spread.

TV'S BAD DAD IS LOVE RAT

Ogg watched as I read the story. Acting on a tip-off that 'the £500,000 a year host' who 'recently interviewed both Prime Minister Lawrence Castle and the Princess Royal' was 'ruthlessly exploiting his privileged position to secure sex and drugs', the *News* had arranged for 'twenty-two-year-old Abbi Pascoe (not her real name)' to work at the programme.

Within weeks, Abbi was invited to 'a sordid orgy in Fleming's BBC dressing room' in which he had 'first engaged her in a perverted sex act' and then 'took part in a foul-mouthed commentary on Abbi's body in terms which cannot be printed in a family newspaper but which would shock Fleming's millions of women viewers'.

The 'millionaire broadcaster' then 'showed no surprise when Abbi produced cocaine, known in TV circles as "celebrity sherbet". But, ever the slick telly professional, even as his perverted dreams came true, Fleming calmly explained that he never took drugs before a show.' Finally, 'after a shower and the removal of the evidence in the bathroom paid for by the licence-payers', the 'super-rich king of chat left for his studio, where he calmly discussed the morality of politics with the Premier'.

Literary snobs assume that tabloid newspapers are sloppy in their use of language. In fact, the twin goals of being totally accessible to readers while secure against suing required hard work with words. 'Engaged her in a perverted sex act' was supposed to make the reader think of blow-jobs, although it also covered what I had done to her. 'Took part in a foul-mouthed commentary' cleverly implied filthy description from me, despite the fact that my only role in the conversation had been a refusal to join in. In the same way, my failure actually to arrest her for producing cocaine was written up as complicity. In its way, it was as complex as a sonnet.

'I know it sounds pathetic,' I said to Ogg. 'But she – I'm not saying I'm a stud or anything – but she really seemed to enjoy it.'

'Richard, that's what rapists say.'

'It wasn't *rape*, Tom.'

'I'm not saying it was. I'm saying that justification hasn't got a brilliant history. Richard, I've talked to HHR about this . . .'

Ogg was famous as a name-dropper but even so.

'You've discusssed it with the bloody Prince of Wales?'

'Not HRH, Richard. HHR. Head of Human Resources. You're a freelance so there's nothing to stop you sleeping with your colleagues . . .'

'If I was on the staff I couldn't?'

'Absolutely. Our recent paper on workplace dating policy states that a staff member sexually involved with a junior employee must inform his head of department . . .'

'Before, during or after? And every time or can you get a book of chits to cover you for the next few screws?'

'DG is determined to be proactive on harassment.'

'This wasn't harassment. And there are senior executives here who've watched more secretaries undressing than they've watched television.'

'As I say, you can sleep with whoever you want to. But even freelance contracts have a clause about inappropriate behaviour on BBC property. What that means is no sex on the licence fee. The sofa-bed you fucked her on is paid for by the public, Richard.'

One wall of Ogg's office consisted entirely of television screens: live-action wallpaper. On one of them, an eight-years-younger version of Richard Fleming was interviewing the King of Jordan on a re-run channel. This was the fantasy of immortality against which north London warned. The King was dead already. How long before I was only re-runs?

'So what's going to happen, Tom?'

'We're taking you off air for two weeks.'

It is the unbreakable belief of freelances that the holiday relief will take the job. I offered to top and tail two Best Ofs for the television Fridays, but Ogg explained that they were keen to look at Cornelius Raven in a chat-show context. Ruthia would drive the radio show alone.

'But Con's one sneeze away from finding his septum in his lunch and Ruthia's fucking her boss.'

'I can't get involved in gossip about your colleagues, Richard. All I can say is that it's the rat closest to the trap which eats the poison.'

A second wife is forced to be more realistic than a first, but adultery and redundancy are still not two pieces of news to bring home even separately.

'Look, Tom, I'm under a lot of pressure at the moment. I have at least two viewers threatening to kill me. I'm getting fucking e-mails from someone claiming to be me.'

'Yes, we considered that. But the view of DOTS . . .'

'Dots?'

'Director of Talent Security . . . his view was that it

wouldn't be a sensible response to such danger to lock yourself in a dressing room with someone you didn't know.'

*

The conversation with Rachel was inevitably harder than the one with Ogg, given that the level of my mistress's pleasure was even less of a defence. My wife was unlikely to sympathize over the paper's omission of cunnilingus from the account.

It was hard to argue with Rachel's view that the wound was deeper because I had recently seemed, for the first time in months, to be trying to make things work. What could I say except that – as with Isabelle and Sophie so many years before – I seemed to be so terrified of rejection that I turned away first? But that was pop psychology only fitting for the morning sob shows. The truth was that a monster of vanity and ambition had kicked over another obstacle in his path.

Tash and Paula cried when they saw the bulging sports bags in the hall. I hoped it was because they didn't want me to leave, but thought it was probably because this was the second time in their short lives they had seen tears and hastily packed cases: emotional baggage.

My last three phone calls from the house we had shared for six years were to an airline, a car-hire firm and a hotel on the west coast of Scotland. I had gambled that the triumphant spirit of Scottish nationalism would encourage the papers there to torment Caledonian celebrities and so it proved. The editions pushed under my door next morning relegated my story to later pages, with no photographs.

I had offered the hotel staff £10,000 to share if no reporters found me during the fortnight. You couldn't hope to beat the media; merely to outbid them. I mainly used room service. The chef had an international reputation, and it almost seemed an insult to sick up his dishes.

On my laptop, I watched the progress of my implosion in the English papers. Someone – Mendip and Ruthia, I guessed – was feeding malicious details to the diary writers. I was alleged to have called my co-presenter a 'Nazi million-airess' but could hardly ask for a correction because it was true that I had used the phrase 'Kraut heiress'. I reportedly claimed my morning coffees on expenses even when they had been given free by admirers.

It was claimed that there had been a daily sweepstake among BBC staff on the time I spent in the Gents. Even Ogg seemed to be briefing against me. One of the Sundays reported that, when a 'senior executive' passed on 'praise for Fleming's presentation from an advisory group of BBC viewers', the 'loose-canon talent' had 'responded with a bewildering volley of four-letter invective: "F*** off and die, you little piece of s***".' How decorous the press were in sparing their readers from swearing even as they destroyed people's lives.

It's common to say that such crises leave you on the other side with a neat list of true friends. My foolscap stayed blank. I could blame the fact that I'd changed my mobile number in order to silence Bannoch, but my agent was giving the new one to anyone she felt was medicine.

Lucy rang twice but she sounded dutiful and bruised. In that dressing room, I had convinced myself that Abbi didn't matter – in regard to Rachel – because sexual infidelity was impossible in a celibate relationship. Now I knew – through Lucy – that you could physically betray someone you'd never slept with. The only flash of her familiar animation was when she said, 'Rich, for the last show in the run, we've been offered Jacob Goldman.'

'Fuck. I mean, I'd love to. But a writer – a serious writer – in peak-time . . .'

'Ogg's wobbling. I've told him we'll go big on the divorces, the drugs bust, the three-in-a-bed stuff with the President. I've told him only the brighter viewers need even notice he's written books . . .'

As a ten-year-old in 1965, I had read my father's copy of *Jailbait* – in the first uncensored post-Chatterley Penguin edition – ten priapic pages at a time, stealing it from his bedside table during my homework hours, careful to return it with the bookmark in place and the pages unstained by my drying fingers.

But, though Pardon-like in my personal admiration for Goldman, I was terrified of him professionally. Apart from the Pennington débâcle, on a fabled Dick Cavett show in the 1960s the novelist – to demonstrate his ambiguity about the interview as an event – had put his fingers in his ears and hummed during twenty minutes of questioning.

'He's a bugger to interview, Luce. When Pennington did him, he pretty much just nodded and shook his head during an increasingly hysterical monologue from our host.'

'Yeah, yeah. But apparently he was coming off mescaline then. The publicist says he's a pussycat now. And he's funding another divorce. They're flying him over on Concorde, and he knows he's got to play the game.'

'I think, coming back and everything, I should play safe. We want a few after-dinner bores I can just wind up and sit back.'

'No, no. You need to remind people how good you are.'

The only other contact came from the famous with parallel shames. Terry Perry rang to say that Abbi Pascoe was Tanya Griffiths who, as Patsy Chalmers, had picked him up at a party and blown-and-sold to the *Star*. Cornelius Raven e-mailed to say that the Abbey in Surrey was the best rehab clinic he knew. My cyberspace impersonator messaged me several times. Richard Fleming told Richard Fleming that his filthy little dick had let him down, and that no one would ever watch his shows again.

When the computer was off-line, I worked for fourteen hours a day on this manuscript. It was my ambition to write the first truly honest showbiz memoir: the ego, the greed, the insecurity, the treachery, described from an inside which doesn't exist, because we are alive only when the outside is performing.

In the second week, I read most evenings a single piece of paper. It was Isabelle's reply to my letter to the *News*. She agreed to meet, though warning that she might walk out if our reunion proved too oppressive. I sent back five possible dinner dates to emphasize that the choice was hers.

*

My first day back on radio – 19 July – was divided by the three significant meals. Breakfast was wheeled in on a table, extravagantly draped like a statesman's coffin, to my London hotel suite – its lighting offering fifteen colours to suit different moods – where Lucy scoured her eyes with complimentary tissues.

The first time I had been kicked out of a house, I had lived for three months in a chain hotel: harvest-scene print on the wall, trouser press, minibar wired to reception to prevent theft, the double-glazing nightly failing to silence the roar from an arterial blacktop.

Both London and I had more money now. My second spell as an emergency bachelor was being spent in what is known in the papers as a celebrity hotel. The adjective does double duty. The famous stayed here – Terry Perry's second arrest for hitting his wife had brought detectives to the eighth-floor penthouse – but the place itself was also well known, hailed as a serious talent in the tavern world in numerous profiles and columns. Now that celebrity was using up the supply of people, buildings were becoming stars.

The name of Overnights was a play on the word used for ratings and box-office receipts in the media world, which provided most of the customers. The rooms were entirely white: snowy carpet, vanilla walls, ivory curtains, albumen duvet. But this was presented not as utility but as creativity: better to reflect the rainbow possibilities of the illumination system. Imaginative lighting, however, was too much like being at work for me, and I kept the setting on the gentlest yellow.

The minibar was a walk-in cupboard in which the prices made you feel like a character in a futuristic novel. Chocolate cost as much as a bottle of whisky in the shops, while whisky had the tag of a restaurant meal in reality. A restaurant meal was the price of a hotel night elsewhere.

Lucy's call that Monday morning woke me at seven a.m. Fumbling the lights on – the switches were trompe-l'oeil, like the bathroom sink – my gummy eyes were surprised by yellow.

'Rich, I'm leaving the show,' Lucy said.

It was always torture to talk before cleaning my teeth and these words were particularly hard work. 'Oh, Luce. I'm a middle-aged fuckwit of a man but I'm not likely to do it again. The researchers will be lucky if I brush against their clipboards from now on.'

'No, I don't want to. They want me to. Ogg just rang me from someone's yacht. He got the time difference wrong.'

*

It was a no-smoking room but Lucy came in trailing clouds like an early loco. I pulled the battery from the smoke alarm. A celebrity hotel must expect its rooms to be trashed.

We hugged and I thought there was a moment when the embrace might have become more complicated. If we hadn't slept together mainly because we were colleagues, then now that Lucy had been sacked . . . Christ. All the focus groups spoke of my likeability. If they ever gave the audience telepathy spectacles, my career would be over. If it wasn't already.

When we faced each other across the white-draped break-fast catafalque – Lucy couldn't eat, I wouldn't – I said, 'Sacked you? Literally sacked you?'

'Well. You know Ogg. It's all vertical integration bimedia out-reach production schemes. They've offered me exec prod on this heritage / makeover crossover show in which viewers sell all their furniture in a garage sale then use the proceeds to replace it with antiques. It's called *In with the Old* or very possibly *Out with the New*.'

'And did he explain why?'

'Now that you're the bad boy of chat shows, they think you need the smack of firm production and so on. They don't blame me for you fucking the help. How could they? But they think – of course – I should have let the PM have his chocolate bar and that the Archbishop of Canterbury's dick might have stayed off limits . . .'

'Are they advertising?'

'No. Mendip is stepping in till the end of the series.'

'Oliver Con-Well! Christ!'

The atmosphere in the room had been all nicotine and jitters. But Lucy was suddenly serene, decisive.

'Rich,' she said, 'we could leave them. Set up a production company. Do the show for Channel 4.'

What we call conscience is the fear that our character is about to be revealed.

'They've got Pennington,' was the excuse I used.

'He's Saturdays. Let's pitch for weeknights. Maybe even four or five. It's accepted in America but no one's done it here. Or the first on-line talk show. That's the future. The audience mailing questions. We could get in on the basement of that . . .'

'When Raven stood in for me . . .'

'I had to feed him every question in his ear. It was like those aeroplane films where some nun's at the controls because the crew have salmonella.'

'Did the ratings go up or down?'

'You don't want to get hung up on ratings, Rich. The show still had your name on it.'

So Raven had increased the audience. Lucy's was probably not the last name Ogg planned to remove from the credits.

'I can't, Luce. I have a three-year contract. There's another divorce to pay for. I'm living in a hotel where opening the minibar is like playing a casino.'

It felt worse than the end of a marriage, which was not surprising as we had both spent far more time at work than at home in the previous six years. Our conversations had always jousted jokes and ironies, and Lucy tried even now, though throatily: 'Well, maybe you'll come on and flog off your furniture as my first celebrity guest on *Tits Sell Tat*.'

In a radio studio, a silence as long as the one that now followed would have switched off the microphones, the presenter assumed dead. But it was my job to keep conversations going even when the people had nothing to say.

'Luce, I'm really sorry about the Abbi thing. It must seem pretty disgusting . . .'

'It's just the image. The tea-girl on her knees in front of the boss . . .'

'Luce, it really wasn't . . .'

'And you were pretty stupid, Rich. You have to admit it's fairly unlikely that a twenty-two-year-old you'd never met would want to suck you off in your dressing room. You'd think even in the average penis an alarm bell might ring distantly.'

'Was it absolutely unlikely that she'd . . .'

'Yes, Rich, it was zero possibility. I think you may have spent too long on Planet Fame.'

*

If Overnights was a celebrity hotel, Afters was a celebrity restaurant. As my guest walked to the table, it struck me that Matthew Pardon was the only luncher here who would not be known to all the others.

Martin Stark and Alice Jackett – nibbling tapas with calorie-counter frowns at the table of the owner, Joanna Fitch – observed him with some terror as he triumphantly caught their eye. It was years since they'd met anyone they didn't recognize. Strangely, despite his nonentity status, Pardon was the only person present who could identify absolutely everyone else. He had seen them all without them ever seeing him.

My table stood sentinel to the lavatory door. In the hierarchy of renown, television is outranked by cinema, theatre and rock. Only writers get worse tables. Pardon, anticipating a dress code, was in pinstripe suit and pseudo-regimental tie. Job interview uniform. He took his place in a room of men in open-necked leisure shirts: media interview uniform. Cornelius Raven ('Respect, you wicked motherfucker, I enjoyed warming your seat,' he had greeted me earlier) was wearing a kind of sarong. It is common to speculate how earth might look to a Martian, but it could be no stranger than the London cultural world must seem to a Midlands accountant.

'Mr Fleming!' he said.

His handshake left me in need of discreet dabbing with a napkin under the table. Perspiration was the sincerest form of flattery in a fan. The true believers looked as if they'd walked through a storm.

'I thought I'd have to go on a waiting list!'

'Sorry?'

'To meet you. I thought it must be like MPs. They see a few of their constituents at the House for tea. But you have to go on a waiting list! Fiona and I waited four years. I thought maybe you invite a few viewers at a time . . .'

'No. It doesn't really work like that. I was sort of impressed by your letters.'

'The hardship committee can't believe I'm here! Oooh, crikey, I can hear your signature tune!'

'Sorry, I'll switch it off after this. I was waiting for a call from the radio . . . Hello?'

Anna ran through the afternoon's main items. She asked if the cuttings about the Child-killer Disco had arrived at the hotel. They had. I said I'd see her at one fifteen.

Pardon, looking up dejectedly from his watch, said, 'So we haven't got very long?'

'Oh. Look, it's nothing personal. Just we're on air at four. I hardly ever do lunch.'

During my two weeks in Scotland, the fashion for newspaper-sized menus seemed to have passed. The dishes here were written in tiny italics on parchment the size of a credit card. We were given them by a young woman wearing a wide-brimmed black hat trimmed with feathers and a flowing black dress which exposed plump *décolletage*.

'Oh,' said Pardon. 'What nationality is this place?'

'Low-fat Organic Retro-English. But she's dressed like that because she's the Rubens.' I left room for his puzzled look. 'Joanna Fitch – the owner, who you see over there with Marty Stark and Alice Jackett – is, as you may know, an artist. Afters refers to the traditional pies and flans and steamies on the sweet menu – a pulling point for the many public-school boys in public life – but it's also an artist's joke. All the serving staff are based on paintings. Our waitress was after Rubens . . .'

I gestured to a central table, where Lord Haydon of Hitchin was lecturing the Defence Secretary as a woman in a headscarf with pearl earrings poured them wine.

'Vermeer,' I explained. 'The restaurant's almost entirely thematic. You'll notice that there's a jug of sunflowers on every table. Of course, if they really took their art history seriously, most of the food would be served by virgins carrying infants, but there you go. Personally, I want my waitress to be the Degas or the Lucien Freud. But they seem to have ruled out nudes.'

The Laughter Injuries Clinic would soon be admitting Mr Pardon to the split sides ward. I knew that I was putting on a performance, but it was TV's Richard Fleming he wanted. As I waited for Pardon to subside, Cornelius Raven passed us on his way for a piss to the door marked Duchamps. Ignoring my unrecognizable guest, he leaned over, giving me a close-up of his blistered nostrils.

'Trust me, man. I congratulated our bloke on his Picasso and it turned out he'd had fucking reconstructive surgery. Car crash. Apparently you were supposed to guess from the old-fashioned apron and the crew cut he was the Edward Hopper.'

When he'd gone, Pardon said loyally, 'I thought he was

best on your show being interviewed by you. He wasn't
as good actually presenting it.'

'No, well. Different gifts . . .'

'I did enjoy your interview with him, Richard. But what's
he really like?'

People always ask interviewers this question, and no one
understands how rude we find it. If a broadcast conversation
has any value, it's to reveal character. Yet there's a general
cheerful assumption that our subjects gull us. What was
infuriating was that every interviewer knew there was some
truth in this. Television shows you a percentage: usually
the most flattering fraction. Sitting here with Pardon, I was
careful not to give him the whole sum.

'Oh, Con' – the diminutive suggesting easy familiarity –
'can be difficult and he'll be using something else for smelling
soon the way he's going' – my snorting mime made Pardon
look satisfactorily scandalized – 'but he can play an audience'
– suggesting that he was not so much actually funny as
cunning in his manipulation of Black Country executives –
'although there is a view that the whole anal sex thing was
done earlier and better on the club circuit.'

By the time the Rubens woman served Pardon's humanely
killed steak pie, the silences were of a length Lucy (poor
Lucy) would have quartered in the edit. I toyed with white-
bait, grandly declaring that it was better to broadcast on a
mainly empty stomach. What was the woman's name he had
used earlier?

'Is, um, Fiona – was it? – your wife?'

'Was. We split up. She didn't have anyone else or anything. We just . . . she didn't really like my job. Hey, she
should have stuck around! No, I live alone now. There's
been no one else really.'

'I'm sorry . . .'

'No, even Britain's top TV interviewer couldn't have been expected to guess that!'

'Are things financially very bad?'

I had thought about giving him money. At least 5,000 licence fees from people like him were paid into my bank account each year. Perhaps I would refund him a few. He might be my penance for Abbi.

'You're easy to talk to, Richard. I suppose that's why you do what you do. I'm, um, well, through my, er, lump sum. I lost the house. Live on an, um, estate now. It's pretty rough. You more or less take it for, um, granted that the kids have guns. It's surprising how easy it is to get them. People always say we're not, um, America but . . .'

'Things travel . . .'

If only de-umming were available in life as well as radio. There was a sequence now which especially called for the razor blade: 'Um, um, um . . . by the way . . . Richard . . .' He paused slightly each time he said my name, as if afraid someone would stop him. 'It's, er, me that should say I'm sorry for your troubles. It's, um, bad enough for anybody but, er, having it all over the papers . . .'

'Oh. It's what we call fame tax.'

'Gosh, yes, I suppose it is like a tax really. And there's no Monaco you can go to!'

'Well, there is. It's called being forgotten.'

I thought of Tony Andrews, clinking across Shepherd's Bush Green, who had once payed fame super-tax. But west London was his Monte Carlo now.

'Um, Richard?'

It was the way a child held a conversation: requiring confirmation that they held your attention before continuing.

'Yes?'

'Um, I've had, um, a fabulous day today already but I

just can't quite believe that's Alice Jackett over there. Say no obviously, of course, but would there be any hope of an introduction?'

'Yeah, sure, we'll go over in a minute. I'm afraid – paradoxically – we've run out of time for afters in Afters. But I should just say that I will be able to do the benefit evening' – the speech synchronized with the passing over of a business card – 'E-mail me on this and we'll sort out the details.'

Or did Matthew Pardon already have my electronic address?

'That's terrific,' he said. 'And, um, look, I know you've . . . but . . . is there any way you'd ask Martin Stark for me? He does do protest songs. I was wondering how to get hold of him and he's *over there*. Do you, um, think I could ask when we, um, go over?'

This was an unexpected development. In saving the Plasco 500, I had taken it for granted that I would be Pardon's trophy star among a line-up of unknown strummers and single-voiced ventriloquists.

'The point is, Matthew, that not all celebrities' – oh no, calling yourself a celebrity, like telling someone you were a good lover, invited disagreement – 'are as cool about the general public as I am. If I get time, I'll e-mail him for you.'

In a suit of slices of primary colour, like the flag of a new country, the waiter at the owner's table was an easy one: Jackson Pollock. I introduced my viewer as my friend Matthew Pardon. You could tell Fitch and her guests were agonizing to remember the profession in which this pressing, sweaty little man must be an alpha male. Both rock star and actress slyly drained their hands against the tablecloth after Pardon shook them. I was frightened he might never let Jackett's go.

'Hey, man,' said Stark to me. 'We're doing your gig again.'

'Are you?'

'Friday after next?' He looked at his lover, who confirmed the diary detail with a nod. 'Together. With Jacob Goldman . . .'

'Oh, Goldman!' enthused Joanna Fitch. 'I taught myself to orgasm reading *Jailbait*.'

Fitch had been short-listed for the Turner Prize for Still Life 2000, embryos sculpted from her deep-frozen menstrual blood. 'Your producer booked us,' Stark continued.

'Lucy?'

'No. Oily guy. He says our show got the biggest ratings of the ones *you* did. So he's asked us back . . . for what he called the first new-style show . . . would that be right?'

'Crikey! When is this?' asked Pardon.

I was worried Pardon might ejaculate, giving the restaurant an unplanned moment after Mapplethorpe. I worked out the answer they both wanted: 'He must have booked you for the 30th.'

'That's cool,' Stark told me. 'Between legs of the tour.' Then he turned to Pardon: 'Man, it's bugging us. What do you actually do?'

'Oh, um, I'm not actually working at the moment!'

'There you go, doll, I said he was an actor,' the rock star jubilantly informed his girlfriend.

'In fact,' said Pardon softly, and I knew what was about to happen, 'I worked for a firm in the Midlands. It's really too boring to go into, but we all got sacked! We're having a benefit night for the families. Richard here has kindly agreed to be the MC, and I know you've done a lot of protest songs, and . . .'

When I saw Stark's eyes slide sideways, I thought he was going to blank him but it was a more sophisticated fame-evasion. The rock star's slippery look summoned from the bar a heavy with a fixed stare. 'I think it's time we left Mr Stark with his friends.'

Pardon's eyes appealed to me, but I shrugged as if to telegraph that this was the kind of celebrity to which I was an exception.

Needing to use Duchamps, I left him by the front desk. When I came back, the poor alien on Planet Fame was trying to book a table. For what? It surely wasn't possible that he was mad enough to ask me back?

'And what's your name, sir?'

'Pardon.'

'I, er, asked for your name, sir?'

The humiliation he had known since school. That, and his classmates rhyming his name with hard-on. Apologizing for the confusion, Anthony murmured that there was a table in early December but he'd need it back by eight p.m.

I really wasn't making a point when I said to the *maître d'*, 'Any hope of squeezing me in again at eight tonight, Anthony?'

'I think, in fact, we just had a cancellation, Mr Fleming.'

'It's a Miss Fleming. If I'm late, settle her in.'

On the pavement, Pardon called me Mr Fleming again, as if signalling the return of the division. Then he said abruptly, 'Your show? It's *live*, isn't it, not recorded?'

There seemed no point in troubling a fan with the technicalities of as-live recording. It was also vanity. My fan would think less of me if I admitted to the safety-net of taping.

'Yes. I prefer live. The adrenalin.'

'Crikey! And you hardly ever make a mistake.'

Hardly ever. I wished I'd made him have the cheap set menu.

'Are you going back to Birmingham tonight, Matthew?'

'No. I'm staying in London a lot with friends. It's where the jobs are. Or, in my case at the moment, the interviews!'

'Oh. Whereabouts do they live?'

The risk was that he would invite me to dinner. But Pardon was a star-struck man living alone, and I had to consider the possibility that he was north London.

'Oh, worse luck, I'm back and forth across the river. Battersea!'

It was possible that job interviews took him frequently to Islington. A professional interviewer, however, is above all a judge of character. I guessed that Toby Double was gay long before the gossip in the Tory Party. And I was sure now that Matthew Pardon's puppyish enthusiasm hid no Alsatian of hatred. He was too weak to be one of my hate-mailers. It was my job to understand how minds worked.

*

The reason that people are told, after falling off a bike or horse, to remount as soon as possible is that the body is best tricked out of fear by repetition. Delay permits reflection on how perilous the activity is. It's the same with broadcasting. After even a fortnight away, you face microphone or camera with the mechanical apprehension of a teenager on a first driving lesson.

UK Today – With Richard Fleming and Ruthia Hortenwurst – Monday 19 July

First Hour – Draft Running Order

16.00 – GTS – Jingle – Menu
16.01 – News Headlines (Sally Raven)
16.05 – Interview: Dame Felicity Hatch – RH
16.15 – Sports Desk (Barry Accrington)
16.17 – Travel (Lavinia Eldersbury)
16.18 – Child-killer Disco – RF + 2
16.24 – Sheep-Shagging Donut – RH + 2

'*Just clear your throat, could you, Richard?*' asked the techie when I gave them level. My other recent troubles had distracted me from that one.

'We hoped all that Scottish coastal air might kill the frog,' said Ruthia, the first reference to my exile and her interregnum. Our iciness was more than usually disguised because the first guest, Dame Felicity Hatch, was already in the studio.

'*The guests have arrived for the child-killer disco. GTS coming,*' Anna advised in my cans.

The green light. The steady pulse of the Greenwich Time Signal. The faster rhythm of my heart.

'Hello. It's four o'clock' – going an octave lower to lose the croakiness – 'on 19 July. From the BBC this is *UK Today*. I'm Richard Fleming . . .'

'And I'm Ruthia Hortenwurst. Coming up in the next hour . . . death behind the net curtains: best-selling crime writer Dame Felicity Hatch on murder in suburbia . . .'

'The parents of Kenny Cole tell Brussels: don't free his killers . . .'

'As top soap Rosemary Close plots a bestiality storyline: are there any taboos left in TV?'

'And – in sport – the curse of Terry Perry's left leg hits England's chances against Austral—' Shit, not Australia. '. . . Er, Austria. But first the news headlines from, er, Sally Raven . . .'

'Can we talk now?' mouthed Dame Felicity Hatch. The floral two-piece and noose of plump pearls suggested a classic English evanescence of jam-bottling and church flowers, but, in her books, she stood knowing and unflinching in the darkest rooms of sex and death.

'The mikes are dead,' I reassured her.

'The Child-killer Disco,' she exclaimed. The magpie eye

of the writer had drawn her to the running order which she read upside down through spectacles worn on a chain around her neck and now held half-way between nose and desk. 'Good heavens. One's dread, of course, is that it refers to the provision of entertainment in secure hospitals. I read a story in the *Telegraph* recently about a serial killer "dating" a nurse who'd done away with a dozen patients. They were allowed to share a cell on Friday nights.'

'Nothing so much fun,' I said. 'Round here, "disco" is short for discussion. We're doing the Kenny Cole case today. Should his killers be released now they're eighteen?'

'How morbid the terminology of broadcasting is,' the crime-writer observed. 'Dead mikes. Child-killer discos.'

'*Cut-throat,*' added Anna as the green light flashed.

'Thank you, Sally,' Ruthia picked up. 'Well, our four o'clock guest today is a lady – sitting in front of me now – who looks like the respectable grandmother and Dame of the British Empire she is. But her dark imagination singles her out from other members of the WI. Felicity Hatch has been described as the Granny of Gore and the Duchess of Death because of her best-selling crime novels. The latest, *Until I Die*, is published today. A very big hello to Dame Felicity Hatch . . .'

'Good afternoon.'

'As I say, you don't look like the kind of person who would write the books you do. How do you know so much about murder and so on?'

I wanted Hatch to look bewildered and savage Ruthia's grammar and assumptions. The problem with the buddy-buddy format – apart from shared attention – is the possibility of watching a rival succeed. Terry Perry had told me it was the same in football when you were substituted. You hoped that your replacement would fall over. If he scored, your cheers for the team covered screams inside.

'People often ask me this,' Dame Felicity was saying. 'And I think, you see, people misunderstand the process. A novel is a kind of laboratory, but the experiment taking place there generally isn't cloning. You stir the mixture, introduce a catalyst. Alan Fanning's campus novels are set in an institution which resembles the university where he teaches. But, if he really behaved like his fictional lecturers, he'd have been sacked thirty years ago. Male novelists, I think, are often asking: What might I be like if I had more fame, more hair, more, er, sex? So with crime novels. We all carry within us the potential to be a victim or a murderer. Good luck saves most of us from the first, conscience from the second. In the laboratory of my novels, I take luck and conscience away from me.'

'*Stalking*.'

Although there had been voices in my head for ten years now, this word disturbed me. Ruthia accepted Anna's prompt: 'In the new book, *Until I Die*, which is a terrific read, I must say' – all she would have read was an A4 reduction from a researcher – 'you write about stalking. Your central character – a teacher – is getting threatening messages from someone: maybe an ex-boyfriend, a colleague. What, er, drew you to that theme?'

'Well, any police officer will tell you that there are really only three new crimes – felonies fresh to the late twentieth century. One is the so-called Rolex muggings, which come from the desire people seem to have in cities now to show how rich they are. The second is the theft of mobile phones. The last is stalking. That, it seems to me, is because sexual liberation means that people have far more former lovers than they used to and therefore there's this vast new seedbed of the rejected. And stalking – in shorthand – is love which turns to hate when not returned. We've had to bring in new legislation recently to stop the menacing of women – as it usually is – by men. Of course, my book is about what you might call *civilian* stalking. There's this whole other area of those who become fixated on the famous. That, in my view, results from the huge cultural delusion that the famous like us as much as we like them. But perhaps that's another book.'

'Dame Felicity Hatch, thank you. *Until I Die* – which had me nervously turning the pages until three a.m., I can tell you – is published in hardback by Quinney. Richard?'

Quinney. I helped to plug books published by the company of a man whose newspapers had tried to ruin me. But what could you do? An invisible God was said by his supporters to be everywhere. Lucas Quinney really was.

'Thanks, Ruthia. It's four fifteen on *UK Today* and here's Barry Accrington with the sport. Barry, Terry Perry's fighting the battle of wounded knee again?'

As soon as Accrington was talking about the England coach's midfield options, I told Anna on talkback that I needed the loo. Her bright smile and lifted fist told me that she had taken fifteen minutes in that sweepstake.

Dame Felicity was waiting irritably beside an X-X lift.

'Oh, Mr Fleming,' she said. 'That seemed to go all right. In somewhat less depth than our recent television encounter. Although I had some curious letters after that. You seem to have some rather intense viewers . . .'

'Yeah. Look, I'm sure this is like people showing doctors their legs at dinner parties but . . . if someone thought they had a stalker . . .'

'Oh. Oh, you poor man. Well, the conventional advice is to contact the police. But the women I interviewed rather felt that the constabulary were better at catching the killer afterwards than anything else. Those poor women had them on the phone, outside the house. With your kind, you're protected from that. I suppose the best piece of advice I could give is to avoid an obvious moment of rejection. Rejection is the engine. Be as gentle as you can . . .'

*

The waitress wore a long and high-necked dress but also a sort of full-body veil of dotted gauze which was tied in a knot at her head, as if she were a bottle wrapped in cellophane. She had difficulty in swinging our plates of swordfish from within this drifty contraption.

'Seurat?' I checked.

'That's right, sir. Who ordered the rare?'

When the server left us for the kitchen or to bathe at Asnières, I said to Isabelle, 'The restaurant is almost entirely thematic. Note the bowl of sunflowers on every table. Of course, if they were strict about their art history, most of the food would be served by virgins carrying infants, but there you go . . .'

The line which had made Pardon guffaw won a weak smile from my daughter. Comedy always works best if the audience wants to like you.

The restaurant was quieter tonight. In fact, I had chosen it because no one I knew would be there. Celebrity London obeys rules of heraldic pedantry, and Afters was designated a place for lunch. Tonight Raven and Haydon and the rest would be at Restaurant. In the six months that Afters had existed, word-play had given way in commerce to ironic simplicity. Overnights and its affiliate Flophouse were already rumoured to be losing customers to the newly opened Hotel.

The sight of my own face circled by the dark brown hair of a young woman was more unsettling in the flesh even than it had been on the front page of the *News*. Isabelle carried it better than me.

Most weeks on the radio show we did at least one piece about genetics. Thinking about this evening in advance, it struck me that our generation's obsession with physical inheritance – our version of the Victorians' concern with financial bequest – may be of benefit to careless parents. If love will not bring our children back to meet us, they might be lured by the puzzle of DNA.

The early conversation was slow. This other person has your blood but is a total stranger.

'Do people call you Izzy or Isabelle?'

'They have. Bel. Iz. Whatever . . .'

My daughter was working for an e-commerce estate agents. She twice rearranged sentences to avoid mentioning the part of London in which she lived. It was like a first date where the girl was leaving herself easy exits in case you got too intense.

'It must have been strange, Izzy. Worse, I mean, even than for other children who don't see their father. Because I wasn't there but I was there . . .'

'You've lost me.' An ironic smile. 'As it were . . .'

'I was there on television . . .'

'That's a rather vain assumption, Richard.'

'I think you could probably call me Dad.'

'I think I probably couldn't. You know how – in the middle classes – you sometimes meet people who, when they were growing up, weren't allowed to watch TV. Or weren't allowed ITV. In our house, we weren't allowed to watch Richard Fleming.'

'Oh.' I tried to hide the pain of this. It had been a consolation – although an arrogant one, I can see – that I had not been invisible to my children. 'And you weren't curious about me?'

'Well, Mum had filled us in pretty well. She was your biographer. Heavily unauthorized, it has to be said . . .'

There's an odd thing in families with voices: an accidental ventriloquism which gives relatives identical delivery. Numerous boyfriends, phoning the family home, blurt something suggestive to the mother or sister who answers. Isabelle, though, had lost my voice. Only her mother's slight Cornish inflection disturbed her Generation X drawl. This was one of the debits I'd paid for desertion.

'It's so strange knowing nothing about you, Izzy.'

'Well, interview me. Isn't that what you're supposed to be good at?'

'Are you serious?'

'Try me.'

'Where do you live?'

'London.'

'Er, could you go further?'

'I'm happy where I am at the moment.'

'What's your favourite television programme?'

'*Peter Pennington's People* on Channel 4.'

'I asked for that, I suppose. Favourite book?'

'It's a tie. Sylvia Plath's *Collected*.' Christ. Why guys make you gas yourself. 'And *The Great Gatsby*.'

I waited to see if she was teasing me. But it seemed unlikely that the unauthorized biographer had bothered to knock my literary tastes. It was the most important answer I'd got since the Leader of the Opposition admitted he'd go to court to stop his daughter getting an abortion. Emboldened by our shared reader-genes, I asked, 'Do you have a boyfriend?'

'Well, no, Richard. I mean, I'd hate men, wouldn't I, given the main example available to me? No, it's girls for me. Or animals. I'm a sort of bestio-lesbian. Female Rottweilers give the best head.'

She watched my blush of patriarchal dismay through an agonizingly long stretch of dead air before giggling. Laughs are also often shared in families, but it was little comfort to discover that Izzy had mine.

'Oh, come on, Richard. I think you gave up your right to moral concern quite some time ago, didn't you?'

By the time our pointillist server replaced the plates with dessert menus, both versions of my face at the table were strained, the female one also resentful.

'Isabelle, I was thrilled when I got the letter . . . a genuine second chance is how I felt . . . but if you don't want to be here . . .'

'My therapist thought it was a good idea.'

I thought of my twins in analysts' consulting rooms, slandering their father. In fact, not slandering. Most of their accusations would be true.

'You're not eating?' queried Izzy, a welcome flash of filial concern.

'It's the show. Adrenalin. I usually eat later. Don't take it personally.'

'Believe me. It isn't high on my list of things.'

There was a speech I'd worked up in the taxi.

'Look, Izzy. It's like the Aborigines, the Native Americans, the Irish . . . all these governments everywhere suddenly apologizing for the past. And the victims say an apology's not enough. And it's not. But an apology *is* something. And I *am* sorry. Seeing the two of you seemed to make you so unhappy back then that I tried not seeing you for a while. And a divorce felt more of a total failure then than it possibly does now. But I thought of you all the time. I'd look at girls of fourteen, eighteen, whatever, twenty-two, the age you'd be, and think – maybe her . . .'

'Yeah. I read about that in the papers . . .'

My prepared speech had given way to improvisation at the end. The reference to twenty-two-year-olds had clearly been a mistake.

'None of the pieces mentioned Sophie?'

'No.'

'But she's OK?'

'Sophie's a bit different about this. The paper went for her as well but she wouldn't.'

My other daughter's loyalty triggered paternal pride, long dormant.

'That was kind of her.'

'Kind? I don't think you get it, Richard. She wouldn't want to be mentioned on the same piece of paper as you. She even uses Mummy's surname.'

When the Seurat beauty brought the bill, Isabelle insisted, 'I'll pay my half.'

'That's ridiculous. I must earn twenty times what . . . Money is what I always *did* give you . . . even during all those years. It's stupid to stop that now when – hopefully – the other stuff might start . . .'

She signed her credit card slip with neat looping handwriting which gave me another tremble of recognition and not just because it resembled my own.

'How long has Sophie lived in Exeter?' I asked, as we left the restaurant.

'What?' Her look of suspicious hostility ended my swagger about the domination of my own DNA in her face. It was her mother's signature grimace. 'I never said . . . oh, you fucker. Oh, God. I suppose TV's Richard Fleming can afford private detectives.'

'No. That wasn't how . . .'

My daughter, my stalker.

'Trust me.'

'Oh, yeah, right.'

'You don't live in north London do you, Izzy?'

'What? No. Couldn't afford to. The deepest south. Why?'

'I've been getting letters. Really quite scary letters. Anonymous. Exeter . . . and north London.'

'Richard, I don't hate you. Not like Sophie does. I just don't know you . . .'

My expression at that moment – mouth half-opened in hopeless preparation for a reply, eyelids flickering as the pricking begins – was caught in the photograph which illustrated two days later the account in the *News* of how I had spent most of the reunion dinner with my daughter soliciting her opinions on my television shows.

*

In the taxi going home to Overnights, I was surprised by the sound of my own voice saying, 'If you really want to learn to talk, try a Feather 141.' The background track for the Great Communicator's message was baby-chat.

There was a jam on the Embankment and the cab driver cruised through the music stations. Most were playing the same song: the single which Martin Stark had previewed on my show four months before.

> I'm in your head with you
> I'm in your bed with you
> I'll be dead with you . . .
> When you smile I know

When you sigh I know
When you lie I'll know . . .

At Overnights, two e-mails awaited me.

From: rgfleming@freetalk.net
To: rgfleming@newtalk.com
Subject: Blood
Time: Monday 12:35:22

Oh, your poor daughters. You're not good with blood,
'Richard'. Not good with blood.

I was relieved to see from the time-line that the message
had been sent while Pardon was at lunch with me. My viewer,
though, had been at the keyboard later:

From: pardon@freetalk.net
To: rgfleming@newtalk.com
Subject: Pushing It!
Time: Monday 16:23:08

Tell me right away if I'm asking for too much but is there
any chance at all I could watch the programme 'going
out' on the 30th from the 'studio'? I would promise not
to 'get in the way' as far as possible. And the hardship
committee, of course, is thrilled! Yours ever, Matthew.

The recent interview with Castle had merely been the
latest of many with politicians. In common with most in
television, I affected to despise that shallow and vain breed
of opportunistic populists. Yet they dealt with people like this
– and their painful ingratiations – every day, while television
presenters were carefully protected from their electorate.

But my decision was not entirely altruism. The best advice
is to avoid that moment of rejection, Felicity Hatch had said.
And so I told Mr Pardon how to get in.

Interviews 5: The Interview Began

ROLL 98 – DEAD ON LIVE TV – INTERVIEW 09/02/00

Man's voice: Clem Sadley, Washington Bureau Chief for the BBC. S-A-D-L-E-Y. I . . . I . . . if there were any way at all of mentioning *Do You Know Who I Am?* I believe there's a film tie-in paperback about the time this would go out . . . Bless you . . .

Int: What are your memories of working with Richard Fleming?

CS: I and Richard Fleming go back to my early years in television. I think I can say I knew as soon as I met him that I would get on with him. I think if I'm honest I . . .

Man's voice: Yeeeeeeeeeeeeeeeeeeeeeeeeees! F***, I'm sorry . . .

CS: I . . . I . . . I . . . why did the cameraman suddenly cheer?

MP/RI/DPP/CASE 102435678/310799

RI: The interview began at ten fifteen a.m. on 31 July. I am Detective Chief Inspector Richard Irving. Also present is Detective Inspector Julie Fitzsimmons. Surinder Khan is present as the suspect's solicitor. Mr Pardon, I'd like to start by asking how Richard Fleming first came to your attention?

MP: Oh, I . . . *(Pause.)* I heard him on the radio.

RI: Can you remember approximately when?

MP: Oh, yes. It was the day they announced Plasco was closing. He talked about it on the radio.

RI: Right. Now I think it's probably fair to say that the story was quite widely reported at the time. Yes? Mr Pardon just nodded. So what was it about Richard Fleming's coverage of the story that . . .

MP: He was the only one who sounded as if he actually cared. You felt that to the others you were just a story! He was . . . *(Pause.)* The word I'd use is friendly.

RI: Were you also aware of Mr Fleming's television programme?

MP: Oh, not then. You see I didn't really watch television. At home, I was only really allowed to watch the religion and wildlife programmes. Fiona . . .

RI: Fiona is your former wife?

MP: Yes. She used to watch those costume dramas. No, I only started watching Richard's television show when he mentioned it one day on the radio programme. I read later in a book that that's called cross-trailing!

RI: Let's just go back on that. Mr Fleming was really a pretty well-known man at that time. But you hadn't known who he was until Plasco closed?

MP: No. As I say, I didn't really watch or listen much. I did other things.

RI: Such as?

MP: Oh. I read a lot. And, when e-mail came in . . . Someone said once on one of Richard's radio programmes that there were a lot fewer lonely people after they invented the Internet!

RI: What kind of books?

SK: Come on, Mr Irving, leave fishing for your days off. *(To MP)* You don't have to answer if you don't want to.

MP: Biographies. Mainly of film stars.

RI: You hadn't watched television much. But you liked movies?

MP: Oh, yes. My mum used to take me to the pictures. She called them the pictures. I still went after she died. First with Fiona. Then on my own.

RI: And when you started to watch television, what did you think?

MP: I was amazed to be perfectly honest! Because – I know this may seem a bit obvious to you! – but it's not like cinema. They're actually there and they're talking directly to you as if . . .

RI: As if?

SK: *(To MP)* You don't have to continue the sentence if you don't want to.

MP: As if they knew you.

RI: It was a year or so after you became interested in Mr Fleming that you first contacted him?

MP: Yes.

RI: Why did you decide to contact him?

MP: I wanted to get into television.

RI: And was it because of a particular programme?

MP: Yes. The Alice Jackett programme.

RI: The first Alice Jackett programme?

MP: Yes.

RI: OK. I think we'll take a break there.

MP: There ought to be commercials!

ROLL 2 – *DEAD ON LIVE TV* – INTERVIEW 22/11/99

Int: Is it true that you used to send him the same e-mail each week?

LB: Before the programme? Yes. Broadcasting is performance and – though they wouldn't want it said – presenters are like actors. They have their little rituals. Richard used to joke that you, Agnes, could only be referred to in his presence as the Scottish Broadcaster.

Int: *(Laughter.)* Remember. I'm not here. But you didn't send him the e-mail before the final programme?

LB: Oh, I did. From home. I had to change it a bit, of course. Something like: I hope I'll be in your ear in spirit even if I'm not.

Int: That's great. But – just for the top of the show – we're looking at a montage – quick-cut, you know – and we'd sort of like you to say something like 'The 30 July edition of *Fleming Faces* has become the most famous programme in the history of British television.' Obviously here people know the story very well, but for foreign markets . . . could you give us something self-contained like that?

LB: I don't really do requests.

Int: Just to help us in the edit. I couldn't get you just to say something like, 'It's not every talk show which ends up with a murder and a suicide.'?

LB: J****.

ROLL 43 – *DEAD ON LIVE TV* – INTERVIEW 2/12/99

Int: Mr Armstrong, a lot was written afterwards about this, but could you clear up the question of how Matthew Pardon gained access to Television Centre on the evening of the show?

GA: Oh, well, there's no mystery about that. Mr Fleming drove him in his car.

6. HOWL-ROUND

There are two stories which I always use in any talk about the power of television: Wallpaper and Suitcases.

When Tom Ogg was Head of Light Entertainment – in the late 1970s – he approved the first gay scene in British sitcom. In *Any Friend of Yours*, the neighbours of the middle-class matriarch played by Hillary Jackett (Alice's famous actress mum) were suddenly seen drinking morning tea in bed together, having previously been assumed to be flat-mates.

On the Sunday night the episode went out, Ogg cancelled all leave on the switchboard and installed extra duty officers. He waited at home beside his own phone with a career-protecting statement for the press about realistically reflecting social shifts. A single comment was received from a viewer. A woman from Essex wanted to know where the poofs had got their wallpaper because it was exactly what she wanted for her best room.

Industry audiences love that anecdote because it exonerates them. TV is watched lightly; it doesn't give people ideas. In my speeches, I let them wallow in their highly paid powerlessness while they laugh, and then hit them with Suitcases.

A few years ago, the consumer show *Serving Them Right* put out a summer edition of holiday advice. 'You know what's it like,' said the Scottish Broadcaster perkily. 'You're standing by the airport carousel – desperate to get to the villa or the hotel – and all the suitcases look the same! There's nothing worse – is there? – than dragging four or five big bags off the conveyor belt and then discovering they're someone else's. So why not try our Top Summer Tip? Buy a roll of bright yellow masking tape and stick a giant X on both sides of your suitcase. You'll be sipping a drink on the terrace while the other passengers are still trudging through customs.'

Two months later, the National Airports Authority made a formal complaint to the BBC. At least half of all baggage now handled was marked with a vast yellow cross. Instances of people leaving airports with the wrong luggage had increased by several hundred per cent.

In your head, you work in one kind of broadcasting or the other: Wallpaper or Suitcases. On the morning of 30 July, I was still a Wallpaper man.

*

Presenting is about pretence, although, in saying this, I risk sounding like north London. A genius of the art, like Richard Rennie, who makes me feel entirely useless when I watch him on election night, is praised by critics for being 'natural'. But what this means is an ability to disguise fear. Except in very rare circumstances – sexual attraction to a famous actress, grief when a princess is killed – the presenter's art is to avoid showing what he naturally feels. Viewers and listeners should never guess that you are ignorant, frightened, divorcing, dying. Presenting resembles in this sense all other forms of acting.

Waking at Overnights, I knew that today would need to be one of my craftiest performances. The papers forced scratchily under the door at five a.m. contained interviews with both my ex-wives. Rachel claimed that I was so vain that I had once asked, after sex, 'How was it for me?' I had said that once, but it was the punch-line of a joke about Peter Pennington as we lay sated after a honeymoon fuck.

The arrival of these libels had not woken me because I had spent a white night straddling in one direction or other the modish chrome lavatory. A chest infection had been incubating for days. I had begun by coughing up pale omelettes of phlegm. Now lurid jellyfish – bright yellow flecked with black or red – slithered across the shower floor. And food or fear had jumbled my gut so that stomach cramps alternated with acid diarrhoea. Innards which may empty upwards or downwards at any time are a problem for anyone, but it is worst for politicians or broadcasters, who must risk the occurrence in front of the public.

Lawrence Castle told a story on the show once about suffering food poisoning in the middle of the 1992 election. On a morning when he was managing five minutes between shivery shits, he cut his stump speech down to four and dashed from the stage as the clapping began. My programmes, however, had fixed lengths. Like an English tourist in India, I would have to paralyse my intestines with Immodium and check the routes to the loo.

As I walked sorely towards the doors of Broadcasting House – above them, Eric Gill's statue of a naked Ariel, his penis chiselled smaller on the orders of an appalled Lord Reith – a male voice shouted from behind me, 'Richard!'

Turning, I faced a deranged stranger. He was a thin, pallid man with unbrushed brown curls and tired eyes which blinked rapidly as they tried to look imploringly into mine.

'Richard, can you give me a minute?'

Fame is like Alzheimer's. People talk to you who know you – even love you – and you have no idea who they are.

'You've got to tell my story, Richard, on one of your shows. I'm dying. Yes?' His bony fingers weakly clawed my arm and my panicked reaction was not that he might harm me, but that he might somehow bring bad luck. 'Cancer. I've just come from the hospital. The consultant said we're out of options. But this was misdiagnosed for years, Richard. That's the point . . .'

I felt the shivering in my legs and the reflex squeezing of the stinging sphincter.

'I'm sorry. I can't . . .'

'Fucker! Selfish fucker!' he shouted, as I pushed the doors, two-hand-heavy because broadcasting facilities are a favourite target for terrorists.

*

In the middle of the *UK Today* office, Anna was ecstatically exclaiming, 'We finally have definitive objective proof that the listeners are fucking stupid!'

'What's happened?' I asked.

'On the very eve of being dragged before this fucking complaints tribunal, I listened to the tape right through again. At two o'clock this morning, I finally heard it. In the middle of that package about wedding catering, some dame refers to "maiden aunts quietly *forking* their smoked salmon". *Forking*. There are listeners out there so desperate to be offended that they really think we've just broadcast someone confessing to shagging cured fish!'

But what I really needed that day were listeners who were deaf. When the SM inevitably asked me to clear my throat, I coughed as softly as possible because any shaking around waist level might be dangerous. Tentative sips from the beaker of tepid studio water couldn't relieve the dryness in my mouth.

'*Ruthia could do it on her own.*'

Though specific to my illness that afternoon, Anna's

declaration sounded ominously general. It was twenty-four hours since my eyes had looked at food, and there was a blur now as they tried to focus on the running order on the desk or the script on the flat-screen beyond. Able to type only half-sentences between retchings, I had been forced for the first-time ever to let Anna write most of the script.

UK Today – With Richard Fleming and Ruthia Hortenwurst – Friday 30 July

First Hour – Draft Running Order

16.00 – GTS – Jingle – Menu
16.01 – News Headlines (Sally Raven)
16.05 – Facelift Disco – RH + 2
16.15 – Sports Desk (Barry Accrington)
16.17 – Travel (Lavinia Eldersbury)
16.18 – Millennium Cock-up – RF + 1
16.24 – Buggery Donut – RH + 1 + Sadley (Washington)

The glow that showed the microphone live – *Gatsby believed in the green light* – and then the bleeps which would be seconded by England's clocks. 'Hello.' On the screen, the words were sliding away as if ashamed of being spoken by me. 'It's four o'cock – *clock* – on Friday 30 July and this is uck – this is *UK Today*. I'm Richard Fleming and I'm Ruthia Hortenwurst . . .'

Shit. And today this silent curse felt at risk of being transformed from oath into action. Humiliation pushes on the sphincter, and mine today could not take extra duties.

Silences on air feel at least four times their true length and I worried about the mikes going dead before Ruthia corrected my double identity as best she could by insisting, '*I'm* Ruthia Hortenwurst. In the next hour . . . facing up to fame: how plastic surgeons can make you into a star . . .'

Even with smeared vision, I could see my most hated syllables picking up their feet to trip me: 'And the government insists the Manun ... the Manyum ... the Ma ... the Man-any-um *Dome* will attract 10 million vizzy ... vit ... vizy ... *tourists* before it shits' – the classic mistake, I'd been thinking, *Don't say shits* – 'er, shuts.'

In mountaineering, if your buddy tumbles, you'll be smashed in the same crevasse. On double-fronted shows, you can stand on firm rock and watch your partner plummet. Ruthia serenely separated every syllable as she continued, 'We hear from Washington, where President Riley's popularity hits *bottom* with shocking new sex allegations. But, first, a summary of the news from Sally Raven ...'

'I'm sorry. I'm sorry,' I told Anna on talkback and Ruthia by implication.

'We notice more than the listeners, I'm sure,' my co-presenter triumphantly lied.

Anna was worried enough to come into the studio during he tape, although not sufficiently concerned to abandon her characteristic manner of address. 'Richard, I don't want my footnote in broadcasting history to be in the chapter on presenters who stiff on air. I'm telling you, Ruthia could do it on her own.' She turned to the functional broadcaster present. 'Honey, do you want to brief Sadley before the buggery donut or can you go bareback?'

'I'm happy bareback,' Ruthia confirmed. It was a measure of her professional independence that the testosterone vocabulary of the newsroom was quite natural to her now. She had sounded at first like a nun swearing.

Ruthia picked up out of the news and introduced the facelift disco: 'Well, you may have heard that Richard pretended to be me at the top of the show. But if there's anyone out there who happens to want to be Richard Fleming, help is at hand. The European Academy of Cosmetic Surgeons, meeting in London this week, heard this morning from a controversial American doctor who uses surgery to give patients the appearance of a star. He recently operated on the nose, chin, lips, eyelids and breasts of a woman patient to transform her into Marilyn Monroe. But is it ethical to use potentially dangerous medical methods to allow someone to live out a fantasy? Or do these facelifts which lift a face from someone else reflect our society's unhealthy relationship with celebrity? I'm joined now on the line from the conference by the controversial surgeon himself . . .'

She was good. She was worryingly fucking good. As the American doctor defended the human right to buy a famous face, Anna talkbacked me: '*Hard flash. Coup in Namibia. Pick up after this.*'

Namibia. Africa? My knowledge stretched to this single fact, which might not be one. I gestured hopefully at the Munich millionairess.

'*No, mate. You're always coming on as the big honcho journo who thinks we do too much fluff. You take it. We've got this bloke on the phone. His name's coming on screen. No agency copy yet. It was on the World Service squawk-box. But we've asked the library for an atlas . . .*'

As the surgeon described the sensation of watching the face of Alice Jackett take shape under his hands on the head of a New Jersey realtor, my brief – comprising a mere two lines, it emphasized the derivation of the word – clicked into place on the computer screen.

Bloke on phone is Dr Wole [VOLLEY] Adebale [ADDER-BALI] of School of Oriental and African Studies [SOAS]

Ruthia thanked Manhattan's fame-Frankenstein and said, 'Richard?'

'Er, yes. Reports are just coming in' – those ancient phrases of journalism were designed to make an idiot sound authoritative – 'of a coup in the country of Namibia. I'm joined now on the line by Dr Volley Adder-Bali of the School of Oriental and African Studies. Dr Adder-Bali, how much do we know?'

The 'we' was cheeky, given that my single contribution to the fact-pool was a stab at the continent on which the story was located.

'Yes. Good afternoon, Mr Fleming. We know that people believed to be rogue elements in the army stormed the presidential residence this morning and have taken control of state broadcasting . . .'

Yes, it was the broadcasters who really mattered, the world over. Through the glass, I saw Anna being handed a battered brown atlas.

'*One of the SMs thinks there was some big story there last year.*'

'Dr Volley' – fuck, I'd switched his names, making him sound like some tennis coach – 'is there any connection between this coup and the significant events of last year?'

'To which precise events are you referring, Mr Fleming?'

'*Sorry. You're on your own, mate.*'

'Er . . . er . . . er . . . the headline events of last year?'

My voice rising querulously at the end like Abbi Pascoe's.

'Well, it is, of course, part of the problem of Namibia that it makes few headlines in the West. Perhaps I could ask you to be more specific, Mr Fleming.'

'*On World Service, they're going on about something called swapp-oh.*'

My instant guess was that swapp-oh was some primitive form of barter. The currency had collapsed and people had

resorted to exchange. The poverty of the populace had triggered a coup.

'What's the role in all this, Doctor, of the new local
phenomenon known as swapp-oh?'

'Well, Mr Fleming, I'm not sure that one would precisely
decribe the South West Africa People's Organization as a
new local phenomenon. SWAPO was, after all, formed in
1960. But, yes, the story of modern Namibia is the story
of SWAPO, first as guerrilla soldiers and then as elected
governments . . .'

On talkback, I could hear the pages of the atlas flapping
as Anna said, '*Neigbouring reaction? We're trying to find
out what it's next to . . .*'

'Do we know anything about the reaction in the rest of'
– Africa? Dare I? – 'the continent?'

'Well, of course, Africa is a substantial place, Mr
Fleming . . .'

'*It borders Northern Rhodesia, Rhodesia, Bechuanaland . . .*'

Rhodesia? Christ, BBC cutbacks seemed to have prevented the purchase of a recent atlas. But Bechuanaland still
sounded the kind of word you flicked past on the foreign
pages.

'Given, Doctor, the tendency of unrest to spread across
this troubled continent' – the certainty surprised me. Knowledge was a trick of the voice. The listeners might think me
a veteran of the Biafran wars – 'there must be some nerves
in neighbouring Bechuanaland tonight . . .'

'Mr Fleming, I am not sure if you using this quaint col-
onial designation to be provocative. In Botswana, as it has
been called since 1966 . . .'

I looked up to see Anna laughing. Producers always
survive, while presenters are sacked. Behind her, Matthew

Pardon, forehead pouring sweat and chest heaving like a defeated athlete's, stood at the back of the production hutch, next to the SMs. He raised his hand.

When agreeing to his request to watch the talk-show recording, I had – like an absentee father courting a child's attention – suggested a day of it, coming to the radio show first. When he failed to arrive, I had ridiculously felt rejection. Now relief at his appearance was balanced by embarrassment that he would see me as a stuttering, racist incontinent.

Pardon raised his hand again. This time I waved back. He was working on the perspiration with a handkerchief, but the cascade called for a towel. I imagined him dashing to get here, frightened of being turned away for lateness.

'Dr Volley, thank you,' I said, concluding the most humiliating interview of my career. As we began the second hour, premonitions from my intestines drove me from the studio twice, and Ruthia effortlessly took over an abortion disco and a sewage donut. My main contribution was to ask Lavinia during the traffic flash whether there had ever been a day when the M40 north-bound was flowing freely and, even then, I took three starts at 'flowing'.

But, at around five thirty, my eyes felt focused and my bowels closed and I was no longer conscious of urging my mouth into the shapes of words. Towards the end of the show – live football commentary, thank God, shortened it on Fridays – when Anna talkbacked that there was a flash news story, I agreed to take it.

'*Murder. Scone-dropper. Leeds. Pumphrey.*'

'And we're just getting reports,' I ad-libbed, 'of a significant murder investigation in the Leeds area.' Scone-dropper was code for a story which would make our listeners spill their putative afternoon tea. 'Live now to our northern England correspondent, Robert Pumphrey. Robert?'

'Yes, Richard. According to West Yorkshire Police, the body of Angela Shipley, a forty-year-old divorcee from the Alwoodley area of the city, was found this morning by a neighbour. Ms Shipley was discovered in the bedroom. She had suffered what a police source described as "brutal and repeated" stab-wounds and was certified dead at the scene.'

Shipley. Angela Shipley. The address-book section of my memory made a connection. The cerebral search engine whirred.

'*A well-known figure in Leeds.*'

'I understand, Robert, that Ms Shipley was well known in the community?'

'That's right, Richard, and even possibly to some of your listeners. She was the subject of quite a lot of publicity earlier this year. Her boyfriend – a man called Jeff Tims – hired private detectives to find Ms Shipley after they had lost touch, having been childhood sweethearts. They were reunited and moved in together . . .'

'Yes, in fact, I talked to them on *UK Today* just a few months ago . . .'

In every possible way, I was at my worst as a journalist that afternoon. But some instinct had survived, because I understood at once why she had died.

A silence on radio, as I have said, seems much longer than it really is. But this was long. The air was very dead.

'*Move on. Richard, move on.*'

There were later three complaints from Christian listeners who had heard a woman's voice say 'Jesus' in the background. Digital sets of immaculate clarity were just coming in, and so there would have been richer listeners who also heard the whispering as Ruthia skimmed a crumpled tissue like a casino counter across the baize of the table towards me.

'*Pick up, Richard. Jesus, it's Peter Finch time.*'

In her panic, Anna had kept talkback open.

'*I dunno. Has he got howl-round?*'

Howl-round was what I had. But there was nothing a technician could do to stop it.

'*Ruthia, pick up. He's EVA.*'

'Er, yes, there's a slight problem with Richard's microphone. We're talking to northern correspondent Robert Pumphrey about the murder in Leeds of, er, Angela Shipley. Robert, what are police saying at the moment?'

'Ruthia, I mentioned Jeff Tims, Ms Shipley's partner, who located her after all those years apart. West Yorkshire Police say they are very keen indeed to speak to Mr Tims.'

When Ruthia had ad-libbed into a tape package about disabled access in theatres, I said words I would never have expected to speak to her: 'Thank you.'

'You shouldn't be here.'

'I really just feel lousy today all-round. And when you've actually interviewed them . . .'

'I can imagine. And I mean, Christ, to spend all those years looking for her and then to kill her.'

But, with my sudden understanding of Jeff Tims and his kind, I disagreed: 'Or to spend all those years looking for her in order to kill her.'

*

Driving Matthew Pardon towards Television Centre, I tried to turn my disastrous afternoon on air into sit-down comedy: 'We all try to deny that broadcasting is showbiz, but they both suffer from this insistence that you carry on even if your leg's hanging off. And, paradoxically, the public, if I can use that catch-all term while a member of it is sitting next to me, actually likes a few mistakes. Those bloody focus groups will probably say how human the whole thing made me seem. Although I guess I'm just going to have to accept that all my obituaries will mention that "I'm Richard Fleming and I'm Ruthia Hortenwurst" moment. Or the other one. Yes, when I die, the headline on the obits will be Parking Joke Man Dies.'

The doctor called by Anna had found me dehydrated by diarrhoea and with long-term inflammation of the throat, which he suggested should be examined by a specialist. Many actors on my talk show had camply ancedotalized Dr Theatre – the invisible physician who permits arthritic actresses to rise from their wheelchairs in the wings and dance their Act V jig – and so I insisted that Dr Television would see me through and left with my viewer for edition 222 of *Fleming Faces*.

Matthew Pardon was unexpectedly morose. At Afters, he had been like a child at the seaside. Today he seemed bruised and subdued. The juvenile metaphor still applied, but now he was like a kid on an access visit: a comparison I could make too well.

The bouncy gratitude had gone from his voice. I understood why when he said, 'I suppose you got a lot of money for the Feather ads?'

'What?'

'I heard your voice on the radio – advertising the Feather 141.'

That day, I had deliberately used the less smart of my two cars. The public is sensitive about the money paid by television.

'Well, you know, we all accept that the voice-over business is ridiculous. But to be fair, Matthew, if you walked past a shop with a sign outside saying "We buy old rope for loads of money" you'd go in . . .'

'No. You're not listening to me. The Americans who bought Plasco wanted us just for one part or . . .'

'Yes. I know. I . . .'

'The part was for the Feather 141.'

Jesus fuck, beam me up, Scotty. I was too ill and tired to be frightened. There was almost relief. I deserved this.

'You have to realize that, a lot of the time, we're just given stuff to read . . .'

'I can't believe you did that.'

My line to break the silence was precisely that of an absentee father bribing his sullen child: 'You've got a choice tonight, Matthew. We can either put you in the audience or on the studio floor. You can shadow the floor manager. That's often what vis . . . vizzy . . . guests prefer.'

'That would be good!'

My viewer sounded almost himself again.

On the day of your death, according to an old superstition, you will meet your exact double. But the vision I saw that afternoon was a portent of my future. Trapped in the rush-hour crawl at Shepherd's Bush Green – the car congestion which had made drive-time radio shows like mine so successful – I saw Tony Andrews, trudging with his heavy bags.

Many of those in the homeward rush from the tube station were from the generation which formed his massive audiences in the 1970s but, tuning out the wino, they all ignored his once-famous face. As we edged towards the Centre, the former star crossed in front of my car and was for a moment framed in the glass of my windscreen, a parody of television.

Just before the tunnel on Wood Lane, I saw my huge and smiling face looming above me, and looked away.

*

Fiona insisted on shaving my hands. A second management memo had made hairless fingers obligatory for presenters. It felt like being prepared for an operation. Then the colouring of my face seemed to take twice the usual time.

'I haven't used this much foundation since a morning disco show about people whose lovers had just left them,' Fiona said.

'I've had a bug. I'm actually on my way up from it. So . . .'

'Oh, Richard, you'll manage to slit your throat one day.'

The under-chin cuts from my blind shaving stung as the powder hit the still-sticky blood.

'OK if I use the smiley drops?' Nodding, I continued the movement into a backward tilt of the head. Fiona dripped in liquid which made your eyes shine under the lights, first used to stop breakfast presenters looking so tired. 'Richard, it's not for me to say, but I felt for you with the papers and . . .'

'Well, I deserve a lot of it.'

'No one does. I see from the script we're getting the rock star and the actress back. I didn't recognize the other name.'

'Oh, Jacob Goldman. American writer. Don't remind me. He's famous for getting through a whole talk show without speaking once.'

Despite the insistence of his publicists that the veteran novelist was now ready to talk and regretted his earlier reticence, the cuttings from the researcher – Abbi Pascoe's very fat male replacement – had included a recent Goldman piece for *Esquire* headed 'Screw the Interview'. The two dialogues with newspapers granted during his UK book tour

had resulted in articles containing one direct quote amid
dismayed paragraphs of commentary on his refusal to play
the publicity game. A planned interview with Elizabeth De
Mare had never appeared. The rumour was that he had
refused to acknowledge her presence in the room during their
hour together.

In the mirror, I could see Pardon, watching with awkward
awe as he stood at the back of the make-up room under the
clock which showed fifteen minutes to air. Now Armstrong
was beside him. He glided his eyes enquiringly towards the
stranger.

'Oh, this is Matthew Pardon. He's shadowing me today.'

I watched their reflections shake hands.

'I'm sorry to . . . with you so close to going out but . . .
everything comfortable, sir?'

'Yeah. I know who Exeter is.'

'You do?'

'She's harmless enough. I'll tell you sometime.'

'She? I did think that. She's still writing, anyway.'

'She will. But it's sorted, as they say on Rosemary Close.
Is north London still . . .'

'Every day. Same kind of thing. But we've searched them
at the door again tonight. Any e-mails?'

'I don't know. I haven't checked.'

There had been no point: the first show without Lucy's
ritual reassurance. The glance in the mirror after make-up is
always disconcerting: the orange face and outlined eyes seem
alien in room light and now the effect was amplified by my
strangely smooth hands as I flicked at hair stiffly quiffed
by spray.

'It must be a bit like being gay once a week!' laughed
Pardon.

Fiona and I deliberately froze him to show solidarity with

our many homosexual colleagues, although it was a joke we had both made separately.

Barry arrived to lead me to the studio.

'You *OK*, mate?' he asked, the emphasis meaning either that he had read the newspapers or that gossip about my vocal unreliability on the radio that day was already spreading.

'We'll be fine,' I said. 'I'm a great believer in that show-business saying, "The cheques must go on".'

'Live man walking!' Barry shouted as we turned towards the corridor.

'Christ!' said Pardon. It was the first time I'd heard him swear. 'Is that what they shout?'

'It's what he shouts.'

My viewer was excited now. He looked as if he was using Fiona's smiley drops in both eyes. He broke the gaze to check his watch.

'You're going out early tonight?'

'What?'

'The show's going out earlier than usual?'

Was it? It was not that I was no longer vain enough to look for my name on the listings pages; more that my narcissism now demanded larger satisfactions. But I knew that the shifting start-time had been a recurrent spat with management.

'They move you around a bit. Because of news and sport and so on. It's like trains at weekends. Engineering work . . .'

Despite this accessible metaphor, it was amost ten years since I had used the railways.

HELLO

The familiar extraterrestrial greeting seemed to hang in the air tonight with some menace. It was a message not from a friendly galactic ambassador but from a potential invasion force.

AND TONIGHT'S
SHOW YOU WILL
FRANKLY NOT
BELIEVE!

The worm was being pushed into my ear. When the mike was on my tie – 'Happiness,' said sound – I hissed, 'What the fuck's this? I didn't write this, Luce.'

But it was no longer Lucy whispering to me.

'*Hi, hi, hi.*'

Oliver Mendip, who always said hello three times but never goodbye when you wanted him to.

'I'm not going to come on like some nightclub MC.'

'*We're trying to help you to sell yourself more.*'

And I surrendered because, for the first time in 222 shows, I just wanted it to be over and to be asleep.

'*Let Goldman go filthy. We can bleep him later.*'

There was a sinister sting in my bowels and my eyes – already wet from the happy splash – were misted by other liquids as I tried to focus on the Autocue:

PLEASE, SIR. I DON'T
LIKE THIS TRICK, SIR.

I have voices in my ear and urgent messages surge before my eyes in flickering green type. And yet no one thinks I'm insane.

'*His worm's showing.*'

Fingers fiddle at my face again, slipping in the unexpected sweat.

'*Running VT. Ten, nine, eight, seven . . .*'

The band began the anthem – 'Richard's Variations', the

music which my will stipulates should be played at my funeral as the coffin leaves the church – and Barry tapped me on the back. Beside him, Pardon had on his face the ecstatic concentration of a viewer who had broken through the glass.

'*OK, people. Let's fuck them. Fuck them until they come.*'

Yes, fuck them.

HELLO
AND TONIGHT'S
SHOW YOU WILL
FRANKLY NOT
BELIEVE!

The guest list was a compromise between the show originally planned by Lucy and Mendip's audience-courting imports. Martin Stark and Alice Jackett – discussing the love which had resulted from my show – were held back for the top-of-the-bill slots with all three chairs in.

BUT MY FIRST
GUEST TONIGHT
IS ONE OF AMERICA'S
GREATEST WRITERS

Disappointed at hearing the word 'writer', the audience revived as my link outlined the obscenity prosecutions, the White House orgies, the imprisonments for affray and the looming fourth divorce.

Jacob Goldman ignored the applause as he padded down the catwalk like an arthritic emperor. Enthroning himself on the soft black chair, he refused to shake my hand, but it was already shaking enough for two.

'You don't like interviews?' I began.

'I don't?'

The cuttings file suggested that Goldman's answers became shorter as the conversations continued. His first bid tonight was two words.

'*Divorces?*' prompted Mendip hopefully but uselessly because I was determined to punish him for Lucy's absence by ignoring him.

'Well, apparently not. You've just published a magazine article headlined "Screw the Interview" . . .'

'Yeah.'

'Well, why is that you, um, feel so strongly about the interview as a form?'

'I do?'

'*Three-in-a-bed sex?*'

'Well, um, someone, um, could easily get that impression. And what fascinates me is why, feeling like that, you agree to give interviews at all?'

'Why?'

'Yes.'

Even mentally adjusting for broadcast time seeming longer than GMT, the gap felt like dinner in a bad marriage. Goldman's mouth chewed imaginary gum and his rheumy eyes kept up a fixed and chilly inspection before he rasped a single word: 'Manners.'

'*Divorces?*'

'You're, um, obviously many of us have, um, had our troubles but you're, in fact, coming up to your fourth divorce . . .'

The fact that the immense silences were no longer unexpected made them no less frightening. The church and concert sound of coughs brought on by boredom spread through the audience. Suddenly Goldman raised both hands and, like someone beating time, brought one finger down four times hard against another.

'Correct.' He confirmed my arithmetic.

'Um, um . . .' Studio stroke. No further questions for this witness. I looked for the Autocue on 2:

DIVORCES?
THREE-IN-BED?
SEXISM?

Two subjects already killed; and a third it would be suicide to attempt. References to attacks on Goldman's work by American feminists were unlikely to open a flow of anecdote.

'*What's your new novel about?*'

The question I had pledged never to ask was the only one left. And it had been clear from the pieces in the research that, if Trappist on his private life, Goldman was more or less post-mortem on the subject of his novels.

'The, um, American Civil War has produced many American novels from *The Red Badge of Courage* to *Gone With the Wind*, although I'm sure you wouldn't want to be ranked with that, but even so as a subject I wondered why in your new book, *The New Nation*, you had decided to write about the Civil War?'

The bronchitic symphony building among the audience was almost welcome, because complete silence would have been worse. The granite impassivity of Goldman's face suggested that Mount Rushmore was slightly more likely to talk.

'*Rip-cord. Rip-cord. Bring on Jackett.*'

Goldman, though, abruptly nodded and smiled for the first time as he replied, 'That's a very good question. The best I've been asked on this trip. Let me tell you exactly why I wrote *The New Nation*.'

There is only one comparison for the feeling an interviewer has when a notorious tight-mouth opens up. It's the moment in a conversation when you realize that someone is prepared to go to bed with you.

'My wife and I,' the novelist continued, 'had a dog. One day, she goes out to call it in for chow, and the pooch's nowhere to be seen. Now this makes us pretty sad, because it's a cute dog. We're shouting its name everywhere, right through the night. But nothing.'

The coughing had stopped. Goldman knew the story-teller's tricks: the lowered voice, the variations in the length of sentences. My only small worry was that it might be a long anecdote. It was not obvious how this tale of a missing dog would come round to the war between the states. Perhaps the pet was recovered at some legendary battle site.

Goldman leaned forward. 'For a year, there's nothing. We're just starting to think of getting another pet. Then one day there's a letter in the mail box. Cut-out words from newspapers like in the blackmail movies. And do you want to know what the letter said?'

A spokesman for the audience's own greed to know, I told Goldman, 'Yes!'

'The note said, "Write a novel about the American Civil War . . . or the dog dies!" '

No guest had ever done my legs so efficiently.

'*Cut-throat. Cut-throat.*'

Over a silence broken by a few chuckles from those con-fused by a phrase which sounded like a punch-line but wasn't, I introduced Martin Stark, singing what was now his Number One hit, the words which had further inflamed his fame:

> I'm in your head with you
> I'm in your bed with you
> I'll be dead with you . . .

When they killed my lights for a song, the sudden patch of coolness in the studio was always welcome, but tonight it felt like an ambulance arriving: a potential ending to the pain. But it was only Fiona – nurse-surgeon to my looks – who ministered to me.

'It's like painting those long bridges,' she whispered as she tried to make the pancake stay on my slippery face. 'I'm going round in circles.'

When Barry waved her away, Fiona put one hand on my shoulder and rested it there for a moment. This cancer-ward pat made me realize how bad things were. The presenter was finally presenting the truth, although the voices in his head were now imaginary:

'*One daughter's stalking you, the other hates you too . . .*'

Open talkback. There was a handkerchief in my pocket but the lights were about to go on. In July, viewers might assume it was hay fever.

'*Today you dried on radio. Your television guest just did your legs. Six million viewers – or however many you've got left – are about to see you weeping . . .*'

Howl-round. Trying to silence the voices, I searched for the green lights of the Autocue:

MY TONGUE ISN'T
QUICK OR SLICK, SIR.

Martin Stark roared his final chorus of the stalker's warning:

When you smile I know
When you sigh I know
When you lie I'll know-oh-oh . . .

As the singer took his bow, his backing group and my band began to jam the wedding march and Alice Jackett, like a bride along an aisle, came down the catwalk, in a rehearsed joke kept from Stark. When she reached the stage, Stark took her hand and kissed her

In what became the last moments of the show, I saw two things. Through the dream-sequence shimmer of the spill from the lights, I followed Tony Andrews as he stood up in the audience, a bottle swinging from one hand, and unsteadily descended the steps until his face, ghost-pale without make-up under the glamorizing blaze, was on camera again for the first time in two decades.

I assumed this to be a hallucination, induced by sickness and humiliation. But I knew Matthew Pardon to be real because I had seen him in the wings before my eyes became unreliable. His advance across the stage seemed, in my flickering vision, to be playing on a video-tape, but a cassette which had been played too often. The images fizzed and jerked. The fading Pardon held a gun. I raised my shaved hands.

Interviews 6: Doing the Voices

ROLL 104 – DEAD ON LIVE TV – INTERVIEW 15/02/00

Man's voice: Yeah. Yeah, sure. I'm Professor Stanley Rockwell – like the painter (?) – I'm keeper of the Jacob Goldman Manuscript Collection here at this university.

Int: Great. Now Mr Goldman has refused to talk to us . . .

SR: And this surprised you? This, of course, is one of the major ironies of this whole story. Jacob Goldman – one of the few writers to refuse to play by the rules of The Interview – is present when the television talk show implodes. At that point he pledges – making an entry to this effect in his writer's notebook on that very evening – never to be interviewed again. But Goldman's public disdain for the interview masks – as often with writers – an almost obsessive concern with the form. That very night – in his room at Overnights hotel in London, after giving his witness statement to the police – he starts to make notes for a novel about a talk-show host. It is to be called *Live on Tape*. You have that expression?

Int: Sort of. We say 'as-live'.

SR: In that first notebook entry, we see that it will take the form of a mock-memoir. The novel calls for the first person because a TV anchor addresses us directly through the TelePrompTer. Should I say Autocue for a British audience?

Int: Would you?

SR: The novel calls for the first person because a TV anchor addresses us directly through the Autocue. But almost at once Goldman encounters a Wapping (?) technical problem. The I-narrator of a novel cannot, for obvious reasons, die. Unless – perhaps – he commits suicide after writing his account. We see in the notebooks that it really costs Goldman some sleep to think of ways of maintaining the suspense.

MP/RI/DPP/CASE 102435678/310799

RI: The interview resumed at eleven hundred hours on 31 July. Is there anything we can get for you, Mr Pardon, before we start again?

ROLL 108 – *DEAD ON LIVE TV* – INTERVIEW 17/02/00

Man's voice: Okey-doke. I'm Steve Venables and this is Patsy, my wife. We were members of the studio audience at the Richard Fleming show . . .

Int: Could you say *Fleming Faces*?

SV: What?

Int: The series was actually called *Fleming Faces*.

Woman's voice (PV?): Is it? We always called it the Richard Fleming show.

SV: They'll be right, love. *(Coughs.)* We were members of the audience for *Fleming Faces* on what you'd probably call the night in question.

Int: Can you tell us what you saw?

SV: We saw this bloke . . .

PV: Two blokes.

SV: Well, yeah. But we saw the first bloke first. Are you sure you want her in it?

Int: I'll probably interview you separately. Patsy, if you could just let Steve have a go at it.

SV: *(Coughs.)* This bloke stands up in the audience next to us. He's got a bottle in his hand. An empty whisky bottle. I thought I'd seen him somewhere before. Which, of course, I had, although I only knew that when I read the papers. The seats are in terraces, like at a football ground, and the bloke walks down the aisle thing in the middle, swinging the bottle . . .

ROLL 111 – *DEAD ON LIVE TV* – INTERVIEW 18/02/00

Man's voice: Fine. Yes, I'm Christopher Browning. I'm the author of *Dead Air: The Television Life and Death of Tony Andrews.*

Int: At the end, we're going for a kind of relay narration of the deaths. Could you pick up from when Andrews reaches the bottom of the steps.

CB: Yes. If you look at the tape, Tony Andrews stops beside a television monitor. He does a double-take. That's because it's him on the monitor. He's just seen himself on television for the first time in twenty years. At least one of the cameras has swung round to show what's going on in the studio. Then Andrews swings the bottle at the screen. He breaks the screen – smashing his own image into pieces – but hasn't broken the bottle, which was what he wanted. So he swings the bottle again against the hard plastic casing of the monitor. And then – with the top half of the bottle in his hand – he walks on to the stage. We see him glancing round the circle of the cameras. And note that it's number 2 he chooses. The presenter's camera.

*

SV: The point is, Patsy and me, at that stage, we still think it's a joke. I mean, we'd been to a Tommy Rankin show where four frigging streakers suddenly ran on while he was talking. So, you know. But the bloke – Tony Andrews, as we know now – looked straight into the camera and then pulled the broken bottle across his neck . . .

Int: Terrific. And, Patsy, what was going through your head at this time?

PV: Well, to be honest, I've only seen that bit on the tape.

Int: You've seen a copy of the tape?

PV: Yeah, well. I know it's not supposed to be out. But they're everywhere. A bloke at Steve's work had one. He got it off the Internet. Mind you, it had been copied so often it looks like when you watch without an aerial. But, like I say, at the time, I was watching the other bloke . . .

*

Int: On the tape, Mr Armstrong, you seem to hesitate.

GA: I'd been in the wings on the other side. I was trying to get myself between the guests and Andrews when I saw Pardon coming from the other side . . .

*

Int: And what was Richard Fleming doing during this?

SV: He was just sat there. I mean, not being funny or anything, but it was like on a video. Freeze-frame.

*

GA: I'd actually felt sorry for him. Little gimp like a kid on an outing and then I saw he had a gun.

*

MP: Can I ask a question?

RI: Yes. You understand that you can stop this interview at any time? Mr Pardon nodded. Go ahead.

MP: How many people saw it?

RI: What? No, listen. If you're hoping your brief can get you off on identification, there were 500 witnesses in that studio.

MP: No. No, I mean. How many people watched it at home?

RI: What? Well, no one. I mean, obviously it didn't go out.

MP: But it was live!

RI: No, no, recorded. 'As live', I think they call it.

*

SV: Alice Jackett was screaming. She sort of curled up, her arms over her head. Marty Stark stood up and started walking, but he slipped on the blood from the other bloke.

PV: It was unreal. *(Laughs.)* I was going to say it was like watching television.

SV: Richard Fleming just sat there.

PV: He was crying. He was definitely crying.

*

CB: If there hadn't been the other death, then Tony Andrews might perhaps have survived. The bleeding could have been stopped. But the point I make in my book is that he didn't want to. He was determined to die on television. When police went to his flat afterwards, they found nearly 1,000 pages of a book about television. Not an autobiography but a long angry thesis about the relationship between the presenter and the audience and the essential deceit of the medium. And – although Tony Andrews actually lived in north London – he would spend most of his days in Shepherd's Bush, scene of his television triumphs, drinking on the Green and then circling the building which would no longer let him in.

*

RI: Matthew John Pardon, I charge you with the murder – at twenty-one ten in Studio TC7 of Television Centre, Wood Lane, London – of David Anthony Smith, also known professionally as Martin or Marty Stark . . .

*

OM: If MD.BRO and I feel guilty about anything, it's that we got the script wrong with regard to Richard Fleming. We thought it was *Network* but, in fact, it was *King of Comedy*.

*

Int: But Jacob Goldman's *Live on Tape* was never published?
SR: I'm holding the uncompleted manuscript here in my hands. After fifty-two pages of double-spaced A4 script, Goldman nixed it. He tells his notebook he's concerned about doing the English voices. And, anyways, a piece Goldman reads in the *New Yorker* tells him the guy – the real anchor? I've forgotten his name – has written his own book. As therapy . . .

PART THREE

MURDERERS

Nobody can be sure about what television does to the viewer. One opinion holds that television programmes can subjugate whole populations and turn children into murderers. Another opinion holds that television is too trivial a cultural event to be considered. A surprising number of experts have subscribed to these views in close succession or even simultaneously.

Clive James, *The Crystal Bucket*

Interviews 7: The Television Room

DS: It must be a curious sensation for you – being interviewed?

RF: Yeah. I've never liked it. Doctors make bad patients.
Interviewers resent questioning. Hey, why's there a
camera?

DS: It's our policy here now. We use it to review progress.
Is it a problem for you?

RF: It's just that I'm paranoid – not in a medical sense,
I should say rapidly – but there's this documentary – at
least one documentary – being made about me and they'd
sell my daughter to have this . . .

DS: Given the nature of most of our patients, our reputation
depends on our security. It really couldn't get out . . .

RF: I was told that about the final programme. But, from
what I hear, every smart dinner party in London and New
York sits down to watch the world's first ever snuff talk
show with their coffee.

DS: If it helps, you can keep the videos yourself between
sessions.

RF: Thanks. That might be useful for the book I'm writing.
Christ, Dr Sark, I just plugged my book before it's even
finished. I'm better at being an interviewee than I thought
I'd be. *(Laughter.)*

DS: Call me Dennis. Is it an autobiography?

RF: Yeah. I suppose. An attempt to explain myself to myself. I started it as therapy. I'm using that word in its civilian sense.

DS: Sure. Is it for publication?

RF: I tell myself not as I write it. It makes you more honest. What I most like at the moment is the idea of it being found in my papers after my death.

DS: You could happily wait that long?

RF: Who knows how long it would be? *(Laughs.)* Oh, Christ, it's going to be plastic cutlery in the canteen now, isn't it?

DS: Has suicide ever seemed an attractive option?

RF: Well, as I say in my book – I'm getting the hang of this guest thing, aren't I? – apparently it's suggested in the *New Yorker* piece – or so Lucy told me, I've cancelled my cuttings service – that I drove Pardon in that day in the hope that he would be my executioner. Assisted suicide live – *as*-live – on TV. But it wasn't that. The awful truth is that I was flattered. I was carrying my fan around with me as a status symbol.

DS: And yet you did say – speaking to my colleague Dr Cherry – I have the transcript here somewhere – yes, you did say that you were 'almost disappointed when he shot Stark'.

RF: Did I say that? It's funny, that's the thing the politicians most hate. When you quote some speech they made in Swansea when they were twenty-three. 'Did I say that?' they always say. It buys them thinking time. Look – Christ, I sound like Lawrence Castle – look, if I did say that, I was being honest – perhaps recklessly honest – about the celebrity thing. I did have, in the days after, this . . . well, it seems ridiculous to call it a sense of rejection . . . but this feeling of: he wasn't even *my* stalker! He was after someone more famous! Like, when I die, the billboards will say 'TV Star Dead' to trick people into thinking it's some mega-celebrity. I gave him lunch and an awayday in good faith – thinking he was my fan – and it was poor bloody Alice Jackett he was stalking.

DS: Do you feel any guilt about it?

RF: In what way?

DS: That you brought Jackett and Stark together?

RF: Oh. My show did. My show isn't me. Which is perhaps a good thing, as it doesn't exist any more. I've written to Alice. I believe she was here for a while?

DS: I can't discuss patients. Not even with patients. Was Alice on your list?

RF: What?

DS: On your first day here you were asked to make a list of everyone you'd hurt . . .

RF: Oh, yes. Both my wives – my ex-wives, that celebrity plural I once swore I'd never have to use – my daughters.

DS: Are you in touch with them?

RF: No. The paper Isabelle's signed up with at the moment isn't one I read. And Sophie's stopped sending me anonymous hate-mail. You can tell how fucked up my life is that I miss it. But we were talking about Alice. She wasn't on my list. In a funny sort of way, I saved her life. From what I understood from the police psychiatrist, Pardon could have gone either of two ways. Eventually, he would have become angry with Alice. But, when we saw them after that lunch, it was Stark who pissed him off. His anger was directed at his rival. I mean, how pathetic does that make me. I thought I had a stalker but Pardon just saw me as a sort of celebrity receptionist, putting him through to the people who really obsessed him.

DS: Have you been following the trial?

RF: Not much. There aren't many newspapers in this place.

I assume that's deliberate? Because – apart from anything else – what most of us are addicted to is publicity. It's a bad news day if the papers haven't got us in it.

DS: We encourage other entertainments, certainly.

RF: I did see a billboard one day on our escorted walk. 'Stark Killer Heard Voices.' I laughed at that.

DS: Why laughed?

RF: You're good at this. You keep it simple. I was probably too prone to the clever question.

DS: Why laughed?

RF: Black humour, really. Two of us in that studio with voices in our head.

DS: You were also hearing voices?

RF: *(Laughs.)* Well, yes.

DS: What did they say?

RF: Oh, could this be relevant?

DS: Let's see.

RF: Well, time counting down mainly. And 'cut-throat'. Those were the main ones.

DS: Time counting down. And cut-throat. Is death something that you think about a lot?

RF: Oh, I see. No, you don't quite understand. There really were people speaking in my ear.

DS: You believed that the voices were real?

RF: They *were* real.

DS: We should come back to this. The stuff that was in the papers about Pardon, did it surprise you?

RF: Some of it fitted. Only child, Dad died young, smother-mothered. The going to church, I suppose. Outside of broadcasters, it generally is the religious who hear voices, isn't it? The wife who leaves him for some bloke from work. A lonely wanker in the empty marital home, he believes that Alice Jackett is giving him the eye from the corner of the room. I'll tell you what *did* surprise me. I'd assumed, when it happened, that he was someone obsessed with television, a case study for the switch-off moralists. But it turned out that he'd scarcely watched it until the months before . . . He didn't understand the insincerity of television. He really thought that poor Alice was looking at him. What made him dangerous was that he hadn't seen enough. Wallpaper, not suitcases.

DS: You'd have to explain that.

RF: You have to let some references go. Too much information for the audience.

DS: You've talked about Pardon. How do you feel now about Tony Andrews?

RF: I did feel about that one . . . not exactly guilt but that I'd somehow *produced* it. No – not as closely as that. Executive-produced it maybe. I'd see him on the Green and somehow I had this thing that he was my flipside . . . my shadow. That what happened to him would happen to me. I quite obviously didn't expect him to walk down those steps, but when he did there was a moment of: *you* – yes, that makes sense . . . as if I'd willed it through a car window . . .

DS: And he, in fact, had developed a connection with you?

RF: So we now know. Sending me those pages of his *magnum opus* about the small-screen fraud factory. You've probably had enough of us in this chair now to know that any praise – any drip of recognition – is better than its opposite. And so in a strange way I felt flattered that he'd chosen my show to slit his throat. We would actually – I know that this sounds awful – have been massively fucked off if he'd done it for Peter Pennington. It would have been like losing out for the BAFTA Award again. And our bosses would have wanted to know why he'd gone to the opposition. But apparently – according to that *New Yorker* piece – Andrews resented me because he saw me as a cautious corporate man who had sustained his long career by doing what executives told him. Christ, he was trying to liven up my show.

DS: How is the Abbey suiting you?

RF: It gets weird in the television room after chores. I came in on the first evening and there were these four chairs in a corner and Terry Perry, Cornelius Raven and Tommy Rankin were sitting in them and I took the empty one and I was the only one who knew everyone else. And so I was marshalling the conversation – 'Tommy mentions Catholicism, Terry, weren't you brought up RC?' and so on – and I did think, *Isn't this what got me into this place?* And you should see the arguments there are, trying to find something to watch on television that one of us isn't in.

DS: According to the medical report, your throat is clearing up well.

RF: Yeah. For the first time in years I have a perfect broadcasting voice again and I don't have a programme. I did actually ask if you had hospital radio – rehab radio – here, but apparently not.

DS: Well, as you say about the problems in the television room, the last thing that a lot of our patients want is broadcasting experience. *(Laughter.)* But let's talk about the eating now. How long have you had a problem?

RF: Seven or eight years. There's a weird thing about TV. If you meet anyone when you've got a series on – even people you know quite well – they'll say, 'Oh, you've lost weight.' Which you have to their eyes because telly puts seven or eight pounds on most people. It's a technical thing. Mirrors reverse you, flashlights give you red-eye,

TV cameras spread the image. And viewers are assumed to like thin people. For years, there's been a maximum trouser-size in News. So most people diet. Though oddly – for some reason – fat was OK for weathermen. But, for me, food and drink are the way I relax. So it doesn't take long to put your finger on – put your fingers down – the solution.

DS: Did people know?

RF: No. I thought they would. But – as you've probably read – to most of my colleagues, going into the loo a lot meant a cocaine problem. Rachel and Lucy just thought I was addicted to mints. When my throat got bad, I assumed nodules or, worse, cancer. I'd interviewed enough singers who had had operations. I must have ordered fifteen or so books off the Internet before I read about acid damage to the larynx. I suppose it was obvious. If you think how your throat feels after you've been sick – people who are only sick with flu or stomach bugs – then if you're doing that every day or more . . .

DS: Did you want to be famous very much?

RF: That's interesting. You can get away with more non sequiturs than we could. Left-field is a therapist thing, isn't it? Our interviews have to be more structured.

DS: Good try. Did you want to be famous very much?

RF: How honest do you want me to be?

DS: Very honest. Honesty is kind of the point.

RF: I know. It's just strange because – in the kind of interviews I did – honesty obviously wasn't the point. It was about giving the best impression of yourself – making people like you . . .

DS: How much did you want to be famous?

RF: Which is a different thing. The second way you ask the question assumes I wanted to be famous.

DS: Did you?

RF: You'll get your own show. I mean, I know they've already done *In the Psychiatrist's Chair*.

DS: You'd be a nightmare guest.

RF: I know. I *will* answer. I wanted to be on television. I remember watching Martin Stark on *Tony Andrews* in the 1970s and I didn't want to be a rock star – like the people I knew at school – I wanted to be the interviewer. In fact – Christ, I'd be locked up if I hadn't been locked up already . . .

DS: You haven't been locked up.

RF: I used to check who the guests were in *Radio Times* and write out my list of questions. For my twelfth birthday, I asked for a clipboard and I'd sit there on the sofa and tick them off as Tony Andrews asked them. Or – usually – didn't. Because a lot of the guests were people who'd been in films I'd never seen. And – Christ, you'll never let me out of here . . .

DS: Go on.

RF: From when I was eleven – big school, as we used to say – if I finished a piece of homework – an essay – I'd gather the pages together then square them off by tapping them against the desk. Then I'd look at the wall opposite my desk and say goodnight.

DS: What made you do that?

RF: What? Did you watch much television growing up, Dr Sark?

DS: No. I . . . This conversation isn't about me . . .

RF: Don't be so modest. You're the interviewer.

DS: Bookish, asthma. The classic story. My parents sort of thought TV was Satan.

RF: It's a view. No, you see newsreaders – in those days –

always used to square off their scripts against the desk at the end. Now, they pretend to log off their computer.

DS: Ah. I should stay in more. What's the best thing about fame?

RF: The reassurance.

DS: Meaning?

RF: The applause. The entourage. The fact that there's an entire staff whose only wish is to make you feel happy.

DS: Why did you use the word reassurance?

RF: Because that's what it feels like. Celebrities – I have to use that dreadful word because there's no good English equivalent, a bit like *schadenfreude* – are often seen as people with massive self-esteem. But more often it's the opposite. Which is why so many of us end up here in the Fame Hospice. Can I ask you a question, Dr Sark?

DS: Sure. As long as it's not about other patients.

RF: It's about me as well. Do celebrities become addicts or do addicts become celebrities?

DS: That question is my career. I think it's clear – isn't it? – that fame is a kind of high . . . and applause, adulation, recognition are rushes of some kind . . .

RF: And failure is cold turkey . . .

DS: Perhaps. Certainly I'd go as far as to say that artists – or performers – of any kind are answering some kind of need for lift, for reassurance. And that is what booze and drugs and sex provide in other ways. A lot of the people I treat first got into trouble because their lives seemed empty after some moment of release – the rock-concert roar, the crowd's Cup Final chant, the novelist's joy at the final full stop . . .

RF: The floor manager's five, four, three, two, one – off-air . . .

DS: Whatever. Are you a very insecure person, Richard?

RF: That's a good question, he said, the most patronizing thing a guest can say. Sorry. My dad was always convinced he was about to be sacked, although I think it was virtually unheard of for teachers to be got rid of in those days. When there was talk of my becoming a priest . . .

DS: You were going to be a priest?

RF: Yeah. The school had a sort of fast-track scheme. Mum was keen.

DS: And why didn't you?

RF: I thought I would find celibacy difficult. So – ironically – I turn out to have had the gift of prophecy, which might have been quite useful in a priestly career. It used to torment us as teenagers that the word seminary was so close to the word for the substance which obsessed us. To be a seminarian, you gave up semen. I was actually interviewed by the Director of Vocations. He said at the end, 'Your problem, Fleming, is that you don't want to be a priest. You want to be Pope.' And it was entirely true. That morning in chapel I'd actually imagined myself in a white soutane on the Vatican balcony, blessing the world in thirty languages.

DS: But you were saying – about reassurance? When there was talk of you becoming a priest?

RF: Oh, yes. Mum pushed it because of her faith. But Dad just said, 'They'll look after you if anything goes wrong. You'll never have to have a mortgage or a pension.' And I did the opposite. I became a freelance.

DS: Do you still have a faith? A religious faith?

RF: There are still habits. Cue nun joke if this were television. I sometimes think that what turned me off religion was all the recording angel stuff. St Peter and God as interviewers. The Day of Judgement as the ultimate talk show, with no AFM to show the audience how to clap. How could I believe in that? No, I say a prayer each time just before I go on air. Did say. I want to believe and it's always there in the background. Howl-round. Recovering addicts tend to get religion, don't they? Swap God for the bottle. Not that it was the bottle in my case. Can I ask another question?

DS: Of course.

RF: People here with drink or drugs problems – Con Raven, Terry Perry – the point is that they have to give up completely. There is no such thing as social drinking or recreational drug-taking. But my problems are eating and working. I mean, do I get an intravenous drip and the ultimate sick-note? I think I'd go mad – oops, do a lot of people sitting here make that slip? – if I could never work again.

DS: You're not mad. It's an interesting point. With some of the problems we have here – eating disorders, workaholism, sex addiction . . .

RF: There are *sex addicts* here? Checked in now? Give me their room numbers. I see from your face I'm not the first to do that joke here.

DS: No. With those problems, recovery cannot mean total abstinence. The aim is to make you feel as other people feel about their meals, their jobs. You could – you should – return to work under the right conditions.

7. AS-LIVE

The questions rolled slowly in front of my eyes:

HAVE YOU EVER REALLY LOVED A WOMAN?
DO YOU BELIEVE IN SHAME?
WHAT IS LIFE?
HOW MUCH IS THAT DOGGY IN THE WINDOW?

Lucy's voice in my ear was tenderly encouraging: *'Feeling OK? Like we never went away, isn't it? Bit for level?'*

'How much is that doggy in the window?' I asked.

'Fine. Did you see the papers, Rich?'

'I'm not really reading them.'

'The BBC have signed Peter Pennington. Given him our slot.'

'Yeah. Piss in our time.'

It was a very Richard Fleming remark. But envy was slowly going, along with the other urgencies of which my personality was being purged. Driving to the studio from the room at Hotel, which was now my home, I had for the first time heard *UK Today* with Ruthia Mendip with the casual attention of a normal listener.

It was a fortnight since my final session at the Abbey with Dr Sark. Confused by my references to voices in the head, he had wasted time trying to prove Multiple Personality Disorder. But we had finally agreed that the problem was Media Personality Disorder.

'Con's coming in.'

As Cornelius Raven joined me in the oblong of bright light – like an illuminated grave – the crew clapped. My own entry had provoked a similar ovation. It had become an industry ritual for recovering addicts returning to work.

We slapped hands, two burned-out stars now trying to reverse our journey through the black hole. Fiona had made up Raven's face so heavily that his new plastic septum was invisible, but his skin made me think of the fourth form: adolescents tangerine with acne cream. Tom Ogg appeared from behind a camera and patted us both on our backs like a boxing referee.

'Back where you belong,' MD.BRO told us.

'And this is for the new digital channel?' Raven asked. 'BBC Has-Been?'

'Er, BBC Replay. Essentially, it's a niche nostalgia channel for the graduate forties to fifties. *And Why Not?* taps into pop nostalgia obviously. It's the flagship show among the originations. The channel's mainly re-runs. The focus group was most excited by 1970s editions of *The Tony Andrews Show*. There's been shedloads of interest in him since . . .'

My conversations were filled now with comments suddenly stopped by the other speaker. People were always almost talking to me about Martin Stark or Tony Andrews. When Lucy or the team reached for a greedy last sandwich at a planning meeting, they cut off their usual observations about its potential fattening effect. Everyone looked alarmed when I went to the bathroom and, in deference, I pissed as quickly as possible and jogged back along the corridor.

'This isn't a stupid show, is it?' worried Raven. 'I don't think my Lazarus programme should be a stupid show.'

'*And Why Not?* isn't stupid at all,' Ogg insisted. 'Clearly it's not the classic chat-show format. But I'd call it post-classical. Populist television with a bedrock of intelligence. It works because of Richard's journalistic baggage.'

'I like that baggage, Tom,' I pointed out. 'It's taken me decades to collect and it's Louis Vuitton.'

'And we booked you for that baggage, Rich. But we also wanted the sense of those cases being checked into a slightly unexpected hotel.'

'A roadside motel which calls itself the Ritz,' sneered the comedian.

'*OK. Camera rehearsal.*'

If I used to feel like a novice again in the studio after a fortnight's holiday, I felt now like a teenager on work experience. It seemed impossible that there had been a period when this charade felt natural.

'Hey! What's your name?'

'Cornelius Raven.'

'Can I trust you?'

'Er, yeah. Yeah, probably.'

'So you want to save the world?'

'Ideally. Yeah. If I could.'

'Ever fallen in love with someone you shouldn't have?'

'Too often.'

'How many miles to Amarillo?'

'From here? Nine, ten thousand?'

At the end of the rehearsal, Ogg sprang out of the shadows again. 'You understand the format, Con?'

Raven stroked his smooth skull, producing the sandpaper rasp which was the sound-effect of the first generation of elective-slaphead men. The shaved scalp had been part of his remaking of himself in rehab.

'You're seriously saying that every single question is the title of a chart hit?' he asked. 'I mean "Amarillo" and stuff obviously, but . . .'

'As soon as we read the proposal, we said the whole nine yards or time-out. When Richard asks, "Hi, how are you doing?" it's a Kenny G single from 1984. The question "Hey, what's your name?" comes from a little-known 1992 chart hit for Baby June. "What is life?" is, perhaps surprisingly, Olivia Newton-John from 1972.'

'Yeah. But his follow-ups can obviously . . .'

'Even the follow-ups. If Richard asks, "Why?" he's quoting the title of a 1994 record by Demob. "Was that all it was?" is Kurt Mazure, 1990. "How can you expect to be taken seriously?", a single for the Pet Shop Boys in 1991.'

After I broke my year of radio and television silence in an interview with Elizabeth De Mare confessing my addictions and trumpeting my recovery, many comeback projects had been offered. But, though I craved escapism from my recent past, I was mainly promised imprisonment in the publicity.

Producers proposed television and radio documentaries about the last edition of *Fleming Faces*. One of them was later presented by Clem Sadley under the title *It Could Have Been Me*. Ogg volunteered a peak-time series about stalking, beginning with John Lennon and Mark Chapman and ending with Pardon-Jackett-Stark.

Although I considered myself the last person to be trusted on the subject of stalking, mine was now the number stored in every journo's mobile for love-spurned murders. So, when Jeff Tims went on trial at Leeds Crown Court for the killing of Angela Shipley, I flew to a Milwaukee sister clinic of the Abbey's.

A series of terrible decisions had created my need for these wards of disordered celebrities but this move proved to be good judgement. Lucy later told me that the tape of my radio interview with the childhood sweethearts reunited by the Internet had been played on every news bulletin reporting the guilty verdict against Tims.

The prosecution evidence confirmed my intuition during my last day on radio about what had happened. The Crown case was not that Tims had turned vicious after relocating his first love but that he had set out to find her with the intention of killing her. He was 'always a stalker posing as a lover.'

I was offered two documentaries and a book about Tims. But the first invitation to appeal was this post-classical chat show in which every question was a pop lyric. Ogg thought I was doing *And Why Not?* – the series title taken from an obscure late 1980s rock band – because digital was the future. In fact, this fresh edge of the medium attracted me because, in the present, almost no one watched it.

While being stripped of my other addictions, I also seemed to be losing the need to be seen. Only the most hagiographic get-well messages and letters about allowing Jesus Christ to be my doctor were now sent on from the BBC – and my e-mail address had been changed to a formula which included neither of my names – but I knew from the police that the various silencings of Pardon, Exeter and north London had failed to disinfect my in-tray.

The padded photograph albums still arrived, now presenting images from the television coverage of my crises and a bootleg video of the snuff show. And the other rgfleming – or someone else pretending to be him pretending to be me – continued to send messages to my former log-on, which a cop now monitored. Like everyone else who had frequently appeared on TV, Matthew Pardon now had his fans and imitators. And those who copied the format most exactly would want to include me.

'Ten ... nine ... eight ... seven ... run VT ...'

Television for me now was like sex at the end of a marriage: the moves familiar but the feelings gone. Live man walking. Christ over Rio. What did you have for breakfast. I regret to inform you that no such reply. His worm's showing. Coming.

'*Cue, Richard.*'

'Hey, what's your name?'

'Cornelius Raven.'

'Have you ever really loved a woman?'

'One. And one out of a hundred ain't bad for a lad.'

'Do you remember the first time?'

'Yeah. I was fifteen. Which means I was fifteen and two seconds when it was over.'

'Do you know the way to San José?'

'Turn left at Heathrow? Planes, right? Have you ever shagged someone in an aircraft khazi? Fucking uncomfortable. Or, indeed, uncomfortable fucking . . .'

'*We can bleep those.*'

'The only reason I bother is that making penetration take place as we actually cross the international dateline is the only way I can make it last an hour.'

'*And any chance of a smile? It's going well.*'

'How much is that doggy in the window?'

'Who cares? It's pussy I want.'

This must have been the first time in a decade that Raven had performed without the cheerleader of cocaine. And yet he was entirely his public self. The drug of television still worked on him. I, though, was recovered. On the monitor – where the sight of my face no longer frightened me – I still looked like TV's Richard Fleming. But inside I felt like a recording of myself. As-live.

'Who put the Bomp (In the Bomp-a-Bomp-a-Bomp)?' I asked Cornelius Raven.

'Bomp? It sounds like one of those euphemisms for shagging, doesn't it?'

'*Cut-throat.*'

Because the pride of the devisers was that the presenter's script would consist entirely of song lyrics – even the opening and closing pleasantries – my outro had occasioned much debate. A music hall solution was found:

GOODBYE-EEEEEEEEEEEEEEEEEEEE!
GOODBYE-EEEEEEEEEEEEEEEEEEEE!

Wipe a tear, baby dear, from your eye-eeee. Don't seem to be reading. Look through the words. Imagine a person out there who loves you, listening to what you have to say.

'*Cut-throat.*'

If you are reading this, then I am dead.

Lucy's voice is frightened now. They think I've dried. Dry on live TV. As-live. But there is nothing left to dry.

GOODBYE-EEEEEEEEEEEEEEEEEEEE!

I have voices in my ear and urgent messages surge before my eyes in flickering green type.

GOODBYE-EEEEEEEEEEEEEEEEEEEEEEEE!

But what I say – the word firmly end-stopped so that those above me can be in no doubt that I've defied them – is: 'Goodbye.'

I'm sorry. I'm sorry that's all we've got time for. Cut-throat.

Author's Note

I have some experience of television and radio presentation and of publicity. This novel, however, also draws on the stories of colleagues with far more exposure to both and I am grateful for my conversations with them. Given the nature of the subject, they would prefer not to be named.

None of the BBC job titles featured in the novel – except Director General – exists in reality.

One line from F. Scott Fitzgerald's *The Great Gatsby* is quoted in Chapters 3 and 6. Lines from *Fox in Socks* by Dr Seuss appear in Chapters 2 and 6.

I am deeply grateful to Robyn Read, Tanya Hudson and Mark Bell for helping me with details of radio and television production. And Sarah, William, Anna and Benjamin for suffering the long gestation of a book which includes among its themes workaholism.

ML